CELESTIAL BODIES

THE SUN SERPENT'S DAUGHTER

R. A. MOREAU

P&P PLEASURE & POWER PUBLISHING

CHAPTER 1

CELESTE

———

A viper knows only one rule.

Lie.

With her words, her eyes—even her body, if she must. Whatever must be done in the name of duty. But under no circumstance can she allow herself to believe the lie. Succumbing to one's own venom is a lethal bite, for which there is no cure. None other than the Serpent's blade.

———

I settle on my objective for the evening as my mark presses his elbow against a frail wooden door at the back of the crowded inn, dragging me into a stifling little room. It's precisely what's needed for the kind of encounter he's anticipating—quick, no frills or fuss. But he believes the lie too easily. As most men do.

I stumble across the threshold, and the door bounces back,

wood cracking against the wall as it splinters under pressure. My eyes blink, struggling to adjust to the sudden darkness. I can feel him standing close, too close, and when my eyes finally focus, his bloated face is a mere hair's breadth away from my own. But I don't step back. There is nowhere to go. Even at opposite ends of the narrow space, I can reach out and touch him. The intimacy of it is disarming. *Perfect*.

"Come on, darlin'. I don't bite," he says, a distinctly male hunger hanging off every syllable, yielding any power he may have had for lust.

"I wouldn't mind if you did," I whisper.

"Ohh, fuck," he grunts.

His beer-laden breath erupts from his mouth, battering my face in a cloud of malt and yeast, and I resist the urge to pull away as his voice creeps over me. He's wound his arms around me, gripping my ass and using it as leverage to press me closer. As the air grows thick with the heat of his desire, I am confident he will fare the same as the rest.

Moisture beads down his neck as I fist my hands in his uniform and jerk him closer. He responds as expected, eager excitement surging to life between his legs as a single sweat-slicked palm scrapes its way up my torso, aiming for my breast.

I bring my elbows down to disrupt his path and push him onto a stack of crates in the corner. The clinking of glass bottles echoes in the small space as his heavy body jostles the contents.

He isn't an idle fellow by the looks of it. His bulky arms hang limply at his sides, wound tight with the effort of restraint. Admirable, but misguided. His chest is broad and deep, like a drum, and his legs jut out from his hips like two tree trunks to balance it all.

I drape a leg over his hips, using his broad chest to anchor myself until I'm straddling him—the evidence of his excitement pushing against me. I adjust my position without shame, watching as his eyes roll back into his head.

Letting out a soft moan, I call on the breathy pitch most men enjoy, though his desire provokes nothing in me. I've grown used to the response my body elicits, and his erection is little more than a thorn in my side. It means nothing to me.

Decades of training had prepared me for this very moment. Serving at the pleasure of the Serpent means honing your craft to the point of perfection. So when he groans beneath me, I do not pay it any mind.

"By Saturn's rings, you're the most beautiful thing I've ever seen." He hiccups, heavy hands sliding down to my thighs as his eyes strain to take in all of me.

He isn't wholly unattractive. In fact, I might have been persuaded were the circumstances any different. But, as it is, I'd rather lose my light than find myself in this man's chamber.

The Serpent sent me to Venutia with little more than a demand and a description, *"Find the man with five rings."*

Typically, my missions are aimed at silencing those who dare to denounce the message of the Serpent. Those who warn against the so-called "harms" of the Sun's light and those who advocate to dim Mother Sun's light. But this time, I'd been dispatched for a much different reason, and I refused to rest until I'd fulfilled my duty.

I'd spent days lingering in back-alley markets and beer-soaked inns, glancing at every passerby with so much as a hoop in their ear before I finally found this one. He'd been drinking himself under the table in a small pub—the fragrant notes of a woman's musk and cheap Venutian oils still clinging to his olive skin.

It didn't take much to get him here. It never does. Once he'd caught the thin covering of my dress and a healthy glimpse of my hips, he'd pursued me like a sunseeker desperate for a meal.

"I've never had a Solarian before," he mumbles, speaking around a fist full of hot air. It bubbles up and out of his mouth like a foul wind.

I pray to Mother Sun this is true.

I hadn't mentioned my celestial house. But if my attire wasn't telling enough, the sunset golden hue of my eyes was all the evidence he needed. The mark of the Sun is burned into them. The brightly colored center surrounded by a vibrant copper ring. Paired with my deeply shaded skin, I am unmistakably a child of the Sun.

I sway in his arms, letting him catch me by the waist as I throw my head back, giggling. But my laugh feels too loud when it bounces back to meet me, and I quiet.

Men do not prefer boisterous women. The Serpent's lesson rings in my mind as I correct myself.

"What's a Satúran man doing in the land of Venus?" I ask, lowering my voice to a whisper and offering him an innocent smile.

Deep within my core, sensing the familiar course of an interrogation, my magic begins to uncoil, reading itself for our inevitable conclusion. But I dampen it. We aren't there yet.

"Oh, darlin', I can't say. My captain would have my head if I spoke a word."

I drag my lower lip between my teeth, flashing him a suggestive smile as I finger the black bands inked onto his left forearm. There are five of them. Each one is slightly raised and thicker than the last. The Satúran military brand—a representation of his rank. A foolish practice, in my opinion, wearing your status on your sleeve. It makes their high-ranking officials easy targets. You couldn't possibly miss them. Rings stacked from wrist to shoulder, like the brightly colored hide of a Mercurian antelope—ripe for the picking.

But the man beneath me is only a mid-tier commander, responsible for no more than a small battalion. And for leading his men against unarmed women.

My teeth grind together in white-hot rage as I'm reminded of why the Serpent sent me.

"Hmm." I pout, running a hand across his pounding chest and watching his body stiffen as my fingers trail lower. "Perhaps you're looking for a girl to spend those cold Satúran nights with?"

The words come easy. The lie that carries with them even easier.

My nipples harden as I lean into him, scraping my chest across the rough fabric of his uniform, and as he grabs at me, I half wonder when this sinful art became so second nature.

"Something like that." He chuckles, moving his greedy hands to my hips.

The viper in me wishes to cut his fingers free, but instead, I let him hold me for a moment.

The natural potency of lust is far more effective than feigned trust will ever be. And I'd discovered long ago that a man would bare his darkest secrets at the slightest show of interest. Women tend to require a bit more effort. But I've found that, in either regard, those who resist the viper's lure only need a little...encouragement.

I push my fingers into his hair, fisting it in my hand and yanking his head back, exposing his thick neck. A deep chuckle pours out of him, and I laugh in earnest at the fool in front of me. Too dim to realize he's wandered willingly within my grasp.

His even breathing turns shallow as his arousal ratchets higher, and I lean back to watch his face as I ask, "Or are you looking for nice Solarian girls to sell in the outer ring?"

My smile fades, but he's still grinning like a fool when my magic begins to fill the room. Sunlight stretches to life inside my limbs, pulsing through my chest and radiating down my arms to settle just beneath my skin. I watch, unblinking, as his gleeful expression dies. Magic courses through my veins until my entire body glows a dim yellow-gold, and the light of my eyes illuminates his face.

I smile as realization sets in, and his confusion is replaced with unbridled fear.

"Y-y-you..." He stammers and squirms beneath me, but I center my weight, shifting my hips to keep him from dislodging me while I encircle his body with ribbons of searing hot sunlight.

I lock his head in my grasp, my nails digging into his scalp as I grip his hair by the root.

It's too late now.

I reach for the blade I use to keep my hair out of my eyes and pull it free, letting my dark, sunlit curls fall around my shoulders. I hold the needlepoint blade to his quivering throat. Blood draws forth where I press it into his skin, dripping slowly down the hilt until it coats my fingers and stains the sandy-colored canvas of his uniform.

"Where are the women you were transporting from Solaria?" I ask, the dulled edge of my voice sharpening to a point.

He answers my question with a strangled cry, forcing me to tighten my hold, hissing as my light burns through his uniform to reach his skin.

I decide to dangle his freedom in front of him. "Answer me, and I'll let you go."

"I-I...I can't. Please." He writhes beneath me, and I clamp down around his thighs, pressing my boots flat into the floor as I wait with thinning patience.

"You don't have much time left," I warn.

My eyes flick from his face to the crimson color on his collar, and a haze of nervous sweat pours out of him in waves.

I sigh inwardly. *This is taking much too long.*

I don't typically opt for this approach. I much prefer to meet my marks quickly, without the back and forth. But the Serpent requires an answer. So here we shall sit until his lips manage to work again. Though, after another long moment of silence, my irritation surmounts.

I shove my forearm into the crook under his jaw, crushing his windpipe.

Sweat-drenched fingers claw at the light that holds his arms, and his hips buck uselessly beneath me.

"I will not ask again," I snap, watching with mild satisfaction as his lips gradually turn a lovely shade of blue.

"Th-the firs-t r-r-ing." He wheezes out the words between his desperate attempts for air, and I loosen my hold. "The crown. They're...in the...first...ring. In...the palace," he confesses, each sentence punctuated by his sharp inhales. "P-p-please," he begs. "That's all I know."

Violent coughs rack his body as I release him, stepping back into the furthest corner of the little room.

"Please," he pleads, frantically waving a hand.

But mercy doesn't come to me as I stare down at him.

My mind wanders to the women he's already stolen. Twelve of them. None older than twenty. Mere babes in a world where we live well past five hundred years.

Who had found mercy for them? Certainly not this brute before me.

The memory of his deep chuckle cuts into my thoughts.

Did he laugh when they pleaded for freedom? Did they all survive their journey? Or were some surrendered to the Sun along the way?

I don't ask him. Because I don't care. This man, this *monster*, would see no mercy from me.

"Thank you," is all I offer him.

Hope darts across his features as I step back. But in a single breath, it's gone.

His eyes widen. His feet scramble as he rushes to stand, and I watch his mind turn. Too slow to prevent it, but keen enough to know it's coming.

Sunlight bursts from my palms, knocking him back, cutting a bright arc across his chest, and burning him from shoulder to hip. His mouth lolls open. A scream dies before he can force it free, and the charcoal-scented smoke of crisped flesh fills the room as his body sags, dragging down his chin until it rests on his chest in defeat.

I straighten and run my hands down my thighs, trying to purge the memory of his skin from my own.

"And I'm not a '*thing*,' I'm a woman," I declare, turning to leave his charred body for someone else to find.

When I step into the poorly lit pub, I'm met with the overwhelming scent of sweat, beer, and cheap perfumes floating through the crisp evening air. Early evening light burns low through the windows lining the walls, illuminating the dank and sticky interior and lighting my path as I step gingerly around the men already piled on the floor, most of them too drunk to stand. I keep my blade in my hand as I push through the crowd, and I don't hesitate to place a small cut on the brooding man who has the gall to grab at my hips.

A warm breeze picks up the dust around my feet when I finally reach the door and step out into the street. The rhythmic trot and bump of horse-drawn carriages float up from the cobblestones, followed by shouts from their drivers, cutting through the singsong cadence of marketeers luring in unsuspecting visitors.

Belloir, the capital city of the Venutian kingdom, is the epicenter of beauty. Made so by the Venutian's unique gift for shifter magic. As such, their talents tend to draw a diverse crowd. Uranians, Nepethesians, Solarians, and the like. All vying for the elusive promise of youth and beauty.

I watch as a Martian woman puts up a good fight with the Venutian vendor across the road, only to see her shrug and shell out much too many pieces for a bottle of cut-rate oil.

Someone should have told her the oils worth arguing over are at least four roads to the east, closer to the palace.

"Well, I'm only in Belloir for a short while," a voice sings, breaking through the symphony of the busy streets.

I recognize the telltale sounds of Raye's quiet flirtations, and I turn to see her propping her short frame against a wall, head tilted up at a confused Venutian woman.

My eyes roll with a huff—*every damn time.*

"Vrey, ti mae venus!" I call, stepping in close and looping an arm around Raye's waist, careful to hide my blood-crusted fingers in the folds of her blouse.

She stiffens at the sound of my voice and visibly deflates as she realizes I've ruined her game.

The woman blinks, stone-white eyes darting from my face to Raye's and back again before landing on where my hand rests on Raye's hip. A delicate frown ripples across her polished skin before she crosses her arms in front of her, cursing.

"Vejera! Ti tae shaevé!" Her long, blond hair sweeps over her shoulder as she turns in a frenzy, stepping onto the road to be carried away by the current of people shuffling by.

"Ugh!" Raye pouts. "What did you do that for?"

Her hands scramble, clawing at my fingers as she twists out of my grip, and I can't help but laugh as she breaks free. Her clenched fist comes charging forward, and I sidestep, leaving her arm to swing aimlessly through the air before dropping back to her side.

"Please." My eyes roll as she folds her arms in front of her. "She doesn't even speak the common tongue. She probably thought you were begging," I tease.

Raye sucks her teeth in disbelief.

"A language barrier has never stopped me before," she says, lifting a dark brow and cocking her head.

She's not wrong. Raye has successfully bedded every woman she's ever so much as looked at. All the way from here to Uranom. She may be short and spry, but she's tenacious to say the least. Except we no longer have time for her wandering eye. The corpse I left searing in the pub behind us means our time in Belloir is over.

My eyes instinctively move over her head, marking the posts where the Venutian scouts watch over the market square. Their bright-white uniforms stand out like beacons amongst the sea of blond hair and sandy skin, and I count at least ten gathered in the courtyard, eyes pouring over people as they pass.

"What did she say?" Raye's voice jolts my concentration.

"She cursed you and called you a little scoundrel," I reply without turning.

My answer is met with silence, and when I glance down at her, Raye's ears are tipped with a bright red that clashes with her soft brown skin. Embarrassment threatens to swallow her as her softly hooded eyes squint at me in irritation.

"Damn you. Why do you insist on ruining my chances? Just because you're not interested? Have you seen these women? Why can't you just..."

Raye's words stop forming sentences in my mind as I return to surveying.

Venutians clutter the road, moving in an orderly fashion. A scout barks an order as a tall Mercurian man disrupts the flow of traffic, but I don't stop to watch as they jerk him to the side. There is a tall white-capped head bobbing up and down as it pushes through the crowd, moving in our direction.

"—you know, maybe you just need a man to give it to you good—"

Raye is still rambling about the opportunity I've stolen from her, but her words stop when I whisper, "The Sun is setting."

Her mouth clamps shut, and with a singular nod, we peel apart.

My feet hit the cobblestones, caking my boots in a thick layer of what I can only hope is mud, and I lower my head to a less conspicuous height. Venutians are rather tall by other standards, but I still tower over most of them. So I keep my eyes fixed on the ground and let the crush of bodies carry me forward.

I don't dare look for Raye. She will choose her path, and I will choose mine, and we will convene at an old abandoned stable near a large breach in the city wall where Suri and Strega sit saddled and ready. For the next few moments, we are as strangers are—unfamiliar faces in a foreign place. Neither willing to risk the other.

But I need not worry about her. She may not be a viper, but

she is smart. And she has her own motivations for avoiding the scouts.

The bony edge of a shoulder jerks my body back, pressing me into the rough exterior of the man behind me. The intruder, a visitor moving against the grain, stumbles as I shoot him a piercing glare, but when I twist to separate from the man behind me, I'm confronted by the alarming color of a scout's uniform barely an inch from my nose. I ready myself as his hands come around my shoulders, bracing my weight.

"Mae porovaé, venus," he mutters. *Pardon me, beautiful.*

My eyes soften, calling on the viper's skill as I let him inspect me.

"Mae á zevere." *It is my fault,* I offer, bowing at the waist to hide my face.

Another hurried pedestrian jerks the scout's body backward, separating us and prompting him to whirl with a shouted order. I use the distraction to slip through a gap in the line before he can turn back for me.

Cutting across the market square and darting down a darkened alleyway, I wind my way toward our meeting point. When the stable finally comes into view, Luna is high in the sky, bathing the city in her light, and Raye is leaning against Suri's hip, arms crossed with a haughty look of victory on her narrow face.

She cheers when she spots me. "I win!"

"How many times must I tell you? It's not a race. Focus on making it out. Not how fast you get there."

Her eyes roll. "Yeah, yeah. I still won."

I stroll past her, flicking her in the arm before plunging my hand into Strega's saddlebag to fist a handful of oats.

"Sorry I ruined your chances back there," I mutter over my shoulder. "She was beautiful."

"Eh." Raye shrugs, waving off my apology.

A sour, twisted feeling settles in my stomach, and I hope she means it.

Raye is so well suited to the life of a viper that I sometimes forget she isn't one. That my mission isn't also hers. Or that she has space in her mind for things other than the Serpent's orders.

Suddenly, as if called into being by my thoughts alone, a small scroll of parchment tumbles from Strega's saddlebag as I pull my hand free. The four of us watch in silence as it flutters to the earth.

Raye sighs. Suri snorts beside her, swishing her tail, and Strega stamps out an angry hoofbeat as if voicing his frustration.

You wouldn't know from looking at him, but the big stallion is a celestial breed. Taller than any standard horse, with a golden mane falling over a russet hide adorned with a smattering of braids. Ordinarily, his tail and mane would be dipped in sunlight, but a few months ago, I buried his light deep in his spirit so as not to raise suspicion.

It took a while for the magic to move away from the surface. First, his eyes dimmed, then the soft iridescence of his coat grew fainter until, one day, he appeared to be nothing more than a rather large horse.

I pat his rump, trying to soothe him before snatching up the scroll and picking at the blood-red seal stamped into the shape of a coiled snake.

"What's it say?" Raye asks, unable to hide the tired look in her eyes.

We've been in the field for months now. Neither of us can remember the last time we slept in a proper bed, and Suri and Strega are growing tired from our long journeys. Even *I* am praying this note will call us home. But I'm met with disappointment as I read.

"It only lists a location." I shrug. "A valley in the Venutian plains."

Raye's shoulders sag as she slumps against Suri, defeated.

I say nothing for a moment. I consider telling Raye to abandon me, but we've had that conversation before, and it always ends with Raye's magic slamming into me with unbridled force, followed by an involuntary fit of rage on my part.

She knows she doesn't have to accompany me. But she does anyway. And she'll only shout at me if I try to dismiss her. Which isn't really a problem in itself. But the trouble with having an untrained Plutonian by your side is that her spirit magic tends to creep out on its own. Infecting the emotions of the people around her. And there is never any knowing if she'll be able to rein it back in. So after a moment of silence, we both swing ourselves into our saddles and settle in for another long ride.

The location the Serpent sent is not near. It's farther east than we've ever gone. Through the volcanic valleys and past the salt flats, just before you reach the Lunar border. A place very few dare to cross. We're both slumped in our saddles as the heat of the valley grows thicker, and the horses turn skittish when the ground shakes beneath their feet, but we're careful to stick to the outskirts, avoiding the seismic center.

The heat only lifts when we cross one valley into the next, and by the time the Serpent's banner comes into view, we're both stooped low in the saddle, trying to make shade from our extra garments.

The Solarian royal crest, my family's crest, waves in the distance as we top the hill. The bright gold fabric stands out against the night sky like a false sun on the horizon, gleaming with a sigil branded in the center—a viper coiled around the base of a skull, slithering out of one hollowed eye. Beneath the banner stands the faint outline of thirty Solarian soldiers mounted on horseback.

General Kefu's familiar build becomes clear as we draw closer. He sits atop his horse, though I'm shocked to see the Serpent's most formidable general is out of uniform. Actually, they're all out of uniform.

Their usual reflective armor has been replaced by simple black canvas from head to toe. Together they look reminiscent of the

Lunar legions, and the viper in me begins to uncoil at the prospect of a new mission.

"Princess Celeste," Kefu calls, crossing his fist over his chest in greeting before dropping from his horse.

Before I can do the same, he extends his hand to help me out of the saddle. I ignore it. But once my feet are firmly planted on the ground, he sweeps my hand up anyway, planting a soft kiss on my knuckles.

"May the Sun never set on House Solaria, and may her light touch every plane," he recites against my skin.

I repeat the creed dutifully, then stiffen when he adds, "It's been far too long. You are a vision as always."

He offers me a brilliant smile that I'm sure has struck down many women, but unfortunately for us both, I'm rather immune to his charms.

Kefu has always been affectionate toward me, and he's more than attractive, with a perfect age, rank, and status to boot. We would be a "well-matched pair" as my sisters used to tease. But something about his perfect teeth and well-kept hair makes me feel as if I'd be ruining him were I ever to take him up on his offer. Not to mention his persistent need to call me princess and treat me like a wilting flower—even knowing I could cut his head from his shoulders in a single stroke. So, rather than sink my teeth into him, I hold him at a distance, never offering much more than a half-hearted smile.

"General," I say with a curt nod. "To what do I owe the pleasure?"

I think I see his shoulders sag as he registers the familiar barrier I place between us, but then he straightens, and my rejection is forgotten. Or rather, ignored.

"The Serpent requires your service," he declares.

Doesn't it always?

Kefu's big hand juts out in front of him, fisting a small scroll identical to the one that sent us here—tightly wound and bound with the Serpent's seal. I make quick work of it, too tired to burden myself with anticipation.

I tear the seal open, drop the wax into the dried grass, and unfurl the parchment to find a single sentence sweeping across the page.

Nest in the House of Luna and await the order to strike.

My eyes dart to Raye, then Kefu, and words tumble from my mouth before I can stop them, "But King Sevah has no need for a woman by his side. He refuses to take another."

Everyone knows that. Even after the Council demanded he wed again, King Sevah denounced their order, flouting the rules of the treaty. The Council allowed it out of fear of a greater conflict. And so place of La Luna's queen has sat empty ever since.

"King Sevah is dead, Princess," Kefu declares. "The Demon Prince of La Luna is to be crowned. But first...he requires a bride."

Raye gasps beside me, the shockwave of her excitement rolling off her.

I can see the moment her magic hits Kefu. His eyes grow wide, and his voice pitches higher. "We are here to escort you through the Night Forest!" he exclaims, much too eager to appear natural. Several soldiers raise a brow as he continues, "We must leave before tomorrow evening if you wish to make it for the selection ceremony!" He sways on his feet like an excited child.

I elbow Raye in the side signaling her to reel in her magic. It takes her a moment, and more concentration than would be necessary for an experienced celestial. But eventually, Kefu's brows fall back into place, and his usual slow and even cadence returns.

Raye shrinks back once she's righted herself, and we both stare at Kefu, praying no one has noticed. Raye's magic is a secret we keep almost as closely as my own. One I haven't even shared with the Serpent. And one that would bring untold horrors to Raye's doorstep were anyone to find out. But if Kefu is suspicious of the sudden change, he doesn't show it. Instead, he barks out an order, causing his men to disperse and ready the camp.

"Rest. We will set out in the morning. It will take at least five days to move through the forest. And the seekers will not be kind to us. Best to go in with as much energy as we can muster."

I nod, pulling my pack from Strega's back and setting the small bundle as far from the soldiers as I can. They won't dare to aim their flirtations at me. But we don't need another incident with Raye's magic when they inevitably come to pester her.

Our small camp is quiet as Raye sets about making a small fire for the two of us. When I drop down across from her she asks, "Are we really going in there?"

She's pointing just over my shoulder at the Lunar border. From where we sit, I can see it blanketing the Lunar territories in darkness, rising into the sky like a wall of night.

I nod, but I don't say anything.

There are true terrors within the Night Forest. Beasts that will not hesitate to lure us to our deaths. Creatures that kill for the thrill of it. And magic that can be found nowhere else. It is a place of mystery, more dangerous than I'm willing to admit.

I take the time to bury my sunlight as deep as I can. In the forest, it will act as a beacon to the sunseekers, and I remind myself to instruct Kefu and his soldiers to do the same.

Lest their light be devoured before they even cross into the night.

CHAPTER 2

APOLLO

The halls of La Luna are relatively empty this evening, with only the occasional groundskeeper or kitchen maid crossing my path, each stopping to bow low as I pass.

Praise be to Luna. I wish they'd stop doing that.

Every dip of the head is like a blow to the chest—a heavy reminder of my failure, striking me like an arrow and punishing me for my misgivings.

If they knew how I fail them each night—if Father knew— they would turn from me. And if not, they should.

It's been weeks since Father's spirit went home to Luna, yet we're no further along than before. The charge sits exactly as he'd left it, and the eastern border continues to erode each night. I am hardly deserving of their veneration.

Water sloshes underfoot as I stalk through the dank and darkened hallways, ducking my head to keep from scraping my horns on the ceiling. The dungeon's narrow corridor arches overhead, forming a rounded tunnel deep under the castle grounds, stretching to the forest's edge. It is wide enough for most men, yet I am forced to hunch my shoulders and drop my head as I wind through the shadows. Even so, the tips of my horns brush the ceiling where the earth above has shifted, dulling the fine points to blunted ends. And every few paces, a crooked stone left jutting out of the wall scrapes my arm, fraying the woolen cloak draped over my shoulders.

But I cannot fault its construction. I doubt the stonemasons had a creature like me in mind while laying this path. I doubt anyone had ever conceived of a creature like me before the night conjured me up. And aside from the inadequate dimensions, the dungeon is near perfection.

The tight, interlocking bricks prevent all manner of sound, light, and in some instances, air from seeping through the cracks, leaving only the purest silence and an unforgiving darkness shrouding my path. But I carry no light with me. I never do. It isn't necessary. Even without the demon's eyes, the heavy scent of copper and salt would be plenty to lead my way.

Blood seeps from beneath the door at the end of the hall. Its scent hangs in the air, thick enough that I can taste the carnage on my tongue. The water beneath my boots begins to run scarlet the closer I draw to my destination, and I need not wonder at its source. It sits at the end of the hall behind a plain-looking door, waiting for me. But the moment I step into the room, it appears it is blood wasted.

Our guest sits curled over his knees, his back pressed into the corner of the too-small room, with his arms wrapped around himself. His head jerks up to meet my gaze as I shut the heavy wooden door and offer him a stiff nod in greeting.

"Evening, my friend," I say.

But he shakes his head, and I can see his jaw clench in anger.

He's beginning to grow tired of his captivity.

I must say I am impressed with his resilience. The Serpent must breed a bone-breaking strength into his men because this one hasn't spoken a word in all his time here. I'm beginning to worry our "conversations" are futile.

Shallow cuts mark his arms and chest, and a bright bruise blooms on his cheek—evidence of our last encounter. He grew bold last night, deciding to test the bounds of my mercy.

He'd slipped out behind a careless guard coming to collect his meal, but he didn't make it very far. Between the nighthounds and myself, he was quickly collected, but not without injury.

Ordinarily, I would give him time to heal before we speak again. He is of no use to me if he is no longer breathing. But I, too, am growing tired of his captivity.

My stomach rolls at the sight and smell of him. He looks sickly beyond compare. Evidently, the healer's remedies seem to be unsuccessful. His infection-filled wounds, and the stench of unwashed skin, fills the room like a rancid cloud. And suddenly, I wish for him to speak, if only so I may put an end to this.

This work is not work I take pleasure in. It's the kind of work that chips away at your spirit, drawing you deeper into the dark with every step. Monstrous work—meant only for monsters. Something I wouldn't dare place on another's shoulders.

But, no matter how he begs, I cannot offer him the sweet embrace of death until I have the answers I seek. My father's honor demands it. My people's survival demands it. So I squat in front of him, watching him closely.

The man blinks a bruised and bloodied eye. It takes him a while to pry it open, the swelling having sealed it shut, and I can barely make out the sliver of fear that flits across his face as the shadow of my horns crosses his eyes. But he doesn't stir. He knows it is fruitless. Instead, he sits silently, waiting.

"Where would you like to begin this afternoon?" I ask, roping a shadow around the thick chain that links his hands together.

He shakes his head, and I jerk hard on the chain, pulling it to the ceiling and forcing him onto his feet. He dances on his toes, barely scraping the floor as he tries and fails to relieve the pressure on his wrists. The bandages beneath his shackles are bloodied from his escape attempts, and weakness finds its way into my heart.

I release my hold on his chains, and he crumples against the stone, making no move to right himself. He winces at the pain, and his mouth drops open, but if he cries out, I cannot hear it.

"I will ask again. *How do I move the charge?*"

My voice rings in my ears indistinctly. The noise I hear is just that—noise. But I can feel the volume as it moves through the walls and floor and surges back into my feet.

Our guest flinches at the sound, and my shadows writhe in frustration. I prepare myself for a harsher approach, drawing shadows from the depths of the darkness around us—pulling them from their place on the floor and calling them out of the corners. My eyes cloud with magic, though I doubt my guest can see them. The light he emits has grown dim in his time, and now it appears to be nothing greater than a flickering candle in the wind.

He scrambles back, pressing himself into a corner at the familiar sight, as if he means to take refuge inside the wall. But before my magic can take hold of him, the Great Mother saves him from his fate.

The unmistakable sensation of heeled boots vibrates across the floor, and I swivel, prepared to berate her. But no sooner do I turn than Evalina bursts through the door, holding her upturned palm in front of her, illuminating the space with her moonlight.

Renwick follows, hot on her heels, and before I can shout at either of them, he speaks.

I can hardly make out the words echoing around me, but the ringing pitch of Renwick's whining is enough to make me bare my fangs at him.

He takes a hasty step back into the hall while Evalina merely rolls her eyes.

When she does not exit immediately, I shout, "Out!"

Evalina pulls back begrudgingly, moving at a leisurely pace, and

I follow them into the hall, abandoning our guest for another night.

"You are forbidden from the dungeons! What about this is not clear to you?" I ask, knowing I will not receive an answer until we exit the claustrophobic tunnel. It is too narrow for us to walk beside each other, and without seeing their faces or Evalina's translation, I will not know what is said. So while neither can offer me their rebuttal, I make my demands clear.

"Neither of you is to come down here again! Should you need me, you shall wait until I return. The dungeons are no place for you."

I can feel them following close behind, and when we reach the tunnel's end and step into the moonlight, I turn on them. "Is that *clear*?" I snap, watching their faces closely so I may read their answers.

"Y-yes, sire," Renwick concedes, bowing briskly.

"Fine." Evalina scoffs, crossing her arms and snuffing out her light.

"Now, what is so important that you insist on defying my orders?" I ask.

We stand in an intimate circle on the outskirts of the castle grounds, far enough from the walls that we cannot hear the dungeons from within, but not so far that we risk the creatures of the forest lurking in the shadows.

We are alone, and Evalina signs freely as she says, *"Uncle has urgent news."*

Renwick shifts on his feet, contemplating whether his "urgent" news is truly urgent at all. I have very little doubt that it isn't.

Renwick's always prattling on about something. Usually, some tedious detail that only he could possibly care about. It makes for quite dull conversation. As a result, I don't much care for his company. But he had served as Father's councilman before my shadow even formed, so I allowed him to retain his position after

Father's death. Too many changes in the palace would make the Council uneasy. And Renwick is a familiar, albeit grating, voice of reason in most circumstances. Although, in this present case, I'd have to disagree.

"You must attend this evening, sire! You..." I watch his thin lips move at a speed I didn't know possible, and I wonder why he insists on shouting. Even to a man who cannot hear him. But I've grown used to reading the people around me, and the demon's eyes make easy work of it, so I catch more than enough to know I am not interested in the rest.

For weeks, Renwick has been herding women into the throne room, trotting them in front of me like cattle, asking me to pick one. And for weeks, he has achieved nothing more than to confirm what I already knew to be true—the night has cursed me—irrevocably and completely.

"I will not entertain this game of yours any longer!" I bark in return, and he flinches at the fury in my voice, growing quiet. But the peace is only temporary as he almost immediately starts up again.

He may soon regret this, I sign to Evalina, whose mouth drops open in a clipped laugh.

Renwick passes a tense glance between us, unhappy he cannot read my words. He never enjoys being excluded from the conversation. His incessant need to know all things weighs on him constantly. But I rarely enjoy having his input, so neither Evalina nor I bother translating for him. Nonetheless, he persists.

"You must select a bride by the full moon. Or the Council will take action! We cannot risk—"

"Let them come!" I shout. Renwick shuffles back a step, giving my anger more room to breathe. "The House of Luna will not be bullied into action by a bunch of driveling old men."

If Father were here, he would tell me I am too rough with my words. That I shouldn't be so harsh with Renwick. But Father isn't here. I am all my people have left, and they need strength, not compromise.

"Old, perhaps. Driveling? Certainly not," Renwick answers, wagging a frail finger at me as if he's taken personal offense at my comment.

He may have. He's at least four hundred and five. I can't be certain of his exact age. He refused to tell anyone other than Father. The only reason I even know that much is due to his constant retelling of his military prowess in the Ennead War.

I never thought to ask Father about it before he passed. I'm sure he would have told me, but it didn't seem important at the time.

"Heavens be, Uncle!" Evalina snips, cutting in and signing for my benefit. *"A bride does not a king make."*

"No—but in the eyes of the Council? It does make a *kingdom*," Renwick corrects. "The other houses will not hesitate to challenge your claim. We must secure the crown. Without your father here, they will—"

A muscle ticks in my jaw as magic pulses deep in my chest, threatening to make itself known. Renwick quiets as my shadows creep across my skin, bleeding into my eyes and swallowing their usual color to replace them with an inky black hue.

"Without my father...*what*?" I ask, daring him to repeat himself.

I watch Renwick's mouth open and shut like a fish gasping for breath, and I'm prepared to wait. But Evalina is too kind. Her hand rests on my shoulder as she tries to save him from his spinelessness by reining in my demons, but it's a useless effort. I shake her off and watch the knot in Renwick's throat bob up and down as he tries to swallow some courage.

Long, silent moments stretch out between us, and when he finally speaks, his shoulders are squared and sure. Evalina signs his words just in case.

"Without your father, the Serpent will look to strike. He

thinks La Luna is weak in the hands of a child. He *will* look to unseat you. Already the Solarian council member has called for Luna's extradition from the treaty for flouting its agreement. He will look to hang you with every councilman so they will not come to our aid."

I stifle a snarl. *Child?* I would hardly label myself a child. Father was three hundred and forty-two on the eve of my birth, and on the day of his death, I marked my two hundredth year. My two hundred years may be a drastic departure from the experienced life of the other househeads, but it certainly isn't equivalent to a child's. Although, Renwick's point is well made—the other corpses who sit on the council will agree with him.

I take a deep breath, hating that his words hold even an ounce of reason, but not so foolish as to deny them.

"Thank you, Renwick," I confess. "Mollifying others is a valuable skill. But it is one I have no use for. Next time you wish to say something, say it. But do be sure you mean it. As you will bear the consequences."

Renwick's mouth returns to its gaping as he glances between me and Evalina, unsure if I'm merely provoking him. But I ignore his skepticism. "How many?"

"Pardon?" he asks, still confused by my admission.

"How many women have you gathered this time?"

"Twelve."

I pinch the space between my eyes, contemplating another tiresome evening of Renwick strolling women in and out. Each one more beautiful than the last, and all of them with a particular knack for telling a man exactly what he wants to hear. But none of them ever willing to so much as look at me, let alone stand by my side. Or, Luna forbid, share a bed with me. My irritation sparks at the thought, and my shadows rise to the surface, causing Renwick to take an almost imperceptible step away from me. But even as he draws back, he interrupts my thoughts to dangle an intriguing prospect.

"This will be the last of them," he says, throwing his hands up. "If you do not find a woman to your liking, I will resign myself as having failed in this regard, and we will abandon it."

I eye him suspiciously. Renwick is persistent to a fault. He is not one to admit defeat lightly. If he is conceding, he must feel truly confident in his selection. Or he has grown tired of playing matchmaker for the Demon of La Luna.

Evalina spins on me, eager for an answer, and they both stare at me, eyes wide, mouths open, waiting for the next words to come out of my mouth.

And they have the nerve to label me *a child?*

I heave a sigh, resigning myself to another night of misery.

"Very well." I groan, rolling my eyes in defeat.

"Oh, thank you, sire! I—"

"But!" I interject, not bothering to read his lips. "I will not meet with them all. If I do not see one that interests me, we will abandon this foolish plan, you will not speak to me of a bride again, and we will take whatever fury the nine houses offer us."

"Yes, yes, of course," Renwick mutters between swift bows.

He retreats, scurrying back to whatever dark corner of the castle he spends his time muttering in.

"Are you truly going to consider a bride?" Evalina asks as soon as Renwick is out of sight.

"No," I answer without thought.

Memories dredge up from the place I've buried them.

Women trampling one another as they aim for the door. A Satúran woman shoving a small Uranian to the floor as they scramble over each other. Both of them screaming as the guards reach out to calm them. I could not hear them. But the strain on their faces is forever burned into my memory.

I don't need even a second to consider it. I do not have the patience to watch some woman cowering at my feet for the rest of my days.

I push a hand through my hair, gripping my right horn and

pulling on it as though it may help free the images from my mind. But it's no use. And I am bound to endure it once more. But *only* once more.

Evalina is frowning at me, waiting for me to elaborate, and I offer her a simple response, "*I am willing to play Renwick's game for one more evening if it means I never have to discuss it again.*"

She hoists an eyebrow as she brushes her stark-white braids over her shoulder. I can't remember what the beads in her hair sound like when they clink together, but I know they do.

"*Any progress with the charge?*" I ask, hoping to turn the conversation elsewhere.

A grim look settles on her face, and she doesn't need to say anything more.

The giant solar energy charge has claimed at least one life each night since it appeared three months ago. Its wild power lashes out each time we draw near, and those that are not burned to death, soon fall victim to the sickness.

"*How many?*" I ask.

"*Another two, just yesterday. One was lost to a seeker. They've been more active the past week. Bolder. The other...the other was hit by a flare. He was crisped within an inch of his life. Mother couldn't save him,*" Evalina signs the words with finality, and I can see the pain on her face as she forms the final sentence with her fingers.

"And the border wall?" I ask.

"*It continues to erode. At least a foot each day. The sunlight is pushing hard on the southeastern border. Less so to the northeast.*" Her debrief provides an easy distraction from the loss of more legionnaires, and the sadness lifts from her eyes a little. "*But the Council is ignorant to it.*"

"Or they are complicit," I counter. "They have already denied us aid when it comes to the charge. They are too fearful of the Serpent to act against him. Or perhaps they wish to see Luna fall," I muse. "Why else enforce an ancient mandate that my own Father refused to uphold? They are looking for excuses to bring the Lunar people to their knees. We are the only house that still stands openly against the Serpent. They are fearful of "the demon" and the trouble I may start."

Evalina nods. *"Either way, the Serpent isn't moving slowly. He will strike soon,"* she adds.

"In the northeast," I decide.

"The wall is strong there. They wouldn't—"

"The southeastern border will fall, but it will not be for the Solarian army. It will be a diversion. One that will occupy our time if we let it. We will need to evacuate the southern border towns. See if the riders can push the seeker packs north. When the time comes, the sunseekers may be an ally to the night."

Evalina chews on her lip in heavy contemplation. *"And if the charge can't be moved before the Serpent comes knocking?"* she asks. *"The legion is not ready. We need more time."*

I almost hate how easily she considers this possibility. Father had dedicated his reign to bringing the Serpent to his knees. He'd staked his life and his sanity on that single goal. In the end, he'd lost them both. He'd become obsessive, paranoid, and reckless, burdened by the sickness. His mania had walked him right into death's hands. Into *the Serpent's* hands.

My gaze narrows as I realize the very thing we need is well within my grasp. Thanks to Renwick, of all people.

The Serpent will come for La Luna. Of this, I am sure. What matters most is when. Our greatest resource is now our most precious—time. And a queen on the throne of La Luna may hold the Serpent off for a while. If we are no longer in violation of the treaty, perhaps the Council will not turn a blind eye.

Evalina stares at me as I weigh my own peace against the peace of my people. But it's hardly a fair fight. They will win every time. And Father's sacrifice shall not be a price paid in vain.

My head feels heavy as I resign myself to doing my duty.

"If time is what we need, then I shall grant us more."

CHAPTER 3

CELESTE

ays without light—sun, moon, or flame—have made me irritable, and the stiffness of my saddle has pressed my patience to its limit. So when the Lunar scouts rip me from Strega's back without warning, I have to clench my fists to keep from singeing their fingers off.

The scouts had descended on us no less than ten seconds after we exited the forest. From their position in the watch towers, we didn't stand a chance. They spotted us before I even heard the first arrow knock into place. And I wasn't so arrogant as to believe we could outpace them, not after the journey we'd had.

The seekers had been on us from the start. The moment we set foot across the darkened border they were circling. They kept out of sight for the first few days, hiding in the thick shadows, waiting to see if they could make a meal of us. At least, it felt like a few days. I couldn't be sure of time's passage once we crossed into the dark.

The forest was shrouded in a magic unlike any I'd ever seen. It was quiet and heavy, so heavy I could feel it sitting on my skin, coating me like a balm. I might've found it calming were it not for the constant chatter of unseen creatures and their disembodied calls. Always coming from just over your shoulder but utterly invisible in the thick night. I'm not sure the others noticed. But I could feel them watching us from deep within the shadows.

Eventually, Kefu's soldiers began to disappear, plucked from their saddles without a sound, only for their bodies to turn up a few yards ahead of us, drained of all light.

It was over after that. Once the seekers had acquired a taste for our light, there wasn't a moment's rest.

I'd heard stories of the sunseekers. Haunting tales that mothers tell their children to warn them against the Lunar territories. But nothing had prepared me for how wrong they were.

The seekers were monstrous, yes, but much more lethal than I'd imagined.

At least fifteen hands high with paws like hounds, bigger than the mitt of a goliath bear. Broad shoulders and heads as wide as crates meant they dwarf the average man, making us all easy prey. But their size was nothing in comparison to their gruesome faces. If you can call them faces.

Long, narrow skulls and hollowed eyes. Gaping jaws, dripping with saliva as they screech into the night air. And grotesque teeth, long and pointed, coated in blood. All of it covered in a coarse black fur that made them impossible to spot.

More than once, I was forced to show my light in order to find the wretched beasts and sever their heads from their horrid bodies.

They'd come racing through our formation, moving like shadows. The flash of white teeth and the ear-piercing howls serving as our only warning.

In the end, Raye and I were the only ones to make it through, and it wasn't until the canopy began to thin and the moonlight started to trickle through the trees that the seekers pulled back, too fearful of Luna's light to push onward. But even we did not make it out unscathed.

"Who are you?" the Lunar scout shouts in my face.

"For what are you here?" another demands.

More voices shout at me as I'm forced down into the wet grass by two meaty hands. My knees buckle under my weight as they push me to kneel, jerking my hands behind my back. Blades are unsheathed, and I smother my instinct as a scout holds one to my neck in a silent threat. Though the viper in me stirs, I do not fight their hold. My eyes are too busy searching.

Suri stands a few feet away with an empty saddle. I strain to peer past my periphery, too mindful of the cool blade pressing into my skin to risk turning my head.

"*Raye?*" I shout, ignoring the demanding voices still cutting through the midnight air. "Raye!"

"I'm alright!" she answers.

Her words are sure, but I can hear the strain in her voice and chance a quick glance at her.

Three scouts—two men and one woman—are pinning her to the earth in a similar fashion, except the woman is gripping Raye by the hair, forcing her face into the moonlight. There's a bruise blossoming on her cheek and blood running down the front of her skirt, but I know both are from our last encounter with the seekers and not these ill-mannered Lunars. Her eyes swim with emotion, but I can see that it isn't fear. If I know her well enough, and I'm certain I do, it's anger.

My suspicion is confirmed when the female scout's face curls into a raging snarl, and her blade presses closer to Raye's neck. The scout begins to shout in Luneer, and my mind tries to keep up with her threats, but I lose track after she lets loose a string of foreign curses.

"Raye!" I snap. "Control your emotions before she cuts off your head!"

"I'm trying!" she hollers back, but then I hear her choke as the woman tightens her hold, and she quiets, quelling her magic so it isn't spilling out of her in every direction.

A scout drops in front of me, crouching in the grass and jabbing me hard in the chest to get my attention. His moonlit eyes look at me in question, and I take it he cannot follow my speech as easily as I can follow theirs.

Good.

"Raye, don't say a word. I will handle this. Just calm yourself!"

She doesn't respond, and I assume her scouts are not as forgiving as mine.

But I speak too soon.

The man in front of me jabs me in the shoulder, this time with the tip of his blade, and I can feel the little nick in my skin as my light rushes to soothe it. I try to stifle it, but before I can smother it, it shines across my chest on its journey toward the wound. The scout jerks back, falling flat onto his ass with wide eyes.

"Solerrjio!" he shouts, waving his blade at me.

That seems to agitate the others, and the cool hands gripping my arms yank me to my feet. But my left leg went numb hours ago, so they're forced to take some of my weight to keep me standing.

"You have purpose in forest?" the scout asks, rising from the earth, his black canvas uniform now caked in mud.

His words come out slightly broken, and I can see most of his scouts don't understand the common tongue. But no one inter-jects. He must be their commanding officer. The one who needs convincing.

Not a problem. I know Luneer.

Rather, I did.

All vipers are trained in all ten celestial languages, but, as with any skill, it requires upkeep. And unsurprisingly, I've never needed Luneer before this night. So my mind struggles to find the words, and I fear my body is working too hard to keep up with the phys-ical toll to spare even a second for my thoughts.

"Unejelo," I say, trying to find the word for "bride" in Luneer.

The man frowns, and I don't think I've chosen correctly.

"Union?" he asks, thickly accented.

Not quite. But I nod.

"Yerro. Ya a la unejelo puro ze regerrino." *Yes. I am a union for the king.* I'm not sure my syntax is correct, but some of the soldiers seem to agree with me as they grunt their ascent.

Their leader peers behind me, glancing at his clansmen, unsure.

Before I can attempt to convince him, they begin arguing with each other. One of them wants to take us to their general. Another wants to place us in the dungeons. One wants to escort us to the village and send us on our way.

For a moment, I say nothing. But then the woman holding Raye suggests they send us back through the forest, and I thrash against my captors. The forest is out of the question.

Lie. The Serpent's voice hisses, and the viper in me is called up with little effort.

I muster up an innocent, pleading look as I beg.

"Tameda mo la regerrino." *Take me to the king.* I ensure my voice is soft and do my best to bring tears to my eyes. When the scout in front of me doesn't immediately yield, I manage to squeeze one free.

"Pejalo. Pejalo." *Please. Please.* I plead.

His thick brows draw together, and it takes a minute before he lowers his blade and the heated words stop flying. I hold my breath as we all wait for his decision. Eventually, he sighs in defeat.

Pulling Raye to her feet, they drag us toward the castle in the distance. Raye stumbles as the scouts set a fast pace, and my own feet struggle to stay beneath me as I'm dragged across the earth. The other scouts continue to grumble about their leader's choice, but he keeps our party pointed firmly in the direction of the castle, and I'm glad he happens to be the one with sense.

Castle La Luna sits like a large stone on the face of the horizon, grey and salient. Its towering spires and pointed arches jut into the night sky, lit only by the blue tint of moonlight. From the valley where we stand, it looks rather haunting. But as we draw closer, its façade softens, and the ornate stones and intricately carved stained-glass windows seem to add a dark charm to its presence.

Its shadowed exterior is nothing like the brightly gilded ornament of my family's palace. And not for the first time since I stepped into the dark realm of Luna, I find myself missing the Sun.

Our captors haul us up the castle steps before dragging us through several moonlit corridors and across an open-air catwalk, where they burst through towering double doors. The hinges groan as they swing open wide, and the image waiting on the other side is an odd one.

Women of every shade and shape stand shoulder-to-shoulder facing the front of the room, where a big, black cloud that moves like smoke sits floating a few feet in front of them. It shrinks and expands before them, breathing, and as I take my first steps into the room, it seems to swell to twice its size.

The women shift uncomfortably, eyeing the dark cloud, too nervous to look over their shoulders. I take a tentative step, my captor's hand still latched firmly around my upper arm, but I stop when I hear the heavy doors close with an echoing thud. Raye's muffled shouts filtering through the cracks.

"Sunspots!" I curse, twisting in his grip. But Raye is already gone from view.

"Found this one at the border," the scout says in smooth Luneer, yanking me forward. "Came bursting through the trees like a nighthound. Claims she is to be a 'union' to the king."

My Luneer may be rusty, but there is no mistaking the disbelief in his voice as he chuckles at my foolishness.

"Does she now?" a man answers in the common tongue, so I, too, can hear his skepticism.

He's tall and skinny, older, but bright-eyed and loud. And when he speaks, the soldiers all turn to listen.

He is of some importance then, an advisor perhaps.

He stands against the wall closest to the cloud, which is now moving in a quiet frenzy—shadows and smoke swirling along the floor and reaching toward the row of women. Some of whom scramble backward before the black tendrils can reach them. Others squirm and flinch but keep their feet planted.

I stumble as the scout hauls me toward the front of the room, lacking the grace the Serpent drilled into me as my left leg now feels like a phantom limb. I can see it beneath my skirt, peeking out of the high slit, and I know it's holding me up, but I can't feel anything below my hip. And I'm only able to take a few shuffled steps before a loud, deep voice rings out through the vaulted chamber.

"Release her!" it demands. The heavy voice shouts, like a drum coming from seemingly everywhere all at once.

The scout stops just short of the women, still standing stiff as weed stalks facing the cloud. His grip loosens, but his fingers don't leave my skin, and I contemplate sending my light to the surface to burn his hand away but side against it. It would not aid in my mission for me to behave so boldly.

"I will not repeat myself, captain." The voice comes again, but I can hear its origins this time.

A few feet in front of me, shrouded in night, the cloud speaks.

Had I encountered a poison of some kind in the forest? Certainly there is no land where dark clouds speak their thunder like men.

"*Now!*" the cloud roars. It shudders and shifts, and I am sure I've not succumbed to some sickness when the other women flinch.

I understand now why they are so silent.

They are fearful of the dark essence swirling before their eyes. Whatever magic it is, it is quite unique. I can almost taste it rolling through the air. Like sun chilis and cinnamon, sweet but spicy. And I absently wonder if it is warm to the touch.

My escort thrusts me into line, wedging me between a slim Mercurian woman and an emerald-eyed Terrarian before making a hasty retreat. The women don't take kindly to my intrusion, and

I'm met with a look of disdain cold enough to strike a Uranian dead.

Vicious creatures, these women.

But I've seen worse.

Glancing down the line, it looks as though a representative of every house has been collected for the prince's selection. A plump Nepturian woman with eyes blue as the Nepathesian Sea heads the line. Following her is a short woman with the telltale signs of Mercury in her blood—eyes and hair as grey as smoke. Beside her is a set of Venutian twins with the same soft, amber skin stretched over identical slender frames. Then there's the Mercurian woman beside me, followed by myself and the Terrarian. A Jupe, a Lunar, and a Martian stand at the other end, shifting and whispering with one another. And a woman of House Satúrn, doused in thick gold bands running up her wrists and neck, marks the end of our line.

Ordinarily, I wouldn't be concerned with the other women. My viper's skill is well-honed, and it has yet to fail me when luring in a mark, but tonight, I fear it will not be enough. Each of them is well-polished, beautiful, and soft, as the Serpent would have me appear. Whereas I look as if I've been run through the mud. Because I have.

Dirt cakes my skirt about a foot up from the hem, blood has crusted the thin fabric to the back of my left calf, and a healthy dose of sweat covers my chest, back, and arms. I wouldn't be surprised if I were standing here with dirt smeared across my face.

I hardly look like the lady I am meant to be.

I cringe inwardly, rubbing my knee, and I'm only mildly surprised when I find it's still there.

The room is empty save for the women, the cloud, and a few soldiers idling in the corners. Light pours in through the glass ceiling, beaming down onto the shadowy cloud but unable to penetrate. Looking at it, I'm reminded of the thick, black night of the Night Forest, and a chill sprints from my head to my toes as I try to smother the memories.

But even as I try, I can't help but stare at it. The inky center, the languid tendrils whipping through the air like solar flares, even the smoky essence creeping across the floor toward my feet. All of it is somehow mesmerizing, and I'm drawn into the void at the center, only to be shocked when I discover two pale blue eyes staring back at me.

They blink—*watching*.

My head swivels to look at the other women, but most of them have their eyes trained on the floor, and the ones who don't are watching the tendrils curl through the air before they shrink back into the darkness.

When I turn back to peer into the void, the eyes are still there, but their subtle glow seems lighter. *Amused*, I'd say, if a cloud can be amused.

A deep chuckle sounds from the center, rising to the rafters as the cloud thins into a sheer haze. Through it, I watch the eyes just as they watch me.

Its gaze fixes on me as the air before my eyes clears. The shadows retreat, sliding back into their place of origin, while some settle in the unlit corners of the room and others pool along the floor. When the haze finally dissolves, I can see the piercing blue eyes aren't just floating in the smoke but sit proudly in the striking, chiseled face of a figure shrouded in night.

A man—no, a demon—sits atop a moonstone throne. Perched along the arm with a black boot propped on the seat and an elbow resting on his knee, staring at me. And I cannot control the shock that washes over me.

Prince Apollo, The Demon of La Luna, is thoroughly inhuman.

I understand why he doesn't sit on his throne correctly. He is much too large for the simply carved seat. His shoulders are broad as a nightshade tree, and his arms look like two solar canons, casting heavy shadows over his throne as he shifts. His legs are long, and I can see his well-muscled thighs through the simple black fabric he wears. Even seated, he may be taller than me, especially if I were to count his horns.

They sit on his head, curling out from his hairline and arching back abruptly before rising to a point like twin towers. The bases lie hidden in a head full of thick, black curls. So thick I can hardly see the silver glinting off his crown, wedged at an angle between his horns as if he'd slapped it on in a hurry.

A black-tipped tail swishes idly through the space behind him, and polished, black claws cap his fingers where the shadows pour free from his palms. A warm, brown complexion surrounds his soft, blue eyes, and I watch them move up and down my body as a small smile creeps across his full lips, revealing the points of gleaming white fangs.

He is beautiful. But he is also the subject of so many stories. So many warnings.

He is a demon, as they say.

Although, if he is a demon, Venus must be the devil.

A shoulder knocks into me, nearly taking me to the floor, and I wobble to find my balance, cursing my lifeless leg. My head whips around for the culprit, only to see the space beside me has been deserted. It is then I realize that the other women are screaming.

CHAPTER 4

APOLLO

———

The women have already begun to panic. As I knew they would. I cannot hear their screams, but I can see their tear-streaked faces and gaping mouths clearly under the moonlight. Several of them reach for each other's hands. Even as they stand beside strangers, their fear tells them to seek comfort in numbers.

The Martian woman is first to find her bearings. She thinks quickly, using her magic to bring forth a flame in the palm of her hand. She holds it out threateningly, even as my soldiers and I remain where we've been from the start. No one moves to cage them. In fact, I can see Renwick waving a hand for the guards to open the doors so the women may flee.

He looks disappointed that he's lost his own game. But I cannot be bothered to care. All I care about is that I no longer have to play. So, I merely watch and wait.

One of the Venutian twins collapses into a pile, and the other rushes to fan her face—her amber coloring having turned the same pallid shade as her eyes. *Shock*. The Terrarian, much too small for me to begin with, jerks back as a ringing tone breaks free from her throat. *Fear.* The Uranian clamors over one of the others as she turns for the door, fleeing from the creature before them. *Panic.*

It is a near replica of every evening prior, and my shadows grow agitated as I'm forced to sit through this spectacle once more. But just as I consider abandoning them to their terror, I notice her. The dirt-covered Solarian standing in the center like a beacon amongst the chaos.

Her light hums low near the surface of her skin, though I don't think it is intentional. It seems to react as she takes in the sights around her. But she smothers it the next moment, dropping to the ground to aid the fallen Venutian woman. A soldier also steps forward, but the waking twin begins to shout and cry in fear. I open my mouth to command the legionnaire leave them be, but my words are quickly made redundant as the bright-eyed Solarian snaps at him to give them space. Her words seem to cut harshly enough that my soldier does not hesitate to retreat, and I wonder what she's said.

I watch her for some time, silently observing.

She looks weary and exhausted. And filthy. Covered in dirt and sweat. Not to mention she walks with a curious limp. Her left leg steps in time with the other, but she hesitates when she sets her foot to the ground, as if she cannot trust it to hold her up. The image of Everet, my scouts' captain, dragging her through the throne room makes my shadows stir, and suddenly I'm frustrated with his handling of her. But I cannot blame his instinct. Were I him, I would have done the same.

Although looking at her, I don't know that this is true.

Her eyes had found mine almost immediately. Not the floor or my shadows, but my eyes. As if she was searching through my magic to find its source. And when she'd seen it, she hadn't let go.

I'd expected her to shy away from me. Even now, I expect her to run sprinting from the hall, but as the Venutian twins rise from the floor to exit, she turns to me with a question on her fine lips.

"What is the meaning of this?" she demands, holding out an arm to the now empty room.

The other women have all gone, no doubt shouting of demons as they flee into the night.

My first thought is to inform her she has not been granted permission to speak in my court, but the words don't reach my tongue. Instead, I find myself wondering if she has an accent. I can read her words well enough, but some of them sit close together in her mouth, and I'm curious about the sound.

She stands there a moment, expecting, and Renwick moves to speak in my place as he usually does, but I hold up a hand.

"You may run now," I growl at her, waving a claw toward the door. "My people will not drag you back."

"That's very kind of you. But I have no intention of trekking back through your forest anytime soon," she says haughtily, though I have a distinct impression that I am missing a tone, and I bare my fangs at her.

She is too bold.

"Are you not concerned that I may devour you whole?" I ask, aiming to intimidate by rising from my seat.

Her brows lift, unable to hide the spark of excitement in her eyes. I think I can see the light sweeping across them, but as quickly as it came, it is gone, receding into a warm flame that flickers beneath the surface. Like the Sun herself has chosen to settle behind her lids.

"I can assure you I am not an easy one to swallow," she bites back, and I can't help the grin that settles on my face.

"I do not doubt it," I say, moving a few paces closer.

I consider her a moment.

She is lovely beneath the layer of sweat and dirt. Tall and bronzed with thick hips and thighs and eyes like the deepest sunset.

It's been over one hundred years since I've seen the Sun. Since their serpent retreated from our borders to slither back into his hole and plot against Mother Luna for another night. But I still remember its rays. The red-orange hue, the warmth weaving through the air. It was mesmerizing at a time. But now, the image in my mind only serves as a reminder of what the Serpent stole from me. Yet, I cannot deny this woman before me is radiant.

Her skirt rests low on her hips, and a thin gold chain hangs around her waist, nesting in the curve of her body with little charms dotting her midriff. Her hair is like a halo surrounding her face, big and curly, with bits of sunlight moving through it. Her brown skin, a few shades darker than mine, looks lit from within, and there's a heavy divot at the crest of her lips that I want very badly to press my finger into.

But there is something else in her eyes as she holds my gaze. Something treacherous that keeps my feet planted. Something daring that I don't find in many.

Defiance.

She is working hard to hide it. But I can see it in the flame-like flicker of her eyes and the way she holds her shoulders. A challenge swimming through her. One I don't have the time to work out of her.

But surely defiance is preferable to fear? To dragging a woman kicking and screaming to the altar.

A battle begins inside me as I look at her. Sense and lust war with one another.

She is beautiful and dangerous—just like I like them.

She will be too troublesome, my logic responds.

As if you would have it any other way, the demon in me answers.

I turn my back on her to face Father's empty throne. It sits sentinel, soaking in the moonlight, and I decide it looks better this way. The smooth, white moonstone unencumbered by my shadow.

What would Father do? Would he take her? Would he risk our people?

I don't need to ask his spirit to know he wouldn't. He was only permitted to remain unwed due to the Council's cowardice. But Father and I are not the same, I remind myself. The Council will not grant the grace of kings to a demon such as I.

I know this. Renwick knows this. And as I see Evalina standing beside the soldiers who have placed their lives in our hands, my choice is made.

I make my retreat, calling out to Evalina with a pointed shadow, "Bring her!"

CHAPTER 5

CELESTE

Shadows cloud around the prince as he moves past the throne into a darkened doorway, and I hardly have time to gather myself before a woman, tall and broad, with a face to rival Venus, steps in front of me.

Her hand wraps around my arm, jerking me forward. But I've had quite enough of being yanked around, so I keep my feet planted as she pulls at me. Her eyes betray her irritation as she tries to will me into compliance, but intimidation is a man's weakness, so we both stand staring at one another until she decides to speak.

"Follow me," she demands, turning on her heel and sweeping a dark cape behind her.

After mindlessly following the scouts and not knowing where Raye's gone, I'm tempted to press her for information. But my entire body aches. The parts of me that aren't numb are now sore from clinging to Strega's wide body, and I'm forced to focus my energy on placing one foot in front of the other.

The woman moves quickly, skirting around great stone pillars, rushing me toward some unknown end, but I keep pace as best I can, only slowing when we come across another open-air catwalk. It is similar to the one I'd crossed with the scouts, but this one faces west, and as we cross over to another wing, I can see the Moon sinking beneath the horizon in the distance. Her light shines bright, catching on the woman's brown skin, where it seems to melt into her like mine does when I step into the Sun. The silvery-white light streaks down her bejeweled braids, and little silver moons and stars hang from her strands, twinkling as the moonlight moves over them. But I hardly have time to take it in before she jerks me forward, forcing me onward.

Keeping myself upright is an answered prayer as we pass through the dimly lit corridors. More than once, I reach for the stone walls to steady myself, though I don't think the woman notices as she carries on in front of me, not caring whether I fall behind. From the looks she's tossing over her shoulder, I suspect she would not mind if I were to become lost and swallowed up by the darkness.

We carry on in tense silence, passing through the empty hallways. Each of them growing darker with the setting Moon. I mark the path we take along with any exterior doors I happen to see. This deep into the castle, there doesn't appear to be many, which makes the information that much more precious.

Eventually, we reach the end of a long hallway that opens into a small, circular vestibule with a set of large, wooden doors at the opposite end. The woman stops just short of the doorway and waves me forward.

"Go on," she snaps, and my fingers itch for the blade I keep tucked into my bodice.

I must idle too long for her liking because she groans dramatically and takes the handles in a firm grip, swinging them open so hard they bounce back a few inches when they meet the wall on the other side.

Before I can move my feet, she snatches my wrist and tugs me forward, thrusting me into the dimly lit room.

My eyes work to adjust, and when they do, my stomach lurches into my throat, squeezing itself into the small space and rendering me mute.

I was expecting a parlor, or a study, or even a cell behind these doors, not the warmth of a bedchamber. And certainly not one with the distinct marks of occupancy.

Blankets and furs are piled atop a four-poster bed three times the size of my own. Parchment is strewn about on every surface, some with hurried scribbles, others left blank, while some lie crumpled on the floor. A woolen cloak rests haphazardly over a well-worn, velvet armchair—the back embroidered with a midnight-colored thread in the shape of an embellished A.

His cloak. His things. *His* bedchamber.

A loud voice snaps me out of my gawking. "Ah!" The tall, slender man from the throne room steps forward, his high-pitched tone sharp on my ears. "Here she is. Miss..."

"Celeste Solém of House Solaria," I declare, dipping my head.

"Right, yes. Lady Solém."

He butchers my name, pronouncing it "solemn," while he waves a wistful hand in my direction as if presenting a prized pony. I have half a mind to be offended before I remember, that's precisely what I am, and this surname is not even mine.

"May I present to you Prince Apollo Alceline of House Luna."

A dark figure moves in my periphery and Prince Apollo steps out of the thick shadows coating the far corner of the room, emerging from the darkness as if he's only just materialized this very second. He stands beside the man, arms crossed, his expression indignant as he watches me.

Immediately, I assume the position. The position I'm meant to play, that is. The gentle lady come to La Luna to offer her hand in marriage. Though I fear nothing can remedy the impression I've left in the throne room.

I drop my head, folding my hands over my chest as I struggle to bend at the knees, mimicking the traditional Lunar greeting as best I can.

Honor him. The little voice in my head commands, and I abide.

My Luneer comes quite slowly, the words trickling down from the far reaches of my mind to supply me with an adequate greeting.

"Yéva malléjéro," I speak softly toward the floor—*your highness.* "Avé na herama." *I am honored.*

Somewhere above me, an amused snort sounds in response, but I don't dare lift my head. I know without looking who stands over me. His heavy booted feet disrupt my line of sight as his big body blots out what little light there is, looming above me like a dark cloud.

I wait for the instruction to rise, but it doesn't come, and my back begins to ache as my left leg threatens to collapse under the weight of my submission.

"Lady Solém," he says, quietly correcting the slim man's pronunciation as he speaks my name with a perfect accent. "Welcome to Castle La Luna. You may stand," he declares, and I hate that my balance wavers as I straighten.

I reach out a hand to steady myself, but before I can latch onto something, Prince Apollo steps in close, gripping me just above the elbow and propping me up. His big hand grasps my upper arm with ease, his fingers meeting on either side as I pitch forward into his chest. My eyes dart up to his face, and he's glaring at me over his wide nose, the wild sea of blue raging with some unspoken frustration as he looks at me.

Who is he to be frustrated? Since I set foot in these territories, I have been grabbed at by every passing person. If anyone is to be frustrated, it is me. The viper, suddenly caged like a bird.

I wrench my arm free. Or rather, I try to. But his grip is unparalleled, and his fingers press into my skin so hard I know they'll leave bruises. He could tear my arm clean from its socket if he truly wanted to.

Speed and surprise will be my allies, I think to myself. *When the time comes.*

His grip doesn't loosen as he rights me, and he doesn't try to separate me from his chest as he holds me by the arm. The deep vibration of his voice moves across my skin, rippling out from where our bodies touch as he mutters, "Leave us."

The woman and the slim man stand frowning, mouths half open as they prepare to question him, but he doesn't give them a chance.

"Now!" he shouts.

The slim man leaves without further issue, but the woman takes a moment to speak her mind, and my head cranes to look at Prince Apollo, stealing a glance while he is otherwise occupied.

His horns are taller than they appeared at a distance, sharpened to a point I couldn't see. They look to be the same material as his claws, which I'm now intimately aware are currently poking into my skin. I squirm a little, but his hold doesn't change.

"I know that Evalina, but you may speak your mind later," he says through gritted teeth. Pinned to his chest I cannot see the woman, but I can see Prince Apollo's eyes heat with anger. "Yes. Fine. Now get out," he speaks again, even though she doesn't say anything in return.

His thick lips flatten as he watches her leave, slamming the door shut behind her.

He releases me suddenly, dropping my arm the way one would drop hot coals—quickly, and with little regard for where they will fall.

"Sit," he orders, peering down at me with his arms crossed.

"Pardon?" I ask, aiming for amenable but feeling the irritation slip in anyway.

I'm not accustomed to taking orders from anyone other than

the Serpent. So it takes another try before I realize that, though *I* am not one to obey readily, Lady *Solém* is.

"Sit. Down." He grunts at me, and if I'm not mistaken, there is a low growl churning in his chest. But before I can take even a single step, he barks, "Never mind. I will do it myself."

I don't get the chance to ask him what he means before shadows surge from the floor and sweep my legs out from under me, sending me tumbling. My body twists instinctually, preparing for the blow and ensuring my butt takes the brunt of it. My light rises to the surface as I reach out a hand to break my fall, but before I can meet the floor, I realize I'm not falling at all—I'm floating.

Prince Apollo's shadows are moving across my body like the enchanted vines in Terra. Cool tendrils lace around my legs, thighs, and waist, propping me up in an odd, seated position before carrying me across the room and planting me firmly in the center of the big bed. My body sinks as his shadows squeeze out from under me, leaving me to be swallowed by the plush fabrics as he comes to stand before me.

I sit up to stare at him slack-jawed.

Does no one in this castle understand the concept of bodily autonomy?

In answer to my silent question, Prince Apollo unleashes another shadow. It moves like an appendage, drifting up my ankle to lift the frayed hem of my skirt and baring my legs to the moonlight.

"Hey!" I blurt, pushing the fabric down between my thighs, but he pays me no mind.

Instead, his eyes glance up at the ceiling.

"What have I done to deserve this?" he asks of the air, and I have to bite my cheek to keep my sharp words from spilling out. "The seekers must have been quite elated," he says as he settles on the edge of the bed to pull my boot from my left foot. "It has been a long while since they've seen the light of the Sun. Seems they were not fast enough for you, though." His lip curls as he rotates my leg, revealing the wide swath of blood staining my skirt and the claw marks running up the back.

I suck in a sharp breath at the sight, completely ignoring his dark essence coursing up my leg.

I knew I'd caught a stray claw in our last encounter with the seekers, but I hadn't thought much of it. The pain had subsided almost immediately, and I figured it was no more than a scratch. But looking at it now, it is much more than that. The claw marks are crusted and jagged, skin held together by mere threads as my light works to repair the damage.

"Heavens," I whisper under my breath as I watch the angry cuts bleed into the sheets. I lift my leg, trying to spare the delicate fabric, but another low growl bubbles out of Prince Apollo, and I still as he grumbles, "Do not move."

I obey. But only because trying to keep my lifeless limb lifted proves to be more difficult than I'd expected.

My eyes find his face, and I'm surprised to see him sneering back at me like he'd rather the seeker had just eaten me whole. Though, I suppose I shouldn't be. Our people have a troubled history. My very presence is proof that the conflict continues. Really, I should be more surprised the scouts hadn't taken my head at the border.

Prince Apollo wraps his finger around my ankle without warning, squeezing, testing.

"I can't feel that," I tell him.

He ignores me—*the brute*—and I resist the urge to kick him as his hand moves higher.

"Can you move your toes?" he asks.

I wiggle them dutifully, and his brows turn down, disappointed. Or confused? I cannot tell. He's baring his fangs in the direction of my leg, but the gesture is rather inhuman, so I can't be sure what it's meant to tell me.

"Huh." He grunts. "Can you feel this?" he asks, squeezing around my shin.

His eyes lift to my face and settle directly on my lips, staring unabashedly.

Typical. Prince, demon, or otherwise, they're all the same, I remind myself.

"No," I say simply, too afraid I will shout at him for his poor attitude if I keep speaking.

He nods, heavy horns ducking toward my head, and moves his hand higher. It wraps around my knee, and he squeezes again.

"Tell me when the numbness ends," he demands, not waiting for my agreement before moving up, up, up until he is clasping my bare thigh. My light follows close behind, chasing after him should action be needed, but I dampen it.

Instead, I watch him closely as he pushes past the slit in my skirt to squeeze my hip. His thumb rests near the joint as his claws prod me, sending a shiver running through my stomach. I jolt, startled by the cool sensation of his skin and the surprisingly gentle touch.

"Your magic must be quite strong," he says when he finally releases me. "Your entire leg should be dead by now. But since it is not yet paralyzed, I take it your magic is working hard in your favor."

"Sorry to disappoint you," I say before my sense can catch up with me.

He jerks back as if I've slapped him, and the angry sneer turning up his face shifts into an almost inhuman snarl.

"I would not wish a seeker's death upon anyone," he corrects me. "They are violent, stupid creatures. It is not a peaceful way to go. I am merely surprised you made it here with nothing more than a scratch."

My eyes drop to my lap. He's right. Kefu and his men had suffered. I can still hear their screams ringing in my ears when I focus on the memory.

"It was not without sacrifice," I say. "Many men gave their light to see me here." My mind flashes images of bodies scattered across the moss, Raye pinned beneath a seeker, hollowed eyes staring at me as it charges forward, and I blink hard, trying to clear it.

"That is unfortunate," Prince Apollo says, resting his hand on my knee. I wait for the inflection of sarcasm, but it doesn't come, and I think for a moment that perhaps this brute is not so brutish. "Though, you should not have been in my forest to begin with," he adds, proving me wrong almost instantly.

"*Your* forest?" I ask, doing my best for a neutral tone.

"Yes. It is within my borders, is it not? Or are your people so used to ignoring those that you've forgotten."

I almost laugh. Not because I find him clever. But because my loss of blood must be turning my mind. How foolish of me to think this demon would hold an ounce of kindness simply because he does not chase women into the night. Especially for a Solarian.

I jerk my leg back, unable to withstand his nearness, and he snarls at me, face all fangs as he pushes to his feet.

"I will send a healer for you. Then you may be on your way," he says.

Fool! Do not push him to discard you! The Serpent's voice scolds in my mind.

"No, wait!" I plead, but Prince Apollo does not slow.

"I have no desire for a woman who is fearful of me," he says, turning for the door with clenched fists.

Immediately I move to my feet, scooting toward the edge of his bed in a rush.

"Please, don't," I beg. But he pays me no mind. "Forgive me. It has been quite an evening. Please." I repeat, swinging myself down from his mountain of a bed, only to knock into a small table beside the armchair. It topples with a dull thud, and the inkwell perched on top comes crashing to the floor, shattering across the stone and sending ink pooling into the finely woven rug.

Fool! The Serpent curses me once more, and I can almost feel the sting of a blade as I recall the Serpent's punishment for my mistake.

But when Prince Apollo shows no reaction to the shattering glass, I think perhaps I am not a fool.

"Your majesty?" I call. But he doesn't react. He does not start, nor does he turn. His muscles don't even tense with acknowledgment.

"Prince Apollo?"

I watch him reach for the door undisturbed and decide to test my theory. If it proves to be true, perhaps it will give me the leverage I need. If not, then perhaps he will just think I've gone mad.

I drop my fist to the floor, slamming it down into the stone three times, hard. My wrist twinges with each blow, but it is worth it the moment he spins on me. His eyes narrow on my face, the table, and then the ink.

Kneeling before the black puddle, I mutter my apology, "Please, forgive me." Then I sign it to be sure.

Please, forgive me.

Prince Apollo's eyes fill with blackness, swallowing the soft blue color as his shadows rise to the surface of his skin. And before another word can leave my lips, the room plunges into darkness.

CHAPTER 6

APOLLO

—

*D*amned.

It takes nearly all of my strength not to speak the word aloud. But there is no other word for it. I am positive Luna has forsaken me. Positive she has damned me to the darkness. Cursed me beyond measure.

Why else would she place such a creature in my path? Why bring me something I cannot have? Have I not suffered enough already?

Celeste's eyes are shining up at me, and her beautiful mouth hangs open as my shadows draw tight around her throat, forcing the air from her lungs. Her hair hangs around her softly rounded face, framing her warm eyes, and I watch her light rise to the surface, illuminating the space between us.

She's stunning. Even trussed up in my shadows, she is stunning—her soft golden light mixing with my magic as it twists across her brown skin. The sight is almost enough to make me forget her words. Or rather, her signs.

My mind nearly cracked in two when I watched her hands

moving in the familiar gestures. For a singular second, it was a sweet relief. I thought Luna had perhaps forgiven me for the demon that I am, dropping a treasure into my lap. A woman who does not flee from me and one I need not struggle to understand. But then I remembered the power she now holds and the house she bears, and I saw it for the curse that it is.

Standing before me is possibly the single greatest threat I have ever faced.

I ought to strangle her for it. Eliminate it immediately. But for some reason, I can't.

I can't seem to make my magic move. My shadows hold her too gently, just enough to keep her fixed but not so much she cannot breathe. Any other woman may have been dead already. But I can't seem to muster the strength, even as she threatens my people with her knowledge. I can't even shout at her. Even as I stand here wishing death upon her, I worry I may bruise her. So I set her on her feet, letting my shadows linger as she finds her balance.

The foreign sensation of guilt pricks my mind as I see her eyes have dimmed to a rusted orange, and for a moment, I worry I've crushed something in her. The defiance I'd seen sweeping through her like a river. Or whatever it is that grants her the gall to face me without fear. But I push the feeling aside, burying it with my other impulses.

She knows of your ailment. She is a threat to you and your people. Cut her down where she stands.

My mind does little to convince me, and we stand staring at each other in silence until she's caught her breath.

"You are more observant than I've given you credit for," I tell her, trying to rein in my anger and failing miserably. It isn't for her, though. It is for me. And Mother Luna. And maybe Father for having saddled me with this fate in his quest against the Serpent.

Rage burns through my chest like flames, sending my shadows billowing out of me uncontrollably, but she hardly blinks.

Yes, your kind tends to underestimate us, she signs back before rubbing absentmindedly at her throat. Her light is rushing to heal the strain, and I watch it move beneath her skin like a wave, rolling across her chest before diving deeper and snuffing out.

"Lunars?" I ask.

Her curls breeze around her face as she shakes her head.

"Men," she spits the word like fire as she signs, and I'm forced to fist my hands to keep from touching her.

I'm not entirely sure what will happen if I do.

"How do you know these signs?" I ask, feeling my frustration build with every passing second.

"There are many in Solaria without hearing," she says. *"From the Solar Wars. My family was not immune to the effects."*

I know the history she refers to. The Solarians fought a civil war some time ago, and the warring factions—the Rising Suns and the Setting Sons—devastated each other with the use of solar charges as the other planes watched on. La Luna was more than familiar with the damage they could cause. Their serpent had made sure of that.

I eye her carefully, searching her face for the truth. I suspect there is more to her story, but I do not care at the moment.

"Was it the ink?" I venture, gesturing at the wide stain still growing as we speak.

She nods.

"And you watch my mouth as I speak," she adds. *"I know what I look like. But not even the boldest of men stare that much."*

My shadows grow agitated at the thought of other men gaping at her as I had mere moments ago, and I groan.

Already she is much too distracting.

I hadn't recognized the thud and subsequent shatter for what it was. I'd felt it ripple into the soles of my feet but thought nothing of it until she began beating on the floor with her fist. I hadn't even registered the indistinct tone in my head as her speaking. All thought had been of her leg, of Shrea, and how much time was left before the paralysis settled in. Even now, I count the minutes. At this rate, she has no more than an hour before it reaches her knee. Two before the effect is irreversible.

I have no time for distraction. But I cannot seem to kill her. That leaves me with two singular options.

Send her back from where she came and hope she speaks nothing of what she's learned. *Or.* Keep her.

I curse quietly under my breath. She has no reason to keep my secrets. Releasing her is out of the question. That leaves only one.

"A guard will escort you to the dungeons," I tell her, collecting my shadows so I may exit.

"Is that where your bride is to reside?" she signs, growing bold in the face of my orders.

My patience frays, and I step in close to ensure she can hear my words as law when I speak them.

"I have no intention of wedding you." Her sunset eyes narrow almost imperceptibly, but I continue. "And you can rest assured I have no intention of bedding you. So, yes, *that* is where you will reside until I decide otherwise."

Unexpectedly, her lips lift at the corners, grinning at me.

"And what will the Council say when they learn you have no bride by your side?"

My eyes grow wide as she levels her threats, but her smile merely widens with satisfaction.

So, this is the creature Luna has sent me. A snake for my garden. How generous.

"The Council need not know what goes on at Castle La Luna," I say through gritted teeth. But she is a treacherous little thing, calling my bluff without hesitation.

"I wouldn't dare tell them a thing. But people will talk. Those women will speak of the demon they saw and how they all fled from him. Leaving him lonely on his throne, brideless. Surely, the Council will come looking."

Her eyes call up a look of innocence, batting her lashes at me like a helpless damsel.

But I get the distinct impression that she is anything but.

"And what do you propose instead?" I ask her, feeling as if my teeth may crack under the pressure of my rage.

"*I stay. Above ground. You have your bride, at least at a glance, and there is no cause for alarm.*" She shrugs as if this is a simple solution. But I know it is not.

"And should the Council come seeking confirmation?" I ask.

"*I shall play my part as you desire.*"

"What benefit does this serve you?"

"*Preservation,*" she answers.

There are words she leaves out. I can feel it. But I don't care to ask because she is right. Renwick had told me as much. My people need more time. And here she is to give it to me.

My claws prick my palms as I form tight fists.

"Very well. You shall remain at La Luna until I am no longer in need of a bride. Understood?"

She nods, satisfied with our tenuous truce.

"You will remain here—" I begin, gesturing around the room only for her to interrupt me.

"*Here?*" she blurts the word as if it's accidentally fallen from her mouth.

She's quick to cover her outburst, but I can't help but agitate her as she agitates me.

"Yes, *darling*. Here."

Light surges behind her eyes, flashing at my flippant use of the term. But all she says is, "*Is this not your bedchamber?*"

"It is," I challenge.

"*And where will you stay?*" she asks, although I suspect she already knows the answer from the look in her eyes.

"Here," I say, and I can see her anger light like a fire beneath her skin. But I say nothing. I do not owe her an explanation.

I'm surprised when she does not question me further.

"And what of my handmaiden?" she asks, crossing her arms over her full breasts and making it near impossible for me to continue looking at her. I realize then she is still standing within a whisper of my chest, and I take a step backward, separating from her.

"What of her?" I ask after a labored breath.

"Where will she stay?" she signs.

"I have no need for a handmaiden. She may return to Solaria."

Before I can even finish my words, her light pours out of her, much like my shadows, except they look like golden ribbons, whereas my shadows are thick tentacles.

They swim around her head menacingly. Were I a lesser man, I would be concerned that she threatens me. Her magic appears to be formidable, and I don't doubt she wields it expertly. As it is, I merely cock a brow and wait for her anger to simmer.

"No," she says firmly, a deep frown creasing her brow. *"She stays as well. I will not send her back through the forest alone."*

I watch the fury in her eyes grow heavy and determined. *She fights for others, but not herself?* Curious woman.

I had not considered the forest. It is far too dangerous for a woman, unskilled and untrained, to risk alone. It's a wonder Celeste made it through after her last man had fallen. Transporting a dead, light-less Solarian through the forest was one endeavor, a breathing one was another entirely. Even the smallest amount of light would draw the attention of the seekers. And though I am a demon, I am not so heartless as to send a woman on that path alone. And my men wouldn't dare leave her unarmed. They would fight to the last of them. I cannot in good conscience sacrifice them for the sake of a child of the Sun.

Again, this treacherous woman has bested me, and I am forced to bend to her will.

"Fine. She may stay in the barracks."

Celeste's brows draw together, dissatisfied with my concession.

But I hold up a hand, and to my surprise, and perhaps my disappointment, she quiets. Though I can see it pains her.

"No harm will come to your handmaiden. My general will watch over her. She, too, resides in the barracks with the rest of my legion."

"Two women and a legion of men? That's reassuring," she mutters but does not sign, so I can't be certain she meant for me to know what she's said. But I answer her anyway.

"I understand you are used to the barbarous life of a Solarian, but trust me. Luna is a freer place for a woman. You will find many in my legion." I bring my face close to hers and speak slowly, as Renwick does when he believes I cannot understand him. "They even lead them. Evalina will see that your handmaiden is safe. You have my word."

That seems to surprise her because her mouth is now stuck, slightly parted, her breathing shallow, and before she can think to argue with me further, I step away.

"A healer will come to remedy your leg," I say, and she blinks. "Goodnight, Lady Solém."

She bites down on her lip, resigning herself to silence, then signs, *Goodnight, Prince Apollo.*

I stare at her a moment, watching as she forms the last symbol that marks out my name, and when she's finished, I wonder if I have made a grave mistake. One that could cost me my life and my kingdom if I don't tread carefully.

I sign my words quickly, testing her proficiency, *Should you tell a single soul outside of this room what you have learned, I promise you will find yourself fighting shadows in my dungeons for the rest of your days, never to see your precious sun again.*

I level my threat with finality, though the image sits like a stone in my stomach.

Her hands fly through the air with a dexterity I've only seen in those taught from birth—faster and more precise than mine or Evalina's.

So captivating I almost miss the heat in her eyes as she declares,
I expect nothing less from the Demon of La Luna.

CHAPTER 7

CELESTE

—

The room is still humming with the remnants of Prince Apollo's energy, prickling at my skin like an electric wind, when the skinny man, with a name that sounds like a foreign bug I can't remember, returns. He comes bursting through the door in excitement, carrying Strega's saddle bag and tugging an elder woman behind him. She pushes past him in a hurry, battering him out of her way with her elbows as she charges for me.

"Ah! My goodness, Shrea!" the bug man admonishes, but she ignores him, hardly even turning when she mutters, "Hush now, Renwick."

Renwick scoffs at her, crossing his arms and sticking his nose in the air.

The elder woman, Shrea, shoos me toward the bed with a fierce look. "You," she says, waving at me vaguely. "Sit. And you," she snaps, turning on Renwick who is still pouting in the corner. "You, out."

She spins, waving him toward the door, and Renwick looks as

if he'd like to stick his tongue out at the old woman, but he doesn't. Instead, he moves toward the door, slow as sap, dragging his feet in defiance. Impatient, Shrea grabs a stack of parchment from a nearby pile and swats him with it.

Renwick yelps, hurrying toward the door with renewed haste. I watch them fuss at each other, and a laugh bubbles out of me without warning.

I smother it behind my hand just as Shrea slams the door shut on a pouting Renwick and turns to me. I drop to the edge of the bed quickly, lest I become her next victim.

"You'll have to excuse my brother," the old woman says, her crinkled eyes bright with a gentle kindness. "He means well. But he worries too much." She shrugs apologetically.

"What is there to worry about?" I ask, glancing down at my leg with newfound panic.

I've sustained greater damage from my own sisters in training. At least then, I'd had the opportunity to repay them. I doubt I'll ever get the chance to thank the seeker that did this to me. I only hope that Kefu managed to take a few of them to greet the Sun. Or Moon. Or wherever such foul creatures go when the light leaves their bodies.

But admittedly, the ever-creeping numbness is beginning to concern me. Apollo said nothing of it after his impromptu examination. But his snarling, brow-bent stare was beginning to worm its way into my mind, whispering stories of a one-legged viper that once was. He did not seem particularly concerned. Then again, my death would be a rather convenient course of events for him.

Shrea shakes her head, her white hair drifting around her shoulders as she stifles a soft chuckle. "Renwick worries about everything, apparently."

But she doesn't elaborate as she pulls a small velvet ottoman from its place beside the matching armchair, dropping onto it with surprising grace.

It's a fluid movement, one that's more telling of her past than her age. A dancer, maybe, or a gymnast, perhaps even a swords-man. I don't ask her what skill her poise is rooted in, but I distract myself by imagining the old woman striking down men on a battle-field, and it is a fitting image, given what I've seen.

Her wrinkled hands latch onto my ankles, jerking me forward until my left heel is propped on her lap.

"Now, let's see what we're dealing with here, shall we?"

I almost grumble as she begins another inspection. But her proficiency is well-honed, and her hands don't linger as Apollo's had. With little more than a squeeze and a pat, she's announcing, "This won't take but a moment, dear."

I chance a glance at my leg, watching with morbid curiosity as she plants her palms on my calf. She must mistake my staring for concern and offers me soothing words to ease my spirit. "Not to worry, dear. I suspect Apollo is correct. You have hours before the paralysis starts. Your magic is doing well."

"Apollo?"

He spoke to her directly? He doesn't seem the type to bother with those beneath him.

"Yes, he said you've had a rough journey. Put up quite a fuss about his bride-to-be," she adds, smiling up at me with a teasing glint in her eyes. "He will be glad to hear it is easily remedied."

I strain, trying not to roll my eyes at the old woman. I suspect it would not end well for me. But her words are hard to believe, given Apollo was choking his "bride-to-be" mere minutes ago. I say nothing as she sets about her work.

Her confidence gives me added comfort, and I settle into the plush bedding, waiting.

"Why doesn't it hurt?" I ask her after she's set out her bandages.

"The moondust," she answers without lifting her head. "When purified, it is used to treat pain. But in its basest form, it is a para-lyzing agent. It works to numb the area so the paralysis can move through the body without disruption. A small scrape like this will take quite a while to progress. But a full blow will bring a grown man down within the hour."

I frown at her words. None of this sounds familiar to me. But it should. I am as well read on all things Lunar as anyone. It was a cornerstone of my training, meant to make my infiltration easier. But I'd never seen mention of moondust as anything other than a healer's remedy. The Serpent certainly hadn't mentioned it.

Shrea catches the confusion on my face. "The seekers nest in forest caves lined with moonstone. As they dig into the bedrock, their claws become coated in the mineral, working as an effective poison for their hunt. They are stalkers, mostly. They only aim to strike once and then wait for the moondust to do its work. Once immobilized, the seeker collects its prize without issue. Although, these days, I suspect they are a bit more eager."

"Eager is putting it mildly," I tell her, remembering the frenzied feeding I'd witnessed. "I did not know that. About the moonstone."

"It is not common knowledge. Very few people encounter the seekers and live to tell the tale. You are fortunate."

Kefu's face flashes in my mind, and I decide that luck had very little to do with it. But I don't tell this to Shrea. I merely nod and force a smile on my face.

Her hands are now gripping my leg with force, squeezing with all her might until pus froths forth into thick white clouds along the back of my leg, filling in the gaps between my torn skin. I gape at the unmistakable sign of infection beneath the otherwise unsuspecting wound, and my sunlight surges to the front, hoping to aid in its expulsion. But Shrea stops me, shaking her head as her fingers prod at my blistering skin.

"Moondust will not respond to sunlight," she explains.

"Then what will you—"

Before I can finish asking, she wipes away the pus and blood with a swatch of cotton, then clamps her hands around the wound. A soft, white light, much cooler than my own, begins to build beneath her palms.

Immediately, the feeling returns to my leg, and I can feel the gentle, soothing light moving beneath my skin.

"You wield moonlight?" I ask breathily, unable to hide my shock.

Those blessed with celestial magic are rare in any regard, but Lunar celestials are even more scarce. Almost as uncommon as Raye.

"Why, yes, dear. What did you expect? Shadows?" She chuckles lightly at her joke, then adds, "No, no. Luna blesses very few. The night even fewer."

The night? How could the night bless anyone?

But I don't get the chance to ask her anything more. She's already wrapping my leg in a light gauze and patting me like a mother would.

"Mo á grobeda yeva," *I am grateful for you*, I say, hoping it comes out as genuine as I mean it to be.

Shrea blushes in surprise, and I can guess that my words are too formal.

"And we are grateful for you," she says in return, bowing her head slightly so her long white hair pools in her lap. "Heaven knows we need you." She mutters her words but makes no genuine attempt to hide them.

When she leaves, I rise with her and am pleasantly surprised to find my balance has been righted.

I follow behind her the few steps to reach the door, and she pauses as she pulls it open, turning slightly to speak over her shoulder. "A word of advice from an old lady—do not believe the tales they spin about our dear prince. He is no more a monster than you or I." The viper in me nearly bursts out laughing, but I manage to rein it in as she adds, "Welcome to La Luna."

She leaves me idling in the doorway, but I don't cross the threshold into the hall. There is a man standing resolute at the opposite end, and he turns on his heel, offering me a stern frown. So I shut the door on him, closing out the echoing sounds of people drifting freely through the halls.

I'm knee-deep in scraps of parchment before the door even clicks shut all the way—sifting and searching for anything of use. Any bit of information that the Serpent may require. I flip through the stacks and even the crumpled pieces on the floor, careful to place them back just as I found them, but find nothing more than what I can only assume are the ravings of a lunatic. I could hardly even call them ravings as there weren't any words on the pages, only shapes, and jagged lines. Even the ones that appeared to be more cohesive meant nothing to me.

Eventually, I drop to the bed in defeat, deciding that Apollo is not so foolish as to leave me in the midst of all his secrets. After all, you'd have to be truly dim to leave anything of value in plain sight. But in my experience, marks are usually stupid. Or rather, they don't suspect a woman like myself to be interested enough to go looking.

Although, I had a feeling Prince Apollo may be different. Already he was much too observant for my liking—constantly staring into my face as if trying to pull a confession from every glance. I'd grown used to the wandering eyes of men, but not ones that paid attention. Most only managed to see what they wanted— or what I *told* them to see. But I could feel the consideration in Apollo's gaze—even as he stood scowling at me.

I was careful not to lie to him outright. While it was true that solar charges had ravaged Solaria in its earliest years, and indeed, *someone* in my line had been afflicted, that isn't the reason I'm proficient in signing. It is a skill imposed by the Serpent and a product of my carefully curated upbringing. Signing is quite common in my line of work, most often used amongst the Solarian armies for quick and quiet communication. Though never before have I used it in casual conversation. I will need to adjust my approach to be less formal.

I explore the rest of Apollo's chambers with a keen eye, even going so far as to check behind the dark, woven curtains. What possible purpose do curtains serve in a land with no sun? I cannot fathom. But it turns out that the moonlight is rather bright in the Lunar territories. In the same way that the Sun burns hotter in Solaria, the Moon beams brighter in Luna.

I push back the curtains to see two expertly crafted arched windows framing either side of the big bed, with a beautiful glass motif resting in the middle. A depiction of a full moon on the left and a crescent on the right, with their images projected across the stone floor as the moonlight streaks in through the panes.

The images are only partial now, as the Moon is nearly gone from sight. But I step lightly over them, feeling for some reason as though I shouldn't pass through them. I try the handle of a simple wooden door tucked into the back right corner. It opens to a plain-looking washroom, and I close it quickly, relatively disappointed by the lack of intrigue it contains.

What a boring monster, I think to myself.

That's when I see my reflection.

My hair has swelled to twice its normal size, the light in my eyes has dimmed, and my blood stains the hem of my skirt where it was stuck to my leg.

I take a moment to smooth down my hair, and then I begin the futile effort of searching through my saddlebag for a change of clothes. Even before I open the flap, I know there is nothing to find. As I turn away from the mirror, I hope a miracle will occur and a nightgown will spontaneously appear. I sift through the bag a while longer before giving up entirely and moving to the chest of drawers set catty-corner to the bed.

I rummage through the prince's things, passing up the pants and vests until I find a well-worn nightshirt in a less suffocating fabric than the rest. I tie the laces tightly at the neck, as tight as they'll go, but it still hangs low across my chest. It wears like a tent, drooping from my shoulders like sagging skin, but I don't mind its size. It makes for a comfortable gown as I burrow into the enormous bed.

I avoid the side that dips down in the middle, marking the memory of Prince Apollo's large body, and nearly moan as the fabric envelops me. It's soft, so soft, and it smells of wet earth and spices, like rain and magic all at once. Like home. Not Solaria—Solaria smells like crisp air and baked earth. No, this smells of home the way Raye smells like joy. Like it has been woven into every fiber with intention.

How can a place I've never been to smell like that? I wonder. But my mind is lost to comfort almost immediately.

This is the first bed my body has seen in months. Not a pallet packed with hay or a cot in the back corner of a barn, but a real bed, and my bones sigh in relief as I pull the blankets to my chin, burrowing further.

I listen for a moment to the sounds of La Luna. Feet shuffling over stone. Muffled shouts in the distance. Hounds barking. It's a symphony to my tired mind, and sleep comes easy. Easier than it has in far too long.

I ignore the quiet rustling when Apollo returns. I ignore the smoky earthen scent he carries with him, like lightning just touched down, and I ignore the moment his magic leaks out to cover my legs. Most of all, I ignore the urge to reach out and touch it. I ignore him completely. But when I dream, I dream of shadows.

CHAPTER 8

APOLLO

———

Evalina is propped up against the wall just beyond my chamber door, and she turns on me the moment it shuts. *"Would you like me to call you a fool now or later?"* she asks, signing with frenzied fury.

"You believe I've made a mistake in choosing her."

I don't stop to address her concern, but when I continue past her, she falls in step beside me, offering her unwanted opinion.

"Yes. A huge mistake! A Solarian? What are you thinking? Looking at her, fine. Craters, I was looking at her. We all were! But selecting her? Choosing her? Have you lost your ever-lunar mind?"

Ordinarily, Evalina speaks freely, but this evening she is treading a thin line. I can only tolerate one woman cursing me at any given time, and I believe that post has now been taken by Celeste—likely permanently. So I stop her before she can say anything more.

"You speak too freely, Evalina," I mutter, turning on her. "I wasn't asking. And you may not call your king a fool. Ever."

Her eyes narrow as she considers my words.

"That's something only a fool would say," she quips, adhering to my order, but just barely. *"How do you expect a Solarian to be named queen of House Luna?"* Evalina continues, as relentless as she is prideful. *"What will people think?"*

I hardly feel the need to dignify such a question with a response, but I know she will not rest until she has her answer, so I give it to her anyway, silently wondering if this persistence of hers is a family trait.

"I do not care what people will think. The Lunar people place their faith in whoever sits upon the throne at La Luna. They would accept her if I demanded it."

Evalina's eyes roll, but she doesn't open her mouth.

"But do not worry," I mutter. "Celeste Solém will not be your queen."

Evalina's eyes grow wide as I tell her of the bargain we have struck, and when I'm finished, she is back to cursing me.

"I suppose you couldn't choose any other for this ruse? After all the women you've seen, it had to be her?"

Yes. The word draws forth in my mind, blocking out all other thoughts, but I cannot offer it to Evalina. She wouldn't understand. I hardly understand it myself. But there is no doubt in my mind. Celeste was the correct choice.

Evalina stares at me, waiting, and my voice is rough and tired when I speak. "She did not run." I shrug, and her arms cross, still discontent. "You know, if I didn't know any better, I'd say you were jealous."

Her mouth flaps open, and I can hear the high-pitched tone of her shouting while she signs animatedly. *"Who wouldn't be? If a woman like that landed in my bed, you'd never see me again."*

She barks out a laugh, and I know exactly what it sounds like. It's been the same ever since we were children. Rough and crass, nothing befitting a lady, as her mother liked to say, and I smother a grin as she adds, *"But I'm not foolish enough to keep a Solarian between my sheets. No matter how pretty they may be."*

I wouldn't describe Celeste as pretty. Pretty is an injustice. Celeste's eyes alone are more arresting than any I've ever seen. Stunning, maybe. Enchanting, definitely.

But pretty? Hardly.

I don't correct Evalina as we make our way through the castle, and she doesn't berate me with questions until we reach the barracks.

Most of the legion has gone to their nightly posts, so the area is relatively empty. But she still signs quickly out of caution.

"I don't see why I can't go with you," she says.

"We are not discussing this again," I growl. "The dungeon is forbidden to you and any others who do not have a need. Do you understand me?"

"We're not children anymore. Why do you insist on treating me like one?"

"The fact that you don't understand this order is proof enough that you have no business there," I snap, feeling my shadows creep across my chest and up my neck, threatening to swallow my patience. It's been worn threadbare this evening, and I don't have much to spare. "If you enter that dungeon, you will regret it." Her face grows indignant at my threat. Though I don't mean it as one. It is simply a fact. One she cannot seem to see. So I ask again, "Do. You. Understand. Me?"

Her arms cross and her moonlight burns bright behind her eyes. She doesn't sign as she grunts, "Fine."

"I will meet you at the charge when I am through. Try to keep them alive until I arrive."

Evalina's sulking lifts as she remembers her duty, and before we part, she rams a shoulder into me, stalking off toward the barracks to collect a regiment.

"I could have your head for that, General!" I shout after her. To which she tosses me an obscene gesture just before the doors slide shut behind her.

I say a silent prayer for the seekers that may cross her path this evening. In her current state, I doubt they'll stand a chance.

When I reach the dungeons, my spirit feels weathered, weighed down by tonight's events, even more so as I greet our guest once again.

But it soon lifts as I squat down to ask him, "What do you know of Celeste Solém?"

Chapter 9

Celeste

—

Blood pools beneath my feet, black and sticky as it splatters across my legs with every step. My blade feels heavy in my hand, and I can see it's tipped with the same black sludge.

I have met my mark. I have killed the demon.

But...where is he?

I spin, sliding across the stone floor, only to find the body missing.

"Did you think you would succeed, darling?" a voice teases, but before I can turn, shadows lace around my legs, winding up my body until my vision goes black and all I'm left with is the cool embrace of night as my light burns out.

"I want to see the p...I want to see Lady Solém immediately!"

Raye's voice comes harsh and wild, jerking me out of my sleep, as she berates the soldier stationed outside my door.

No, not *my* door. Apollo's door. *My* cage.

I've hardly seen outside these walls since the night he locked me away.

He was insistent that I remain in his chamber, even after I offered to stay in the barracks to watch over Raye. He claimed it was to keep with the lie we'd chosen to tell, but honestly, I think he enjoys lording over me.

He even gave me a guard, one I was instructed not to speak to, and a curfew that ended just after his court sat for dinner. He then drew a boundary, confining me to the west wing. As a result, my "days" are spent alone. No company to keep. No information to gather. And hardly any sight of Apollo.

Some nights, I hear him shouting as he barrels through the halls. And others, I wake to find the smell of lightning and earth lingering in the air as if he's been standing beside me. But only a handful of times have I seen his face.

Which, in all honesty, I can't claim to be upset about.

"*Now!*" Raye shouts, and I'm flying from the bed, swinging the door open wide before her mouth can get us into any trouble.

Lucious, the young cadet with the innocent face who has been assigned as my guard, spins on me.

"My lady." He bows politely, and part of me wonders if he is too dense to realize I am nothing more than a prisoner here.

"Celeste!" Raye shouts, trying to push past Lucious.

He sidesteps, blocking her path.

Evalina stands off to the side, and I can see her watching Raye with a close eye. The same overbearing surveillance Apollo seems so fond of. He designated her as Raye's escort, but she seems to spend almost every second projecting an unhappy frown in constant protest. Her eyes narrow at me when we see each other, and I resist the urge to roll mine.

"My lady," Lucious interjects, holding out an arm to keep Raye at bay. "Prince Apollo said you were not to be disturbed tonight."

I frown at him, confused.

Has Apollo been feeding him lies to keep me isolated?

If I wasn't the victim of this treatment, I might compliment him on his approach. It is benign, yet effective.

"The only person to dictate when I may be disturbed is me," I tell Lucious, reaching around him to yank Raye through the sliver of space he left open.

Lucious nods, eyes darting between me and Evalina, asking her to intervene. But she merely pushes away from the wall where she's been sitting like a fixture and declares, "Prince Apollo will hear of this."

I meet her threat, unwavering. "I doubt that very much."

The muscles in her left cheek jerk as if she means to growl at me the way Apollo does, but I close the door on her before she can think to say anything more.

Raye bustles into the room, suppressing giggles as the door swings shut.

I've only seen her a few times since the night we arrived and only after threatening to reveal Apollo's impairment to the nearest soldier who would listen. Not that I would dare. That knowledge is currently the only leverage I have, and I plan on keeping that tidbit to myself until it becomes absolutely vital.

"Busy night?" Raye asks, winking at me as she takes in the expanse of Apollo's room and the rough state of his bed.

The mark of my restless night is clear, but the other side remains relatively untouched, as always.

I guess the demon does have *some* manners.

"Hm." I chuckle dryly. "He wishes."

She giggles again, then plops unceremoniously onto the bed, sweeping her dark cloak out behind her.

Raye took to wearing the Lunar styles almost immediately—heavy woolen skirts, dark colors, and a warm cloak draped over her shoulders. Even the oddly laced chest piece the women seem to enjoy. Admittedly, it suits her color quite well, but I have yet to find a fabric that doesn't feel as if I would immediately catch flame.

"I bet he does wish," she quips, tucking a stray strand behind her ear.

I shake my head at her but don't say anything more.

Raye doesn't know the extent of my and Apollo's bargain. Though I would trust her with my life, she talks more than she breathes, and I won't endanger her with the truth. So before she can think to ask any questions, I turn the conversation in a direction she always enjoys—her.

"How are they treating you?" I ask. "Is Evalina being rough with you? Are the soldiers being brutish?"

Raye's face lights up as she settles into a long-winded explanation.

"This place is so strange! I haven't seen a single person that wasn't Lunar. Besides us, everyone has the same silver-white hair and light blue eyes. It's a little eerie," she remarks, shivering in exaggeration. "But they're okay. For the most part. Some legionnaires don't seem to like me, but I think that's only because they think I'm Solarian. Most aren't rude about it, but some aren't shy about it either. Not to mention the entire legion is talking about you. They're mostly just curious. I've heard them trying to catch glimpses of you on your evening walks. Because of the rumors..." Raye pauses for dramatic effect, and I roll my eyes. "Some of them say the prince has gone mad like his father. Others say he's succumbed to the curse or been 'blinded' by your light. I don't know what curse they're talking about, but..." She pauses for air and a shrug. "Most of them seem to think it's just a desperate ploy to find some peace between Solaria and Luna."

I chuckle at that. What a foolish dream.

The divide between Lunars and Solarians is written in the stars. All the Serpent wants is for the people of Luna to feel the Sun as all the other houses do. The tyrannical insistence on keeping the Sun from the Lunar people is a celestial sin that the Serpent will never forgive. Not until the Lunar people lay down their wards and allow Mother Sun's light to pass through their borders. Until then, the Serpent will not rest. And neither shall I.

"What about Evalina?" I ask, noticing how Raye has conveniently left her out of her rant.

"She's not so bad." Raye shrugs again, but this time there's a familiar twinkle in her eye, and when she doesn't launch into another tangent, I know exactly what she's thinking.

"Raye. No. You can't."

"Says you," she sasses, crossing her arms.

"I'm serious. Evalina is keener than you think. You need to tread lightly."

"Oh, I know," she says, eyes gleaming at her newfound challenge, and I throw my hands up, ignoring her as she mutters.

"Ugh." I groan aloud, but I can see Raye is already calculating her chances. I suspect they are quite low given Evalina's weariness of me, but I won't be the one to tell her this time.

"Any chatter in the barracks?" I ask, crossing the room to drop down beside her.

"I haven't heard talk of any plans, but the legion is well-trained and tight-lipped around me. I have seen them, though. Training— nothing like the Solarians."

I nod. I had seen them too, in passing. Their skill was well-suited for close combat, but not nearly as meticulous as the Solarian soldiers.

"And I've seen groups of them sprinting off into the forest at night," she adds, dropping her voice into a low whisper.

"The forest?"

She nods, shifting closer.

"Dozens of them. Every night. Like clockwork. And they only return just before the Moon rises."

My mouth opens to begin a thorough interrogation of what she's seen, but before a single word can fall free, a sharp rush of cold air breezes through the room. The door swings open wide, slamming against the wall.

Apollo's towering form stands in the open doorway, and he strides in, ducking his horns and barking orders.

"Out!" he demands too loudly for the enclosed space.

I stand, blocking his path and peering up at him. His fangs glare back at me as he snarls in my face.

Raye rises abruptly, eyes wide with shock and mouth hanging open as her fear leaks out of her. To her credit, she doesn't run sprinting from the room. But she does begin to hold her breath in a valiant attempt to cage her magic.

"Excuse me?" I shout back as Apollo tries to move past me.

His eyes darken and his fists clench as his gaze settles on my lips.

"Not you," he grinds out, letting his shadows pool around his feet. "Her."

My head follows the direction of his clawed finger to where Raye stands by the door, her face turning pale as she refuses to take a breath. I nod, and she slips through the door without so much as a bow.

"*What do you want?*" I snap, turning back to him, only to find him standing much too close.

He's watching me with those swirling blue eyes, and they seem to grow darker the longer they linger.

"Many things," he mutters between clenched teeth, and I resist the urge to reach out and burn him with my light.

"*What do you want from* me?" I correct, my patience growing thin.

For nights I have not seen even a glimpse of him, and now he wanders in, growling at me? Perhaps he is no better than a beast.

He pushes a heavy hand through the dark curls that crowd around his horns, and I can see the familiar path his fingers take as he rakes through them.

"Many things," he echoes, and I'm forced to step back as his shadows drift around my face.

"*Do not touch me,*" I command.

Apollo raises a thick, dark brow, but his shadows continue to linger, mere inches from my head.

"What was she doing in here?" he asks, wholly ignoring my demands.

"I don't see how that's any of your business."

"This is my chamber," he says. "Everything that happens here is my business. And I told Lucious you were not to be disturbed. Now, shall I dismiss him for his inability to follow orders? Or are you responsible for his failure?"

My mouth opens, then closes, and I narrow my eyes at him.

"You have no right to decide whether I may be disturbed."

Apollo's arms cross over his chest, and his horns dip down as he bends to bring his face closer to mine.

"You sleep like a wild animal," he answers, frowning at me as if he finds this wholly unacceptable. "Tossing and turning constantly. Your body is still used to seeing the Sun. You must rest if you ever hope to sleep through the night."

"What do you know of how I sleep?" I ask, suddenly conscious of the evenings I've spent sprawled across his bed wearing nothing but his nightshirt.

"As I've said. Everything that happens in here is my business."

Apollo doesn't wait for my smart reply. He pushes past me, shouldering me out of the way to reach the armoire on the far side of the room. His cloak falls into a heap around his feet as he shrugs it from his broad shoulders, and I can't help the gasp that escapes me.

He is covered in blood.

The crisp linen shirt is soaked through to his skin, and it clings to him as he yanks it over his head. I step aside without argument when he breezes past, heading for the washroom. I can hear him grunting and cursing under his breath as he bumps around in the tiny space, and when he emerges, he somehow looks more tired than before. But it's clear he's done his best to wipe the grime from his skin.

Water beads between his shoulder blades as he stalks around the room, and his shadows writhe beneath his skin. They move like thick black bands, snaking around his body from top to tail. Which juts out just beneath his belt where a hole has been tailored for his comfort.

I'm so distracted by the subtle flicking motion it's making that when Apollo speaks again, it takes me a moment to understand his words.

"Have you been for a tour of the gardens?" he asks, but his back is to me, and I have to wait until he turns to face me before I respond. Only, when he does turn, my mind runs blank, and my mouth feels dry.

My eyes are hooked on the broad canvas of his chest and the glimmer of his taut, brown skin in the moonlight.

"Celeste?" he asks again, and I manage to close my mouth. But I can't make the words come out, so all I can do is sign to him in silence.

No, I sign, trying to find his eyes. But it's a slow journey past his chin and shoulders, and even as I find his face, my eyes settle on his mouth, noting the way his fangs peek out over his bottom lip.

He grunts and frowns, frustrated once again by something seemingly inconsequential.

"Lucious will take you," he says, yanking a shirt over his horns, barely keeping from punching two holes through it.

I don't get the chance to tell him off as I've been meaning to. The shirt has barely settled over his shoulders before he stalks toward the door. A shadow reaches out to snatch it open, revealing the little crowd that has gathered outside our door. *His* door.

Renwick has joined Evalina, Lucious, and Raye to stand in weighted silence. They all scuttle for the edges of the foyer when Apollo swings the door open wide.

He looks back at me, fisting the door handle in one hand and his cloak in the other, but all he says before slamming it shut is, "Do *not* disturb her."

CHAPTER 10

APOLLO

―――

Sleep is no friend of mine. It avoids me like a plague. And even when I catch it, my mind is filled with thoughts of sunlit women tossing in my bed.

No, that is not correct.

Not women.

Woman.

A singular sun-blessed woman who knows no bounds. Or if she does, she consistently chooses to ignore them.

Celeste's essence is everywhere. In the air, in my sheets, on my clothes. I cannot escape her. Even at a distance, she has invaded my solitude.

I thought avoiding her entirely would make it easier. Easier to ignore her and easier to disregard the quiet voice in my mind telling me to take her as my own. But I suspect she seeks to punish me for this decision by making it...difficult.

Each evening, I depart before she wakes. But each night, when I return to my chamber, she is there. I return well past midnight when I am confident she is asleep. Yet, even at rest, her presence is overwhelming. Her warm light fills the room, bathing it in a dull glow as she sleeps. And her scent hangs in the air like fog.

Some nights I find the sweet musk of her arousal lingering, and I am forced to lie in the barracks like a slighted lover no longer welcome in his own bed. My legionnaires gawk and think I do not know that they whisper when my back is turned, but I cannot find it in me to care. The aroma of her desire is intoxicating, too distracting to sleep through. But perhaps most infuriating is the sight of her half-bare body sprawled across my sheets.

Every evening it is the same. She lies with her long legs tangled in my sheets and her body draped in the nightshirt she has claimed —*my* nightshirt, wholly ignoring the sleeping gown I have procured in order to vex me. Instead, she swims in the fabric of my clothes, bare underneath. Which I could ignore if it were not for her tossing and turning.

The little heathen thrashes in her sleep, restless, kicking her legs free from the blankets every now and then, baring her ass to the moonlight.

I am not a beast, contrary to popular belief. But I am a man like any other. So though I try not to, I find myself watching her. I sit in my armchair, gazing at her glimmering skin and watching the sunlight with shameful curiosity as it winds up from her toes to her legs and into her chest, where it settles before coursing back down again. It is glorious to behold, and after a few cycles, I stand, crossing the room to peer down at her inlit skin, then tug the hem of my shirt back down around her hips. I do my best not to linger, but some nights my hands move of their own accord, and I brush a knuckle down the back of her thigh to see her light follow the path of my finger.

My success in ignoring her came to a swift end as soon as I saw her last night.

She was still wearing my nightshirt, and her big, curly hair was still mussed from sleep, but her quick wit and sunlit eyes were ready and waiting for me—poised with heated words and cold stares. I was prepared to meet her in kind, but my temper fell to pieces when I saw her standing before me. I decided that, for a moment, I could let my guard down. But a moment was all she needed. And I'd left with her image imprinted on my mind.

I hadn't the strength to return after our early evening run-in. Meaning, last night was another night in the barracks. Which also means my spine is now bent from the too-small bed, and my patience is already worn when I step into the training ring.

I arrive at moonrise, too restless to do much else. The cadets are eager to spar, but Celeste's image clings to me, disrupting my focus and making me more brutal than usual.

She's all I can see as I duck under a young cadet's arm.

He swings wildly, aiming for Luna knows what, and I sidestep, using his momentum to drive him in a circle, jabbing his spine with my elbow. His blade cuts close to my chest, narrowly missing skin as half my mind rests in my chamber, still propped up in the armchair, watching Celeste's deep breathing. But even with half a mind, the young cadet is downed easily. He is too erratic with his movements. Too blunt, no follow-through. His strikes start and end where he meets his mark.

"Do not stop!" I bark, shoving him back and forcing him to reset his feet. "Your energy must pass through your opponent. Meet your mark, then keep going!"

I bring my fist into his chest, striking in the center as if I mean to cut a hole through him with my hands alone.

The air in his lungs rushes out of him, expelled against his will. It puffs out in a cloud flecked with blood as his body hurtles backward, landing hard in the dirt. I watch as he writhes, clutching his chest, and I'm reminded for a moment of Celeste's restless sleep.

"Get up! Or get out of my ring!" I shout as he pulls himself to his hands and knees.

When he doesn't stand, his brethren step forward to shoulder him. He's a hefty fellow, and it takes three men to lift him up and over the metal railing.

Suddenly, I'm left standing there with nothing but Celeste's body branded behind my eyelids.

"Evalina!" I shout her name as another cadet steps over the railing. This one is small and will go down quickly unless she is aware of her center. If she is not, today she will learn.

I wave the cadet forward, and she comes at me fast, using her light-footed nature to move quickly. But as soon as it begins, it is over. I spin, throwing off her trajectory, and sweep out an arm, striking her twice in the side. Without balance to keep her standing, she collapses in a heap at my feet.

Evalina appears at my side as if conjured by moonlight. One moment the space beside me is empty, and in the next, she is standing there, arms folded, both of us peering down at the cadet now passed out in the dirt.

"She needs clothes," I assert.

"She looks fine to me." Evalina frowns, toeing the young woman with her boot and stepping around her body so I can read her lips.

We do not sign in the presence of others. Only Renwick and Shrea are privy to my secret. And now, I suppose, Celeste.

"No. Not this one. Though she does need better training. I was speaking of Cel-Lady Solém."

"Lady Solém?" Evalina repeats, eyeing me skeptically.

"Yes. She needs clothing."

"She has been provided clothing. As you requested."

"Then why does she insist on not wearing it?" I groan.

"I'm sure I don't know what you mean," Evalina says, raising a brow and feigning ignorance.

A growl starts in my chest, and Evalina all but rolls her eyes.

"She sleeps in my nightshirt," I add, to which Evalina merely stares at me. "*Only* my nightshirts."

"I would think you'd be pleased by that," she says, crossing her arms. But the small smile creeping across her lips tells me she is enjoying my torture almost as much as Celeste.

"Fix it!" I tell her. I have had enough sleepless nights.

Evalina drops her arms and her face steels. "No."

"Excuse me?" I ask, holding on to my last thread of patience by a hair.

"I said no. I am already babysitting a handmaiden who talks much too much and smiles as if she will die should she stop. The cadets need constant training and improvement." She gestures toward the woman by our feet as evidence. "And now you wish me to keep *your* bride from terrorizing you? No. I shall not."

"She is not *my* bride," I correct through gritted teeth.

"Yes, well, *you* chose her for this farce. So she is yours as far as I can tell."

I bare my teeth at her.

"And stop growling at me," she reprimands. "If you'd like someone to be angry with, go stand in front of a mirror."

I heave a sigh. She is right.

I hate when that happens. Not for concern of my pride, but for my peace. She will remind me until she is blue in the face and her light burns out.

"Are you aware of who you are talking to?" I ask, wondering if she will ever recognize her place, but knowing the answer is a resounding *no*. We spent too much time together as children. And now she thinks of me as her friend. And, though I'd never tell her, she is correct in that too.

Evalina answers my question by shooting a moonbeam from her palm, striking my eyes, and blurring my vision.

"You are lucky you bring good counsel!" I shout at her as she sprints across the training grounds, and even though I can't hear it, I know she is cackling as she flees.

———————

I abandon the cadets after a short while. Their eager attacks were a much-needed distraction, but I require someone of greater skill to exercise my own, and Evalina is the only one who comes close these days. So I grew bored quickly and left them to lick their wounds, resigning myself to wandering about the grounds.

I move from wing to wing with little intention, and when my eyes finally lift from the floor, I find myself face-to-face with the cadet blocking the door to my chamber.

"Merry midnight, y-y-your highness," the greeting shuffles out of his mouth in Luneer—the words running together as if they are all one.

I recognize him as one of the trainees Evalina favors. From what I can recall, he is quick with a blade and faster with a bow, but he is no good to me standing outside my door. A scout should be stationed here. Someone with keen instincts and an acute sense of awareness. Even I, deaf as I am, can feel Celeste's feet shuffling around behind the door, the featherlight sensation moving quickly from one end to another. Something a scout would know better than to overlook.

"Step aside, Lucious."

He hesitates, shifting from foot to foot, unable to meet my eyes.

"The-the lady is in, your highness," he says as if that fact holds any bearing.

"Yes, I'm aware. Now step aside."

"Of course, your highness," he says, waiting until he's finished speaking to actually move his feet.

I don't bother to knock. These chambers are mine, and there should be nothing worthy of secrecy behind these doors. But I quickly come to regret that decision as I step into the room.

The air is thick with the swell of Celeste's sweetly scented aroma. A heady scent, like firelight and honey—warm but soft, and immediately my shadows aim to capture it. To pull it free from her so I may enjoy it without the constant reminder of who it belongs to. My eyes close of their own volition as I breathe her in, and I stifle an audible groan.

Luna, please, whatever I have done to deserve this, I shall right it. Just free me from this torture.

When I open my eyes, Luna has once again ignored my pleas. In fact, I believe she, too, taunts me.

Celeste stands before me, eyes wide with panic, waving her hands madly, pleading with me. Only she hasn't been caught in some nefarious scheme but by the strappings of her corset. She clutches it to her bare breasts, barely containing them as the ties hang loose around her back. It gapes open like some beast that's tried to swallow her and failed, and the sight is so extraordinary that it takes me a moment to realize she isn't waving at me, but signing with her free hand.

Lucious, slow as he is, bursts through the door a moment too late, and Celeste begins shouting once more, abandoning her signs for harsh words that I can't make out. Her bare feet stomp as she screams and clutches her breasts closer, pressing them up to her neck. She is completely bare save for her cotton underwear and the unlaced corset, and with one look at her, a snarl rips up my throat.

Possession overcomes my senses as I turn to find Lucious gawking like an owl, and I move toward him in a flurry of shadow, bringing them up like a wall to block his view of her. He shrinks back instinctively, clamping his hands over his ears to save himself from Celeste's screeching. But they will not save him from me.

I wrench his arms down to be certain he hears me because I will not repeat myself.

"You shall not enter this room without my permission. Should you make the mistake again, it will mean your head. Do you understand?"

Lucious's face pales.

"Do you understand?"

I can see the very moment my words reach his sprite-sized brain, but I don't give him a chance to answer. My shadows clutch his uniform, and I toss him through the open door like a stone, slamming the door shut just as swiftly.

Light floods the room, and I turn to see Celeste standing before me like a torch. Eyes bright, skin swimming with light. It courses beneath the surface as it does when she sleeps, and I'm so distracted, I barely notice her hand and mouth moving in tandem.

"Don't! Don't look at me! Close your eyes!" she signs quickly, her brown skin blushing with sunlight.

I blink, refusing to believe my own eyes.

I threaten to string her up in my dungeon and receive nothing but blank stares. But now, the threat of embarrassment has swallowed her nerve, and she stands before me...*blushing?*

"I said close your eyes!"

She shouts as she signs—but it is haphazard as she continues clutching her corset to her body.

"I am familiar with the sight of a woman's body. Surely it is not worth all this screaming," I say, ignoring her pleas but doing my best to keep my eyes on either her hands or her mouth. Which proves to be more difficult than expected.

Her arms cross before her, grasping uselessly at the loose ties.

"If you want your eyes to remain in your skull, you will close them!" she shouts at me again.

My shadows reach up from the floor, aiming to strike some fear into her heart, but she doesn't startle. When her eyes meet my own, a stroke of desire grips me.

Never have I seen a person so bold in my presence. Not even Evalina dares to threaten me.

I want nothing more than to punish her for her heated words, but still, I am incapable of it.

I cross the room in three quick strides, standing so close her fingers brush my chest as I curl a shadow under her chin, forcing her to meet my eyes. She jerks her head back, but I hold her tight, keeping her gaze fixed on mine.

"Do not threaten me, darling. We will both regret it."

Celeste stares at me—a plump pout on her full lips and a hint of defiance in her eye, but for once, she's at a loss for words.

"Now, turn around," I command, waiting to see if she will threaten me once more.

True to form, words spill out of her. But her hands are pressed between us, and my traitorous mind is too busy gawking at all the things I cannot see while she sleeps.

The subtle streaks of light coursing through her curls. The faint scar that disappears into her hairline. The dark freckle dotting her left brow.

Eventually, she quiets, looking at me expectantly.

"I don't know what you've just said," I tell her. "And you should know, I'm not one to repeat myself. But I will give you grace this once…Turn. Around."

Her eyes flash a little brighter, anger mixing with a distinct sunlit flush of excitement, but she turns for me without another word. She gathers her hair, brushing it off to the side and baring her smooth back as she shifts impatiently on her feet.

"Hold the front," I direct her.

Her hands move to her stomach, causing the chest to flop open, and I suck in a hissing breath. From my height, I can see her bare breasts clearly over her shoulder. Soft, plush mounds tipped with a dark, ebony brown stare back at me, and I can feel my cock growing stiff in my pants.

Before the demon in me wins out, I wrap my arm around her and press the corset close to her chest, shielding them from view.

She stiffens as my hand cups her breast, but she doesn't fight to be free of me.

"You'll need to place one hand on your stomach and the other here," I say, tapping just over her heart.

She nods, then signs briefly, *Sorry.*

"Do not apologize," I tell her. "It is a lovely view."

Goosebumps sprout up on her skin as my words wash over her, and I lace the corset quickly, trying my best not to linger. But her skin is so warm, warmer than any Lunar, and I have to fight the desire to spread my hands across her back and feel the light beneath. As I finish, my fingers betray me, and I sweep my thumb down her neck.

Then my mouth follows suit, and words trip clumsily past my lips as my mind refuses to heed my orders. "So warm..."

"*Pardon?*" she asks, turning to peer up at me, still clutching the garment to her chest.

"*Your skin,*" I explain, wishing she would stop staring at me with her lips parted just so.

"*Is that a problem?*"

"No," I answer, confused as to why that would ever be a matter of concern.

"*Well, it is for me. Don't you people make anything that isn't so heavy? Or tight?*" she asks, fussing with the corset now laced around her body.

"Is that why you refuse to wear a nightgown? You're hot?"

Celeste's brows turn down into a fierce frown.

"*And how would you know I do not wear a nightgown?*" she shoots back.

I ignore her question, as I suspect she will not enjoy hearing that I have seen her sleeping in the night or that I've seen her bare ass on multiple occasions.

"Finish dressing," I command. "We will remedy this immediately."

She makes no attempt to hide the shock on her face, and her mouth opens to defy me, but I hold up a hand.

"That was not a request, darling."

Her eyes roll with heavy exaggeration, and I hate that all I can feel is desire coursing through me like a river—a bone-breaking need to see them roll back with pleasure.

"*Then, by all means, send for the legion so I may put on my skirts,*" she sasses.

I stare at her for a moment, slack-jawed and utterly speechless.

But then something cracks in me, and a heavy chuckle builds in my chest, rippling through the room as she stands before me, arms crossed and frowning as usual.

My laughter grows louder, crackling out of me like dust flaking off an old, forgotten tome. Slow at first, then fuller as I realize how absurd this is. A demon and a snake pretending to be a natural pair, as if either of us wouldn't hesitate to take a bite out of the other.

I laugh a little harder.

What a cruel, cruel joke the Great Mother plays.

CHAPTER 11

CELESTE

H is laugh is thunderous, roaring, and brash, with no concern for its volume—like the big brute he is, and I love it. I shouldn't. But I do.

It reminds me of my own, from a time before my viper had been born. When I was free to laugh as I please. Now it's nothing more than a weapon in my arsenal.

I can still hear Apollo clearly as he stands beyond the door, chuckling deep in his chest, and I wonder if he knows how at ease it makes him sound. If not, I won't be the one to tell him. He seems the type to stifle his pleasure in the name of strength, and I'm rather enjoying it at the moment.

As I stand listening to him, my own veneer cracks a little, and a quiet giggle slips free before I can stifle it. I worry that I am straying too far from the Serpent's teachings, but then I remember there is no need for the Serpent's methods here, no need to seduce Apollo to secure myself a place in his palace. We've already made our agreement—a "bride" for my "freedom." An arrangement simple enough to abide by—nothing more, nothing less. But that also means that when I smile at the sound of his deep laughter, I know it's genuine, and I work quickly to smother it.

Instead, I try to focus on his barbaric behavior and his persistent need to call me *darling*—as if I were some pet he's keeping. Almost immediately, I remember I am as good as, and that seems to do the trick.

My temper simmers as I finish dressing, but I still slide my blade into my bodice as a surety. Glancing at the small pile of clothing that's left, I think the blouse is meant to be worn beneath the corset, but I'd rather meet the Sun than ask Apollo to relace this contraption.

We do not wear such things in Solaria, and I was not aware I would need four hands to get dressed this evening. Ordinarily, I am not shy about my body. I know what I look like, and most often, I use it to my advantage, but the moment Apollo burst in, I lost all sense. His watchful eyes and easy demeanor made me feel like a doll on display, and my anger won out as he stood staring without shame.

When I step out into the hall, I see him leaning against the doorframe staring daggers at poor Lucious, who's now taken up post at the far end of the foyer.

Apollo doesn't acknowledge my presence as I stand between them, but his shadows leak out from under his feet to curl around my ankles like black fog crawling across the earth. I think to kick at them, but the moment his magic meets my skin, I moan audibly. The cool essence caresses my heat-stricken legs, and the fight in me is quickly smothered.

Lucious turns a bright red shade at the sound I make, dropping his gaze to the floor, but Apollo shows no sign of recognition.

His gaze lingers on Lucious for a moment longer, and before he looks at me, he rakes a hand through his dark hair. But the moment he meets my eyes, the stern glare on his face softens, and I'm surprised his voice isn't thick with rage when he speaks.

"Hm, my colors suit you," he muses as he eyes me from head to toe.

I glance down at myself. Whoever chose these pieces had selected them in the Lunar royal colors. Heavy greys, dark blues, and blacks—an exact match for Apollo's vest and pants, but a far departure from the brightly colored clothing back home.

"Thank you," I mutter. I want to thank him for helping me dress, but my pride gets in the way, and my tongue won't move.

"Lucious!" he barks. "Is there something you'd like to say to the Lady Solém?"

Lucious manages not to jump as Apollo's voice echoes through the domed space. Instead, he turns to me, folding over in a deep bow and speaking to his feet.

"My deepest apologies, my lady. It will not happen again."

Before Lucious can lift his head, Apollo barks out another order. "Go join the others in the ring. You are not needed tonight."

My head snaps up to Apollo's face. Not needed?

Lucious scampers out of the foyer before Apollo can say anything more, and once he's out of sight, I turn on him.

"Do I no longer require an escort?" I ask, hoping he's going to loosen his reins.

A broad smile sweeps across his face, fangs gleaming in the lantern light as he peers down at me.

"Don't say foolish things. Ignorance doesn't suit you."

I level my gaze at him, fisting my hands and clenching my teeth as if that will keep my sharp words from escaping.

"Then who will be my escort this evening?" I ask.

"I will," he declares, crossing his hulking arms over his broad chest, a smile plastered on his face, taunting me.

"And what if I don't want to be burdened by your presence this evening?" I spit back.

My words cut deeper than I mean them to, and the smile drops from his face as his eyes darken to a deeper blue.

"Then you will have to suffer in silence, as I do," he replies stiffly.

"What is that supposed to mean?"

He steps in close, trying to force me back, but I hold my ground, even as his face turns dark, and his shadows reach up to swim around my head. His voice lowers to a scolding tone, and when he speaks, his shadows lift my hair from my shoulders, but he doesn't reach out to touch me.

"I think you know what it means, *darling*."

I know exactly what he means. I've been flagrant in my disregard for his presence, and I know it grates on him. He thinks I don't notice, but I've heard him in the night, grumbling to himself about the space I take in his bed, and I've felt his fleeting touches in the dark. Never more than the brush of the hand, but always accompanied by quiet curses in my name.

Silently, I've been hoping that if I make his chamber unbearable, he will abandon it to me or give me chambers of my own. Most nights, it seems to work, and he leaves after idling in the shadows for a while. But, unfortunately for us both, he is persistent.

I give him a terse grin, abandoning the hope that he would go on ignoring me. Or at least pretending to.

Where are we going? I sign, too angry to speak.

"To the village," he says plainly.

"Won't we need guards outside the castle grounds?" I ask, waving vaguely in the direction Lucious has disappeared to.

Apollo lets out an unamused chuckle, cocking a brow at me. "Do you doubt my ability to keep you safe?"

I stifle a laugh, covering it quickly behind my hand. As if I would ever need him to ensure *my* safety. "No," I begin, shaking my head and forgetting to sign the words. "I only meant—"

"Then why would I need guards amongst my own people?" he interjects, his voice deep and even. But his usual tone of condescension is absent this time, and I suspect he's genuinely asking.

"Oh, I-I don't know. The Solarian royal family never leaves the palace without them," I say.

"Yes, well, the Solarian royal family is a hazard to its people. I'm sure plenty have noticed and would like to remedy it if they had the chance," he answers as if it's a fact, and I cover my sneer by biting at my lip.

"Come," he commands, turning without warning, and I do my best not to drag my feet as I trail after him.

Luna's light greets us as we step out into the night air, and Apollo leads me across the darkened grounds, stopping at the iron gate set into the wall at the front of the castle. It cranks open slowly, parting to reveal a busy street filled with people, carriages, and horses moving about.

"Enjoy your evening, your highness!" a woman calls from somewhere far above us.

When I glance up at the high wall, I can see her waving from her perch at the top. A scout sits atop the wall every fifty feet or so, watching us, and I make a note of the additional guard at the gates.

"Thank you, Midina!" Apollo shouts back without looking.

Before I can take a single step, a cold sensation curls up my arm, looping around and around before tightening ever so slightly. I jerk my hand away, confused, only to see a dark band wrapped around my wrist like a brand.

I turn my face to Apollo, but he's already looking at me, so I waste no time in my protest. "What is the meaning of this?"

"Can't have my bride running off now, can I?" he chides.

"Is this not a bit conspicuous?" I ask, holding up my hand and pointing at the shadow trailing down my arm, tying me to him.

He considers me for a moment, then thrusts his hand out in

front of me, palm up. I eye it suspiciously, then search his face. He merely raises a brow in challenge.

He means for me to take it?

"*Ha!*" I laugh, and his jaw tightens as his fist closes around empty air. "The shadow will do just fine," I assert. "Thank you."

He only shrugs before dragging me down the road—the shadow firmly laced around my arm.

Heads turn as we pass through the crowds, and I tense, expecting people to shout or rush toward us as they do back home. But most people only smile and bow before going back to their work. A few children wave eagerly as we pass, but their elders swat at their hands and hurry them along. Some people seem to duck their heads and disappear through shop doors, but no one approaches as we weave through the busy streets.

For a long while, I wonder if it is me they are running from. But as I watch a young man snatch up his lover's hand and hurry down an adjacent pathway, I realize it isn't me they are wary of. It's *him*. Apollo. Perhaps not all of them, but enough that the walkway clears of people in a matter of minutes.

He walks easy, with his head held high and his horns towering over the crowd. But his hands are fisted at his sides, and I can see the anger settle into his jaw as he watches people scurry from him. Still, to walk freely amongst your people? He must not know the power he wields in such a simple act. It is a feat I have never seen mastered by any royal. Certainly not the Serpent.

He leads me through the crowds in silence, strolling through the village and past the shops and market squares. I spend little time looking at the moonlit shops and more time paying attention to the roads we take, trying to mark an exit route should it ever be needed. But I can't help but notice the marked difference in the Lunar village.

It's different from any village I've ever seen. The shops in Luna don't have awnings like the other cities do. Without the Sun beaming down on them, it isn't necessary. Instead, every shop has a small seating area arranged outside for patrons and passersby to sit and eat or talk. It makes for rather cluttered roads, but the people seem happy and excited.

Usually, you would find many foreigners milling about a village of this size, haggling and bartering, but there are only Lunars as far as my eyes can see. Each and every person is a similar shade of brown with the signature alabaster hair in various textures and lengths. It strikes me then that Apollo is quite different from his people. Demon aside, he's a few shades darker than them, and his curly hair is a deep, dark brunette instead of the same shock of white as the rest. Between his monstrous appearance and my sunlit skin, a sea of blue eyes watches our every step.

I ignore them as best I can, but I don't miss the way Apollo's shadows seem to grip me a little tighter as we pass by a group of huddled people, gaping and muttering under their breath. They stand off to the side of the road in front of an all-white building with the Luneer word for "Sanctuary" carved into the façade. A man breaks away from the crowd, reaching out a hand, and I pause. His eyes are fixed on my face, but somehow, I know he isn't looking at me. His gaze moves up and down as his mouth opens and closes, with nothing but faint sounds seeping past his lips. He stares at me unblinking, and I find myself reaching out in return.

"Celeste!" Apollo barks, snatching me back with a hand wrapped tight around my wrist. "That man is sunsick. Do not touch him."

Almost instantly, the man's face turns sour, and he begins to shout incoherent curses at me. His fists wave in the air, and the others answer in a chorus of rage before a woman dressed in all white hurries the small group back into the building.

"But-what? What do you mean sunsi—"

Words sputter out of my mouth, but Apollo wastes no time. He's already gripping my hand and hauling me off in the opposite direction.

I try to slow his pace, pulling at the shadow looped around my wrist, but I can't grasp the dark smoke the way he does, so I grip his arm, yanking him to a stop. He turns, visibly frustrated by my touch, but I ignore his frowning face.

"What was that?" I ask.

Apollo's brows turn down, and his horns dip close to my face as he leans forward to whisper, "It is a sanctuary for those with nowhere to go. And you shouldn't bother them. They are not well. They don't know what they do," he finishes gruffly, yanking me further down the street.

My mouth opens and shuts as my feet tangle from trying to keep pace with Apollo's angry steps. Eventually, I catch up, gripping his sleeve for leverage. I want to ask more questions, but his back is already turned to me, so I fall into step.

We continue moving through the crowds of busy Lunars until Apollo stops abruptly in front of a small shop a few blocks east. It bears a tailor's mark along the doorframe—a weaverbird carrying a thread in its beak—and piles upon piles of fabric stacked to the ceiling in any place they'll fit.

A shop bell rings overhead as Apollo opens the door to usher me inside. I turn on him before it even swings shut.

"Those men back there?" I ask in a hushed whisper, even though I know he cannot hear me.

He holds up a hand, trying to silence me, but I bat it out of the way.

"What happened to them?" I ask, immune now to the glint of his fangs as his lip curls in frustration.

The Serpent happened, he signs, and I glance around to ensure no others are in view.

But...I don't understand, I sign.

"You don't need to understand," he growls, leaning forward until his face is a mere inch from my own. "All you need to know is that it is not safe..."

The shopkeeper interrupts our quiet conversation, and once again, I'm left with more questions than answers as the elder man steps from behind a swaying curtain—hands full of fabric. Searching for somewhere to set them, he waddles with the unwieldy bundle from corner to corner in search of space.

"One moment!" he calls when it takes him longer than expected.

Apollo and I idle in the doorway. He picks at the pile of fabrics on the counter nearest the front, and I stand there wondering how the old man has managed to wedge material between the rafters.

"Hello, Silas!" Apollo calls back.

The man does a little hop of excitement before abandoning his pile on a nearby chair. Several bolts tumble to the floor, but the old man ignores them as he rushes to Apollo with arms thrown wide.

At first, I think the old man will hug him, but at the last second, he claps his hands on Apollo's shoulders, patting him repeatedly. My eyes widen at the overly familiar touch, and I wonder for a moment if Apollo is a prince at all.

"Your highness! Good to see you," the old man says, fussing over him like grandparents do their young ones.

The tailor's aged hands brush down Apollo's arms before clasping his fingers. "How are you liking the items you ordered? I trust your bride enjoys the gowns you selected?" the old shopkeep asks, and a sputtering cough jumps out of Apollo.

His eyes lighten to a turquoise hue, and I take it the abrupt shift in color means he's embarrassed.

Apollo doesn't offer Silas an answer. Instead, he offers me up as bait. "Why not ask her yourself?" he asks. "Silas, I'd like you to meet Lady Celeste Solém of Solaria. Soon to be Queen Alceline of La Luna."

I blink at the ease with which the lie falls from Apollo's lips, but I don't have time to contemplate it. Silas shuffles toward me with outstretched hands, and when he reaches me, I understand why he touches Apollo so familiarly. He is not merely overly friendly, he is blind, and his wrinkled hands are gripping me tight before I know it.

"My goodness!" he exclaims, hands running up and down my arms as his eyes remain fixed on some obscure point just over my shoulder.

His hands travel up my wrists to my shoulders and neck before he cups my face in his hands, and I stiffen, unused to such a physical greeting.

"Quite a beauty you've found, Apollo," Silas declares. Once again, I'm shocked by his familiarity. Then again, as he circles my waist, patting me. "You were right. This cut does quite well for her shape."

I whip around, expecting a look of embarrassment on Apollo's face. Instead, he is standing off to the side with his jaw clenched tight and his shadows stirring up the fabric along the floor. His fists clench as he watches Silas move to my hips, checking the fit.

The old man pulls and tugs at the skirt, and I don't disturb him. It is a tailor's inspection, albeit more intimate than most, and my blade is well within reach. But the inspection doesn't last very long.

Apollo's shadows are growing in number, spreading from under his feet and threatening to darken the room. Before Silas can inspect the hem of my corset, Apollo's big arm cuts between us, sweeping me back a step and cutting off the old man's examining.

"Silas," Apollo's voice feels heavy in the over-stuffed room, and his cool fingers settle on my hip, keeping me firmly planted by his side. "Please. Celeste is not used to being handled."

Apollo strains to remain polite, digging his claws into my skin as he fails. Shadows crawl across my body as Apollo holds me close, and I squirm in his grip but he doesn't loosen his hold.

I send my light to the surface, letting it grow hot beneath his hand until the temperature becomes too much for him, and he's forced to release me. He grumbles and bares his teeth at me, but I ignore him.

"Ah, forgive me. I am ahead of myself," Silas mutters, bowing deeply. "Welcome to La Luna, dear. What can I do for you this fine evening?" he asks as he stands before us with arms crossed, a wide grin stretching across his weathered face.

"Lady Solem is in need of something lighter," Apollo says. "The Lunar tastes seem to be too cumbersome for her. Too warm."

"They're lovely designs," I add, pausing to glance at Apollo. "But my...sunlight runs quite hot."

Silas startles ever so slightly.

"Sunlight?" he asks, eyes wide. "Apollo did not tell me you were a Solarian celestial." A long pause stretches out between the three of us, and I worry I've made a mistake in telling him this.

The Lunars I've met so far have been rather cordial, but it is no secret that there are those who do not want me here. I can hardly blame them, given our people's history. It is filled with blood and battle, and I would not be surprised if this elder remembers the times before the Council.

I brace myself for his anger.

"Well, yes! Of course, Silas exclaims. "The traditional fabrics would be too heavy for a woman like yourself." He harrumphs. "Apollo should have mentioned such a thing!" he says scolding him. "Not to worry. I have plenty of fabric that should work."

Without another word, Silas disappears back through the makeshift door, muttering something about Venutian silk, and Apollo turns on me.

You will do well to keep your light to yourself, he signs before balling his hands into tight fists.

And you will do well to keep your hands *to yourself!* I snap back, signing wildly.

Apollo nearly growls at my impudence, and I throw my hands up before stalking toward a small sitting area packed in between the mountains of fabric. He follows without invitation, and I groan. But he pays no heed to my anger as he drops down onto a small sofa, returning to our usual silence.

Silas returns with a pile of mixed fabrics and quickly shoves dresses, skirts, and blouses into my arms, directing me behind an ornate folding screen—unsurprisingly, draped in more fabric.

"Most of these are Martian in origin," Silas begins with a bright smile. "But they are built to withstand the Martian flames, so they should do just fine for a Solarian like yourself. I had intended to send them to market in Venutia, but I'd much rather you wear them, your highness."

I translate Silas's words without thinking, and Apollo balks a little, watching me with a small frown.

I may not like him all that much, but his exclusion from conversation does nothing in my favor, so I continue even as he sits brooding in his too-small seat.

Silas breezes in and out of the room several times before disappearing altogether, and I'm left standing there holding the big pile of clothing. Apollo stands abruptly, taking the bundle from my arms, then collapses back onto his seat without a word.

He looks enormous in the little store. Everything made too small for his monstrous proportions. His massive arms are draped over the back of the sofa, spanning the entire length, while his long legs stick out before him, taking up an abnormally large amount of space. His knees are thrown open wide, and he somehow looks more comfortable peeking out over the mountain of fabric in his lap than on his throne.

Laughter bubbles up as I watch him, and I bite my lip, trying to cover it.

"What?" he barks, eyes narrowing.

I shake my head, gulping down air to avoid bursting at the seams.

"Speak! Or I'll leave you to your sweating," he demands.

My eyes roll, but I sign to him, *Nothing. It's just...this is quite an unusual experience. For a person in your position.*

Apollo straightens, pinning me with a hard stare.

"Silas has dressed my family since before you were a thought. He is the finest tailor in all of Celestia, older than you and I combined, with a masterful collection and skill. I would not dare ask him to lug all this to La Luna for me," he says, gesturing at his lap and frowning as if he's disappointed with me. "We go to him." He speaks with the same finality he says all things. As if it couldn't possibly be a topic for debate. "As we always have."

His horns jerk upward as he stares me down, daring me to defy his words, and I'm surprised by the passion my comment has elicited. I didn't mean anything by it. I wasn't suggesting this was beneath him, merely that it was odd to find someone of his rank wandering freely through the streets and shopping at the local tailor as he does.

I doubt he will believe me if I explain myself, so I settle for, "*You're right.*" Though, I still find it strange that a man labeled a demon is more considerate than any other royal I've ever met. Myself included.

"I know I am right." He grunts in return before shooing me. "Hurry up. We don't have all evening."

I snatch up a few items from his lap and shuffle behind the big screen, careful not to drop anything. Immediately, I settle into a fight with my corset ties. Unlacing it isn't nearly as tricky as lacing it. But after several long seconds of tugging and pulling, I take my blade to the strings and sigh a heavy release when it falls unceremoniously to the floor. I take a moment to fan my sweat-slicked chest before slipping into dress after dress.

True to his word, the fabric Silas selected is more than breathable, and I quickly decide I will not be donning the sun-forsaken Lunar garments again. Already my body has begun to cool, taking a bit of my temper with it. But it only lasts until Apollo decides to speak again.

"Come out, *darling*," he calls, drawing out my pet name so it lingers in the air, taunting me.

"Foul brute," I mutter.

Silence falls over the little shop as I ignore him.

"Don't be rude, darling," he says after a few moments pass. "If

I am to supply it, I should have a say. Or do you now prefer the Lunar garb?" he calls, threatening me.

I glance down at my corset, now useless atop the pile of Martian dresses, and release a heavy sigh.

I step reluctantly from behind the ornate divider, arms crossed and jaw clenched as Apollo stares at me without reservation. His eyes roam freely, lingering around my chest for much longer than I would consider polite, and his head cocks as if I am a specimen to be examined.

Again, I'm reminded of my newfound status. Pet.

His shadows reach out to drift around my ankles, lifting the hem of my dress. I kick at them, but he ignores my resistance. Instead, he stands in a shockingly graceful motion and crosses the small space in one step to stand within an inch of my chest.

"What is this chain you wear?" he asks, reaching for the thinly braided metal draped across my waist.

"*It is a waist chain*," I tell him.

I'd worn it beneath my corset. A decision I now regret. Seeing as the metal has left little indentations in my skin where the charms usually sit.

"Does it have a purpose?" Apollo asks, plucking at the tiny sun hanging just above my navel.

"*No.*" I bat his hand away. "*There is no purpose. Are we finished?*"

His hand drops to his side, but he continues looming much too close.

"That depends. Are you still hot?" he asks, crossing his arms over his broad chest.

Yes, I think to myself. But suddenly I don't think it's the clothing.

Apollo's shadows course around my ankles, and his thick arms brush against my breasts, sending little shocks of friction through me each time he shifts. He watches me patiently, eyes now dark as night, and I have to force myself not to take a step back. Though his presence is overwhelming, I refuse to give him the satisfaction.

I breathe deeply, ignoring the way my body presses closer to him when I do, and say, "No. I'm not hot."

His tongue runs over his thick lips before a sly grin settles on his face.

"Wonderful," he whispers. "Silas! Can you craft a few night-gowns from this fabric?" he asks, brushing his knuckles across my stomach and pinning me with a hard stare. "Our lady is in need of some."

This time I do not hold in my laugh. I can't. My antics in his chamber must be bothering him more than he's willing to admit, and I'm too self-satisfied to hide it.

CHAPTER 12

CELESTE

———

"Come," Apollo grunts once I've selected quite an extensive array of items from Silas's collection.

I do not know how much longer I will be at La Luna, but so long as Apollo is supplying them, I will take what he can give.

He takes his time on our path back to the castle, stopping at several stalls for various foods that I'm not familiar with. The merchants don't seem surprised to see his face, but they do not appear thrilled either. Still, Apollo grins politely, hiding his fangs, as he shells out a generous amount of money. By the time we reach the castle gates, he has more bags than his hands can carry, and his shadows are lugging most of his load.

I follow in dutiful silence, sniffing after the confections and trying to quiet my stomach. He hardly acknowledges me as we make our way through the moonlit corridors, and I half expect him to send me back to my cage with no one but Lucious's nervous silence to keep me company. But then we pass the narrow hallway that leads to his chamber, and I can't keep quiet anymore.

I tug on his sleeve, but he doesn't turn. Instead, he grips my hand, pulling me along and grumbling, "I will feed you, and then you may be rid of me."

I don't argue as he hauls me across the catwalk toward the eastern wing, and when he stops in front of a rather plain-looking door, I do not question him. His shadows push past it, swinging the door open wide to reveal a small, intimate table set for one.

"Is this where you've been eating?" I ask.

Raye and I ate with Evalina, Shrea, and Rewnick, who I quickly realized were daughter, mother, and uncle, respectively. But each night, Apollo was notably absent, and I never thought to ask about him. My guess was that he didn't wish to dine with his "bride."

"When I have the time," Apollo answers, pulling out a rickety wooden chair.

He waits until I sit down before pulling out an equally suspicious chair and sitting beside me.

His chair creaks and cracks as he lowers himself onto it, and I watch, wondering if it will snap under his weight. When it doesn't, he empties his load onto the table, then pours a glass of wine from a half-rusted pitcher into a large goblet. He pushes it in front of me, and I take it, even though it's clearly of a size meant for his hands. I take a leisurely sip, and when I'm finished, Apollo takes the goblet and downs the rest before refilling it.

"Why do you eat alone?" I ask as he piles a plate high with assorted meats, cheeses, and a few pastries.

I think he's going to keep it for himself, but then he places it in front of me and sets about making a plate of his own.

"Why do you ask so many questions?" he answers, at which I frown.

"I'm curious," I admit. And not just for the sake of my mission, but because Apollo is quite a strange man, if he is a man at all.

"I can see that," Apollo murmurs. He leans back in his chair, stuffing his face with a flaky bun of some kind. "I will answer your questions if you answer mine," he says, speaking around a mouthful of dough.

I pluck an identical pastry off my plate and bite into it. A flavorful jam bursts across my tongue, and I accidentally finish it before I answer him.

"Fine." I shrug.

A smile curls over his fangs, and I have a feeling I may have just played into his hands, but I can't bring myself to care right now.

"Does your crown know you're here?" he asks, sipping from our shared goblet, peering at me over the rim.

"I don't see why they would," I answer.

Apollo grunts in disbelief.

"A noble lady of Solaria? Engaged to the prince of night? The *Demon* of La Luna?" His eyebrows lift as he looks at me skeptically. "Surely that is of consequence to the Serpent."

I shrug again, letting the lie settle onto my shoulders. *"I wouldn't know."*

He huffs, skewering a cheese cube with a claw and popping it into his mouth. "I eat alone because I am not very pleasant to have dinner with," he answers in exchange.

"Yes, well...if you interrogate all your dinner guests, then I'd have to agree."

His deep chuckle rumbles through the room, and I avert my eyes to hide the light rising in my cheeks.

"Why do you call yourself a demon?" I ask.

"Because that is what I am," he says cooly, leaning back in his chair and propping his arms behind his head.

"But there is no such thing," I counter. *"Your magic is no different from any other being blessed by a celestial mother. Lots of celestials have a second form. I have one,"* I add, at which his eyes lighten to a soft sky blue. *"It only emerges when I need it most, and it may not look like this."* I wave a hand vaguely at his horns. *"But are your horns and fangs so different?"*

His jaw clenches, and his big muscles flex in frustration. His eyes darken quickly as he passes me a warning glance. But I dismiss it. As I do most of his threats.

"That's where you're wrong," he says. "I have no second form. This is all that I am. I cannot shield it from view."

My frown deepens. *And that makes it the work of demons?"* I ask, confused.

Apollo puffs out an unamused laugh, and a dark tendril reaches out to stroke my cheek. I don't shy from it. I won't let him dissuade me from this. I merely cross my arms and sit frowning until he chooses to answer me.

When he finally does, I am surprised by the sadness in his eyes.

"I am not a celestial because I was not blessed by a celestial," he begins softly. "Celestial magic is a blessing from the *celestial* mothers. The deities that rule one's house. Martians are touched by flame, and Venutians shift matter. Uranians wield ice, and in Saturn, they bend the air. *You...*" Apollo taps a claw to the center of my chest, and my magic rises to meet him even as I try to smother it. "Have been kissed by sunlight. But my shadows are not a blessing from Mother Luna. They are a curse from the night."

My mouth opens, but another shadow caresses my lips, hushing me as he continues. "After the Solar Wars had burned half of Solaria into ash, Father knew that one day the Serpent would move past his own borders."

I was too young to remember the Solar Wars. They were long before my light had formed. But I know the history well. Everyone born in Solaria does. From childhood, we are taught the might of the Rising Suns, their plot to bring sunlight to every territory, and how the Serpent defeated the Setting Sons and their mission to stop them.

Many lost their light fighting. Solaria was nearly leveled. Homes were turned to dust and cities to rubble. All while the nine houses watched from the safety of their own borders. None had interfered, and as a result, the battle was prolonged, spanning many lifetimes. Eventually, the Rising Suns prevailed, and the Serpent took the throne after a hard-won victory.

"Father designed a plan that very day. The day your serpent took the throne." I don't miss the way in which he sneers the word "your" at me. But I say nothing. "Father believed that only darkness could defeat the light. Not moonlight. But true darkness. Night."

His shadows fill the room as he speaks. Dark columns snake up the walls to fill in the windows. They pour from his palms to snuff out the candles in the center of the table. His magic continues to swell until we sit before each other, steeped in darkness, and the only light is my own.

"When my mother bore me in her womb, my father took her to the forest. Deep into its heart where the magic that blankets the trees in darkness is born. He asked the forest to bless me. To bring forth their savior, a child blessed by the night. One who could withstand the Sun. A prince of darkness," he says, moving his magic about me and casting shadows on my light. "So, no. We are not the same. I am a demon. And you..."

His words trail off as he decides not to finish his thought.

"If you're a demon, what does that make me?" I ask, blinking at him.

His eyes hood as he traces the light moving beneath my skin with his finger.

"The devil herself?" he quips.

"What's a demon to a devil?" I tease, and Apollo laughs before his eyes darken and he frowns at me.

I bite my lip, trying to ignore the heat in his stare, but my light betrays me as it burns hot in my chest. My breathing grows sharp as he pulls away to level his next question.

"Why aren't you afraid?" he asks, squaring his shoulders, and growing seemingly larger right in front of me.

"Afraid of what?"

"Me," he says as if it's obvious.

A breathy laugh escapes me, and Apollo's eyes darken as his hands ball in his lap.

"I have no reason to be," I sign. *"Why do you expect me to be?"*

"Because all the others are," he says.

"Others?"

"Other people. Other...women."

My heart sinks to my toes as his eyes fall to his plate.

I've spent more time looking at Apollo than I care to admit, and I've recently come to the conclusion that there is nothing truly horrifying about him. Not his towering horns or his gleaming fangs, not even the constant swish and flick of his tail. No matter how I try, I can't seem to see this demon he speaks of. To me, he only appears to be a man blessed by a magic we don't yet understand.

I realize then that Shrea is right. Apollo is no more a demon than I am.

"Fools," I bite back, and the smile he gives me is enough to make me contemplate my allegiances. *"They just don't know any better,"* I tell him. *"People are always afraid of what they don't understand."*

Without warning, Apollo reaches across the table to grip my chin. He holds me gently as he brings his face closer, inspecting me.

"You're a rather unusual woman," he muses, and I find myself enjoying the cool touch of his claws.

"Says the unusual man."

He's looking at me as if he wants to ask me another question, and I can't seem to look away until he's said it. So I'm only dimly aware of the door to our little dining room swinging open with a quiet thud when a loud voice screeches Apollo's name.

He groans in response, deep in his chest, and I can feel my light fluttering in my stomach in open betrayal.

Hesitantly, he pulls his hand away from my face, and his shadows begin a steady retreat as he pushes back from the table.

Though he leaves a single tendril draped gently across my collarbones as he moves to block the interloper's path.

"You must be half nighthound. How is it that you always seem to know where I am?" Apollo asks dryly, but I can't see the person he's speaking to.

"Very funny, sire," the intruder replies, and I recognize Renwick's high-pitched tone. "I've come to tell you of the Solarian guard. We believe we've found the last of them."

"What?" I blurt, jumping from my seat as anticipation overrides my manners.

Apollo idles in the doorway for a moment, forcing me to peer over his big shoulders as I push at him. My efforts are useless as he stands like a stone pillar before me. But I am determined, and he eventually growls and steps aside.

"Found them? Found them where?" I demand, signing for Apollo's benefit. But Renwick doesn't speak. He focuses his attention on Apollo, who is hovering behind me like a second shadow. *"Hello?"* I demand, and Renwick's face turns up in dismay, but I think I hear Apollo chuckling softly.

"I suggest you tell her what she wants to know, Renwick," Apollo says, and my arms cross in haughty satisfaction.

Renwick bows his head for a brief second, but when he speaks, he speaks only to Apollo. I sign the words automatically, leaving me too occupied to be upset when Apollo's shadows find their way around my hips and waist.

"They were scattered across the forest floor. It seems the seekers had..." Renwick glances at me, hesitating. "They were dragging them to their dens. But the Solarians fought valiantly. Many of them are not—" Renwick takes a deep breath. "Whole." His gaze falls to the floor, and for a moment, he looks almost...sad.

Damn these Lunars and their kindness. This would all be much easier if they spent their nights cursing me to high heaven. Like Apollo does.

"Take me to them," I order as I move toward the door.

But before Renwick can protest, Apollo's arm wraps around my waist, hauling me backward.

"Absolutely not," he grunts.

I twist in his arms, fighting for my freedom, but he lifts me from the floor, crushing me to his chest.

"And why not?" I ask, trying to focus on something other than the hard lines of his muscular body.

"You have no business with the dead." He counters.

"Well, I certainly have no business with you," I hiss, thrashing against him.

His expression shifts suddenly. One moment there is a playful glint in his eye and the next his eyes are filled with darkness. The muscles in his strong jaw clench and release. Fury hums through him, but he sets me on my feet.

I don't wait to see what he will do. I turn on my heel and rush past Renwick, not caring when Apollo shouts for me to slow.

CHAPTER 13

APOLLO

———

Celeste is hardly a lady. That much is clear. In fact, I'm not entirely sure she wasn't raised by seekers. She's loud and forward—bold. But perhaps most importantly, she is mesmerizing.

Every moment I find myself eagerly awaiting her next decision because I have failed to predict her actions from the second she set foot in my throne room. She does not flee when I think she will, she does not cower when I think she will, and somehow, she does not yell when I think she will. She is an enigma to me. Far too daring and far too curious for my heart to handle. She goes brazenly toward whatever suits her, reaching for sunsick men and marching off to meet the dead as if it were nothing. How am I meant to protect such a wild thing? Particularly when she disregards my orders every chance she gets.

I watch now in mild awe as she sweeps past Renwick, lifting the hem of her skirt around her knees as she takes off at a jog.

Savage woman.

Renwick gapes at me, confusion clouding his usual tense

expression as he wonders why I allow her to behave in such a way, but I say nothing. Firstly, because I do not owe Renwick an explanation for my actions. But mostly because I do not have an answer for him. Were it anyone else spitting their words at me and sauntering off without warning, they would find themselves facing down the demon. Yet I do nothing but fight the ache growing in my groin as I watch her leave.

When I look at her, all I can think is—*mine*. And I hate her for it. Because it seems there is nothing I can do about it.

Her presence is already a poison to my heart, and now her every passing glance holds me hostage, while the sight of her leaves my stomach feeling empty, hungry for something I can't have. Even the sight of Silas's gentle inspection of her sent me into a frenzy. And now his handiwork is driving me near to madness.

The Solarians may be right in their traditions, with their thin coverings and scarce fabric. The memory of Celeste dressed to her toes now strikes me as a sin. I am loathe to admit it, but I cannot help myself. She is radiant in the Martian style.

It is not nearly as sheer as the Solarian garb she arrived in, but it clings to her like skin, framing her plump ass and flaring at her full hips as she stalks down the hall. I curse myself for my weak mind, burying the thought of her sprawled across my bed as my sense returns.

I hurry through the empty corridor, catching up to her quickly despite her speed.

"Celeste," I call, grabbing her hand to halt her progress.

"*Were you going to tell me?*" she shouts, and I'm forced to step back as her light burns hot.

"Excuse me?"

"*Were you going to tell me you were* collecting *their bodies?*" she yells, yanking her arm free.

"*Collecting* them? What kind of monster do you take me for?" I shout back.

Heavens, what is happening to me? I am the master of this

castle, of this land. There is no reason for me to tolerate her shouting. But even as her eyes burn bright and white, I can't help myself. She is fearless in the face of my anger, and I adore her for it.

"What were you going to do with them, Apollo?" she hollers, sunlight shifting to a searing white light, forcing me to shield my eyes.

"Whatever you wished me to do with them!" I bellow, then watch as the heat leaves her eyes and dims to its usual golden yellow.

Her chest heaves as she stands before me, panting from the effort of restraining her magic. My shadows swirl around her, desperate to latch on, but I hold them back—just barely.

Me? she signs silently.

"Yes," I grunt. "They are your guard, are they not?"

"But-but...the Serpent. You hate—"

"The Serpent. Yes, but I am not heartless. I would want peace for my men if someone were to offer it. I had Renwick recover the bodies in case you'd like to give them a proper burial."

"Oh," she mutters. There is a quiet apology that she leaves unsaid, but I accept it anyway.

She turns, prepared to march off, but I catch her by the arm again.

"I have to—" she begins, signing with her free hand and speaking quickly. But I interrupt her before her mind runs away with her again.

"I know. I can see the determination on your face. I will take you to your guard. But I must warn you. It is not a sight suitable for a lady." Her face turns up, insulted, and I correct myself. "It is not a sight suitable for *anyone*. I *will* take you. But I will not let you wander in unprepared. A seeker's kill is rarely clean. They are stupid creatures. Destructive when desperate. People are often left in *pieces*. It may not be a sight you wish to see."

"I know," she says, more reserved than I've ever seen her. *"I've seen what they do. I've seen what they are capable of. That is why I*

must see my guard. They gave their lives for me. I at least owe them my thanks."

She doesn't lift her eyes from the floor, and I don't force her to look at me. I suspect there is something in her expression she does not wish for me to see. Instead, I take her hand and fold it into the crook of my elbow.

"Very well," I say.

To my dismay, she does not argue as we walk arm-in-arm, and I take the quiet moment as a small blessing amongst my new curse.

The empty grounds are cluttered with legionnaires the closer we get to the barracks. Some of them sit idle in the wet grass, while others mull about, training and moving supplies. But all of them stop what they're doing in order to watch us—no, watch *her*—as she passes through the barracks' doors.

The simple building is not an elaborate construction. It has several main corridors that connect to single-occupant rooms and smaller social halls, as well as a large infirmary wing at the far back. Heads poke out from open doorways the deeper we roam, but the halls are curiously empty.

I need not guess where my legion is. They are a nosey bunch, and they'll have found their way to the infirmary by now. I'd bet my crown on it.

Sure enough, when we arrive at the infirmary doors, I can see soldiers crowding the room on the other side. They are all standing between the narrow cots, staring down at the dead as though they might rise again. Someone had sense enough to cover the bodies, but I can see the eager curiosity on their faces as they try to peer past the fabric obstructing their view.

Celeste steps into the room, breaking away from me only to come to a stop as she reaches a knot of people too enthralled in their gaping to notice her. I wait for her to demand that they move. To shout at them as she does me. But she stands there, silent, shifting on her feet. I think she will holler or unleash her light, but then she wrings her hands together, uneasy, and guilt quickly catches up to me.

I *am* a monster, truly.

Here she stands, preparing to face the death of her comrades, and I deny her. Meanwhile, my men look on as if it is entertainment for their eyes. No wonder she thinks so low of me.

A sour sensation settles in my gut, and my shadows reach ahead of her, smacking several soldiers on the head.

"Hey!" I shout, my voice filling the room.

Celeste doesn't so much as flinch at the sound, but the others jerk around, heads turning toward me, ears trained on my next words. "When the Serpent cuts off *your* heads, shall I let his army gaze upon your bodies until they've satisfied their curiosity?"

My voice ripples across the walls and floor, and several soldiers drop their heads, too embarrassed to meet my eyes. Some take a moment longer to understand, staring at me with blank faces before shame catches up to them, and they, too, bow their heads.

"Out!" I demand.

The mass exodus is quick. Feet shuffle and bodies shift as Celeste and I wait by the entrance. Most of them manage not to sneer at her as they pass, but I note the faces that do. It's a similar look to the ones I receive from passersby in the market square, and I decide they will find themselves in my training ring come midnight tomorrow.

I step forward, only to bump into Celeste, who stands stalk still, watching the soldiers filter out until we're all that stand between the rows of covered faces. Her head swivels from side to side, looking for something to take comfort in, and she finds it at the end of the hall, standing beside Evalina. The short, tan woman, with hair black as shadow and red-rimmed, swollen eyes. Raye is her name. Supposedly a handmaiden, though I have my doubts about that. Evalina's hand rests on her shoulder, but Raye breaks free to sprint down the aisle, throwing herself at Celeste.

Handmaiden my tail.

Evalina joins us in the center, standing over the sobbing handmaiden as I hover near Celeste, the two of them embracing between us. I lift a brow, to which Evalina merely shrugs.

Raye buries her face in Celeste's hair, weeping, and I can feel Celeste speaking in low tones as her voice ripples across the floor.

Is she always like this? I ask Evalina, taking the moment of distraction to sign to her. I gesture with my tail at the weeping handmaiden.

No. But I'll take this over the incessant talking. Evalina signs. *She speaks too much.*

Evalina smirks, but I don't miss the spark of amusement as she refocuses her attention on Raye.

This one as well, I sign, tipping my horns toward Celeste.

Evalina laughs short and clipped, and the women pull apart to glare at us. The handmaiden eyes my horns and fangs briefly before dismissing my presence. She returns her attention to Celeste, who all but ignores me as she takes in the bodies spread before us.

Her eyes are curiously dry, but I can see the tension mounting in her shoulders when she turns to her handmaiden and asks, "Have you seen them?"

She does not sign the words, but she angles her body in my direction so I can see her lips.

I realize then that Celeste has yet to leave me out of conversation. Even when she has no reason to, she accommodates my impairment. Always giving me a view of her beautiful mouth or signing when she is able, and I absently wonder if perhaps this woman is both a blessing *and* a curse.

Eventually, she breaks away, moving through the room. She lifts the sheet from the vacant bodies to peer down at their faces. I watch her visibly start when she pulls back the first one. Her hand goes to her chest as if she's trying to still her heartbeat, and I know the sight is horrid when she buckles at the knees. She bends forward, propping her hands on her thighs before righting herself. Her handmaiden swipes at her own tears, gathering herself to help, but Celeste waves her off, and we all watch as she winds her way through the rows of men.

She moves slowly and methodically. Each time she lifts a sheet, she folds it over the man's chest before placing a hand on him and muttering words I do not try to read. I know it is a quiet goodbye, not meant for me. I leave her to mourn on her own. But eventually, the little startled movements she's making start to weigh on me, and I move to her side despite her protests. She shoves at me, but I ignore her, draping my shadows around her like a cloak while cautiously tucking her under my arm. Her light heats then cools as she abandons her anger.

We can return to our begrudging silence later. For now, I walk beside her, offering her what little comfort I can.

She stops at every bed, unveiling every man and peering into his face even when some are half missing. She does this thirty times and each time, her face grows even more troubled.

As I watch her, a stroke of unbridled jealousy whips through me.

What is she searching for? A lover among these men?

The thought makes my shadows rise, and I swallow hard, forcing my instinct back. But I still feel a wave of relief wash over me when she doesn't seem to find who she's looking for. With any luck, her lover has been swallowed whole by the beasts of the night.

When we reach the end of the last row, she turns to face me, signing quietly as I shield her from view.

There's one missing, she signs, eyes shimmering with a dull light. *There are only thirty here. Our party held thirty-one guards.*

"Are you sure this is all you've found?" I ask, turning toward Evalina. "She says there is one missing."

Raye speaks, but I only catch the question at the end as she chokes on a sob. "Who?"

"Kefu," Celeste says before a stony look clouds her soft features.

I can't tell if this Kefu is a lover or a friend. But Evalina shakes her head, and all I'm able to offer her is, "This is all."

Celeste does not cry, but she does deflate a little further.

Evalina speaks up as Celeste and Raye remain downtrodden.

"The scouts said the scene was..." Her eyes flit to Raye, still swiping fiercely at her cheeks, trying to clear away the tears. "Violent. The blood likely drew out the other creatures."

Raye sucks in a breath at the thought, but Celeste merely nods and says, "Thank you. For letting me bless them."

Ah, so that is what she was whispering. A prayer.

"What will you do with them?" she asks quietly, signing when Raye's eyes shut tight with emotion once more.

"What would you have me do with them?" I ask.

Evalina's brows rise, but I ignore her. As does Celeste. She thinks for a moment before glancing at Raye and steeling her decision.

"We will send them on to Mother Sun," she says with a certainty I find oddly fascinating.

She is not asking me. She is telling me.

The realization makes my shadows stir, and I have to concentrate to keep my tail from twitching like a fool.

I nod, even though I know not what such a thing entails.

"Very well. Renwick can see to the arrangements. Tell him what you require, and it shall be done."

Her blank expression fractures, leaving behind a look of surprise that has me aching.

She still thinks I am a beast, I am certain. But perhaps she is not wrong. Because as we stand surrounded by fallen men and the stench of rotting flesh, I have the urge to wrap her in shadow, carry her off to my chamber, and drink from the well I know lies between her thighs.

Celeste's lips part, and her chest heaves as she prepares to speak, but her words are cut off as Raye declares, "I can do it! Evalina will help me, won't you, Evalina?"

Evalina looks as if her patience is being held together by a single hair, but she merely rolls her shoulders and bows her head in silent agreement.

As I look at her, I can't help but wonder what poison these women have planted for us both to be so complicit in their demands. But the thought dissipates as Celeste meets my eyes, offering me a sight I won't soon forget.

A wide smile, teeth and all, beaming up at me like the Sun herself.

CHAPTER 14

CELESTE

———

I feel foolish, trailing behind Apollo all afternoon, letting him lead me by the hand like a child. But our visit to the infirmary weighs heavily on my mind.

The bodies were as expected. A ghastly sight. Unlike any I've ever seen.

A viper's work is discrete. My kills precise. Quick and effective. Rarely do they end in such a violent manner. Some of the men were still whole, with not an ounce of light left. Most were missing pieces. And at least one was missing entirely.

The sight of it was more than I was prepared for, and guilt overcame me almost instantly.

Kefu gave everything for me. His light, his life...there isn't even a vessel to send his soul home to Mother Sun. The Serpent should reward his mother and father handsomely for his service, but I know they'll see nothing. Not even his ashes.

Anger slices through me like hot iron, and I don't have the energy to argue with Apollo when he reaches for my hand to lead me out of the barracks. At least, that's what I'm telling myself. But somewhere, buried beneath the viper's bloodlust, I'm starting to question whether I truly dislike Apollo, with his dark shadows and brooding stare.

He is harsh without a doubt, but only as necessary, and he doesn't take sport in pain as the Serpent does. I struggle to imagine him as anything other than unyieldingly fair. Even when others may view his fairness as unjust.

I saw the scowling faces as we entered the infirmary. And even though our union is a farce, Apollo demanded they treat me with equal regard. As we exited the barracks, half the legion was crowded around the entrance, glaring at me, and Apollo took the time to make his position known.

"Celeste is to be your queen!" he shouted, so loudly that I am almost certain the ground shook beneath my feet. "You may not like that fact, but I do not care what you like! If you take issue with her place at La Luna, you are free to address it with me directly! In the training ring! I welcome your challenge. But be prepared to lose your rank because I will not tolerate traitors in my midst."

The cadets scattered before the last word passed between his fangs, and I was left standing beside him in awe.

He is shockingly evenhanded, but I have no doubt he does not know mercy for those who would do him wrong. In this, we are the same.

Apollo leaves me in his chamber for another lonely evening, bowing briskly before sweeping out of the room to disappear down the hall. But I have no interest in being caged tonight. I planned on spending my night gathering what little information I could. But that was before Apollo stole me for the evening. Now, as I peek outside my door and see his shadows lingering like smoke in the hall, I decide it's best to see for myself what his legion does in the forest at night.

Lucious is standing in the center of the foyer, pacing back and forth, and he startles when I call his name.

"My lady! Do you need something?" he asks, rushing toward the door.

"I was wondering if you could help me with the ties on this dress?" I ask, batting my lashes as I uncoil the viper that has been dormant for the past few weeks.

"Oh, I-I-I don't think. Prince Apollo would not approve," he stammers, and I almost feel sorry for what I'm about to do.

"That's alright. It will only take a second," I appeal, gripping him by the hand before he realizes he's wandered into my bite.

My light surges, passing through him in a rush, and I watch it move beneath his uniform, up his arm, across his neck, and behind his eyes, before pulsing once and bringing him down to the floor with a hard thud—his head bouncing lightly off the stone floor.

"Thank you," I coo as he falls into a deep slumber.

He'll be fine. I'd done little more than stun him. He'll rest peacefully for a long while and wake with nothing more than a bruise. Assuming Apollo doesn't find him in the meantime.

I step quickly over Lucious's limp body sprawled across the floor and take off sprinting through the halls.

Apollo's path is not hard to find. His unmistakable fragrance —the scent of rain and earth mixed with smoke, carries through the halls on a stiff wind, and I follow it through darkened corridors, drawing into the shadows whenever the sounds of people draw near. Which they rarely do. The vacant nature of the Lunar castle is even more prominent after the Moon sets. So I move undisturbed through the dark night.

Apollo's trail leads me past the gardens and beyond the barracks to the far side of the La Luna, where the Night Forest butts against the castle grounds, then disappears between the nightshade trees.

"Sunspots," I curse aloud.

What could he possibly want in that heaven-forsaken forest? It offers nothing but darkness and demons. True demons. Not handsome ones with ebony horns, thick lips, and beautiful eyes.

I groan, kicking a tuft of damp earth. Memory strikes me as I stand staring at the tree line. Gurgling screams and swallowed light. The desperate wailing that poured from Kefu and his men. Raye's tear-stained face.

I'm forced to squat in the grass, gulping air as I try to find myself.

Testing the fate of the forest a second time seems like a fool's errand, and I idle just before the trees, peering into the pitch-black night as my courage splinters.

The Serpent demands it, I tell myself, standing abruptly before creeping toward the forest boundary.

As I draw nearer, I can see the scouts' towers sit empty, dark, and unmanned, but I don't stop to question it. Mother Sun must be on my side this evening. I only hope she sticks close.

As if conjured by my presence, howls spring up in the distance, and a stinging ache shoots through my left leg in memory of the seekers' hunt. I bury my light, trying to hide it deeper than I had before. But a bone-chilling shiver runs from my head to my toes as the sound of their calls echo through the trees. And with my light gone, the cold night creeps into my bones, making me regret my decision to abandon the cloak Apollo procured for me.

I swallow hard before burying my fear alongside my light and starting down a well-worn path.

I follow the winding trail, creeping at a snail's pace, and stiffening at every sound. The seekers may dominate this forest, but they are not the only beasts that reside here, and I have no desire to meet the others. So I tread lightly.

But the deeper I go, the louder the forest becomes, and soon the sounds of men and women shouting along with the thrashing hoofbeats of a dozen horses battering against the earth come charging in my direction. I pause for half a breath, considering my options.

Being found is absolutely out of the question. Not only would my mission come to a swift close, but Apollo would likely take my head if he discovered a viper curled in his bed.

A chorus of hounds looms behind me, and a panicked throng echoes their cries somewhere far ahead. The legion must be close. I've ventured too deep into the forest to turn back, and the noise of seekers creeps closer with every breath. They will reach me before I reach the tree line.

Another screech, this one like the cry of something desperate and dying, rings out, closer now, and I turn for the nearest nightshade tree.

The base is wide, too big for me to wrap my arms and legs around, but sturdy enough to hold my weight. I heft myself up its trunk, tucking the hem of my skirt under my chin while squeezing my thighs around its wide berth. I scramble for purchase as I haul my body onto the branches and cling to the dry wood.

Perched among the narrow limbs, I hold my breath, not daring to make even the faintest sound as I strain to hear the seekers cutting through the forest.

A rumble starts in the distance, growing louder by the second. The ground shakes, and the nightshade I've chosen trembles. A thunderous roar of horses, seekers, and soldiers explodes into the night air, passing directly under me, shaking my hiding place like a leaf in the wind.

"Push them east!" A man shouts in Luneer, and I watch the riders streaking by on horseback.

Voices strike up in a chorus.

"Hya!"

"Hya!"

They yell, "Allera, allera, allera!" as they fly past, blending in with the dark night as they move across the forest floor.

Whoops and hollers rise to the treetops as the Lunar scouts and riders race through the forest, pushing the horses to their limit as they force the seekers east. The seekers do not look up as they pass, and I wonder if they are hobbled by their short, thick necks—*valuable information if it proves to be true.*

I scale the rest of the way up the tree until I sit amongst the dense leaves, peeking out over the canopy. My eyes follow the seekers' call and the answer of hoofbeats, peering over the trees from my perch above the darkness to see the object of their desire. *Light.* But not just any light—sunlight pouring out from a grove a few hundred paces west.

Orange and yellow flares burst through the meadow before being swallowed by the surrounding night. I bite down on my tongue to stifle a gasp and watch the trees shake as the riders cut close to the meadow, steering the seekers in the other direction.

Heavenly Mother! A silent curse passes through my lips.

A solar charge sits in the center of the clearing. Tall as ten men and wide enough to eviscerate a large city. Its light lashes out in every direction, but the magic of the forest keeps it from piercing into the sky like a beacon.

Sunlight...In Luna? Is that even possible?

I twist around. I can't even see La Luna from where I sit. The light is coming from deep within the forest, deeper than I'm willing to wander tonight and deeper than anyone can see from beyond its borders.

I waver, wondering if I should head back.

A charge is a powerful weapon. All-consuming once detonated, and this one looks close to erupting. I can tell from its color it is nearing its final stages. But how did it get here? Only a Solarian celestial can form and set a solar charge. And by the looks of it, this one was set by someone of great ability.

Certainly the Serpent would have told me if there were ongoing operations in Luna. Especially one as devastating as a solar charge. But as soon as the thought enters my mind, I know it's not true. The Serpent values victory over all else, and there are no limits to the lies told in pursuit of it.

The prospect of seeing the entire eastern half of Luna burned to a crisp turns my stomach. I imagine Apollo's people in a similar state as Kefu and his men, and bile rises into my throat, forcing me to look away.

I drop silently to the forest floor, resigning myself to my assigned mission and nothing more. Crouching, I feel for the rumble of seekers and riders before moving back down the path to the mouth of the forest. I move quickly, more familiar this time with the twists and turns, but my mind feels numb to the sounds around me as I run.

When I break through the tree line, I continue sprinting across the castle grounds, long after the darkened wood is behind me.

CHAPTER 15

APOLLO

———

My mind has grown treasonous, burdening me with distraction.

Try as I might, Celeste's face is at the front of my mind. Even as I stand among the light of the charge and my legion works to rein it in, I can see her. Her soft lips brushing over the wineglass we shared, her big, bouncy curls whispering over her shoulder, the light in her eyes as she shouts at me.

My inability to ignore her grates on my nerves and my sour mood follows me into the dark of the forest, calling the demon to the front.

I push my legion hard as a result. Too hard, perhaps, as we gather around the charge for the near hundredth night in a row. I do not know how many nights we have gathered here, hoping to save our people from the surety of death at the hands of the Serpent. I have lost count of our failures. All I know is that it has been months without progress, and my men grow more discouraged with each passing night. But there may be no reprieve. The charge had grown larger once more, nearly doubled in size from when it was first discovered. It stands at a staggering height, and the flares have grown violent—almost *hungry* in their attacks. And we work tirelessly as we try to move it.

My soldiers drip in sweat and squint at the bright light in the center of the clearing. Some of them hunch over on their knees, catching their breath and gathering their moonlight while the others continue their efforts. They rush around me in a frenzy, magic pouring from their palms as they try to subdue the charge. Evalina stands by my side, shouting her orders. My shadows fly like whips through the air, shielding them all as best I can. I cannot hear their shouts for help, so I must watch closely for the signs of a flare, a flash snapping free of the charge to strike at them.

I watch as a flare breaks away like a bow strung too tight, severing under pressure. The tendril of blinding light flies through the air, writhing like an injured creature before whipping down in a menacing arch directed at Evalina.

She's standing too close, too busy making demands of the riders to notice. I release my magic, yanking her off her feet and jerking her backward as I intercept the flare with a wall of shadow. Against my magic, the light is harmless, and it feels like little more than air when it touches down. But for Evalina, it would mean certain death. And she's still yelling out orders over the call of seekers and the shouts of riders. So I take the blow and set her back on her feet.

The riders do not have an easy task tonight either. Something has riled the seekers, and they rush through the forest in a frenzy, searching for something that may feed them. It makes our work harder as some of them peel off to head for the charge, disregarding the direction of the pack. So much so that the scouts have come to the riders' aid to drive the pack in two directions at once.

Between the flares and the seekers, it is another night of sweat and agony. And I can only hope that this night does not end in blood as all others have.

After what feels like several hours of failure, I shout for a halt despite Evalina's insistence. She whirls on me, prepared to challenge my word, but I pin her with a stern look, gesturing at the soldiers who are straining with effort. Two of them lie in the dirt shielding their eyes, and I know already they have been before the light for too long. They will need to see Shrea immediately if there is any hope of saving them from the sickness.

Evalina nods, her face turning down in disappointment as she sees our legion crumbling under the weight of the light. Even she is beginning to look weathered. I can see the tired look in her eyes even as she urges me to continue on, and I worry her repeated exposure will soon be too much for her.

"Leave it for another night!" I command. "Find the riders. Follow them out!"

Some cadets glance at me with the same pained expression I see on Evalina. They know that another night left means another night we will return. But then the soldier to my right collapses in a heap, and I disregard their pleas, shouting at them to turn back.

The riders circle the group, pulling the soldiers into their saddles before cutting through the trees. I stand by, combating the white-hot flares as they make their retreat. I can feel the rumble of horse hooves as Lupin, my chief rider, races through the clearing to collect me. I cover him in a blanket of shadow, shielding him from the flares, before taking up a run and launching myself onto the back of his horse.

He pushes the riders hard as well, demanding a breakneck speed until we break through the tree line.

But his efforts are not for nothing. Evalina signals the "all clear," a fist held high in the air for me to see as we streak past the empty scouts' posts.

No one has been lost. Not tonight. Not yet.

———————

I trudge through the castle in grim silence. This night may not have ended in death, but a soldier lost to the sickness is a loss just the same. Two had fallen ill this time. A price I'm not sure I should have paid.

Evalina manages to hold her tongue until we make it to the residential wing, but not a moment longer.

"Out!" I shout at Lucious as we enter the foyer of my bedchamber.

He's sitting slumped beside the door with his head in his hands, and he flinches as my voice meets his ears. I almost feel sorry for startling the young man. But then I remember how much he's seen of Celeste, and the feeling dissipates.

He scurries off, and Evalina turns on me, her moonlight raging behind her eyes.

She doesn't shout as she cuts in front of me, signing excitedly, *"Tomorrow night, I think we should—"*

Her words are cut off as I hold up a hand.

"Enough," I say, but it comes out more like a plea.

"Enough?" she asks, confusion cutting into her train of thought.

"No more. No more pushes. That is enough."

"That's it?" she demands, the vein in her neck coming to life in silent anger.

"Yes!" I bark, unable to rein in my own frustration. "That is it."

"But!" She gestures beyond the walls of the narrow corridor. *"What about the charge? We can't just leave it there! It will swallow the entire city if it's detonated. We can't just give up!"* Her arms fly through the air, and moonlight seeps from her skin, filling the space and casting shadows of her own.

"Give up?" I scoff. "It is not giving up! It is preservation. Plain and simple."

"Your father didn't give his life for preservation! He gave his life for victory!" she signs, and I can see she's shouting now as well.

"My father was mad!" I bellow, gripping her shoulders and trying to shake the sense into her. "He knew nothing of what he found in the forest. All he saw was hope. And like the poison that it is, it carried him over a cliff. He gave his life to madness!" I declare. "I know you cannot see it. It is easier to be the one pointing fingers, calling out 'fool' whenever you feel like it! But I do not have that luxury. *I* am the one who must live with their loss. Not Renwick! Not you! *Me*." Her mouth closes, and she takes a step back. "I am the one their mothers will curse when their bodies are returned home!"

I pause, trying to control my anger.

"How many more, Evalina? How many more must we lose to the charge? How many more must we watch sink into madness? Or die consumed by sunlight?" She swallows hard, blinking, shocked by the tone I've taken. But I've had quite enough judgment from her. This kingdom rests on my shoulders, not hers. "Do not accuse me of being careless because I will not continue down the path my father laid."

I turn from her, but she must be taking lessons from her uncle because she rushes past me before I can reach my chamber door.

"One more," she pleads. *"Just one more try. I think we can move it! We just need to change our approach."*

I bare my fangs at her.

"Evalina..." I growl in warning.

"No!" she barks. *"Do you think they follow you into the forest simply because* you *ask them to? We have never forced them to confront the charge. They volunteer. Every single one of them."*

"Your point?"

"My point is that you are not the only one who's lost something to the Serpent. They confront the charge because they want to. Because they need a win just as much as you do."

She jabs a finger against my chest before dropping her hands to her sides in defeat.

I cannot deny that she is right. My legion has known many sorrows at the hands of the Serpent, and they deserve the chance to spare the rest of Luna from a similar fate.

"Fine." I huff, and Evalina nearly bounces right out of her boots. "One more. But the mission shall be yours from start to finish." She nods eagerly, and I worry she isn't listening to what I'm saying. "If we fail, we will abandon this, and we will evacuate the nearby villages. We will meet the Serpent on the battlefield. With blade, shadow, and moonlight."

Evalina's eyes narrow in anticipation, but I ignore her, aiming instead for my bed. She does not block my path as I reach for the door, and I release a weighted sigh when it swings shut behind me. But as I drag my half-beaten body into my chamber, my temper heats past its point of erupting.

Celeste is sprawled across my bed, legs and arms twisted in the sheets, her sunlight coursing through her hair as it drapes across my pillow. The sweet fragrance of honey wafts off her in waves, and I breathe her in, savoring the balmy aroma.

She is still wearing my nightshirt, and it pools around her, threatening to reveal every inch of her as she rolls toward the center. A nightgown lies neatly folded atop the bureau, in the same place it's been since I placed it there, untouched and ignored.

Ungrateful woman.

The thought comes from my distaste for her arrogance, but the smile I feel pulling over my fangs comes from a twisted pleasure deep in my spirit. From seeing her bathing in my essence—my clothes, my bed, my scent—even as she flouts boundary after boundary. It is a crude pleasure. One I don't claim to understand but is undeniable as my tail thrashes against my leg.

I grip the end in a tight fist to keep it from drumming a beat across the floor, but the effort does nothing for my shadows, and they writhe as I watch her, distracted once again by her mere presence.

She shifts, spreading her legs, and I groan.

She's been out of the castle this evening. I can smell the midnight air on her, like mist and grass, like the forest. I take a deep breath as worry settles in my chest.

If she's entered the forest, she must be foolish. Even wandering near its border could mean death for her. Why would she do such a thing?

I run my fingers through my hair, trying to soothe the anxious feeling and block the lewd thoughts now filling my mind. This torture may be more than I can bear. But I refuse to spend another night in the barracks, with my feet hanging over the edge of my bed and my horns scraping the wall. The seekers and Evalina have run me ragged, and I am not here for her. I am here for sleep.

I drop onto the bed, shrugging out of my clothes and lying on my back like the dead. Immediately, my eyes slide shut, and I reach for the sweet embrace of sleep, trying not to think about Celeste resting mere inches from me. But then she rolls and crashes into me, her head ramming against my shoulder, startling herself awake.

Her plush lips fall open, and she makes a deep, muffled sound as she rubs at her forehead. Light moves to the space between her brows and then behind her eyes as they flutter open, settling on my face.

What are you doing? she signs.

Trying to sleep, I sign back, too tired for words.

Must you do that here? she asks, frowning.

I'm beginning to enjoy her frowning face. Her beautiful eyes always seem to burn brighter when she's frowning at me.

Part of me wants to give her an equally smart reply, if only to see her frown some more. But I do not have the energy for our usual back and forth. Instead, I reach out a hand and brush it down her arm, watching her light surge to the surface. It radiates from beneath the heavy blanket we now share, rippling across the sheets each time she moves.

"Are you hot, darling?" I ask, watching the tension lift from her shoulders as my fingers graze her skin.

She pauses, contemplating whether she, too, is too tired to continue our little war games. After the evening she's had, I can see that she wants nothing more than rest. Same as me. So when she nods sheepishly, I don't hesitate to drape her in my shadows.

I send them winding up her warm body, curling around her waist and between her legs, gripping her lightly until nearly every inch of her is covered. Her lips part as she releases a soundless sigh, and I can feel her light dim beneath my magic as I hold her.

"Better?" I ask.

She nods, but her eyes have already slid shut, and I don't bother to make any space between us. I leave her pinned close to my side as I, too, reach for sleep. Tonight, it comes easy. Easier than it has in many moons.

CHAPTER 16

CELESTE

Magic courses through me, and I'm spinning. No—I'm floating. Or hanging? Hanging from what?

My body jerks as a dark tendril eases up my bare body, twisting around my legs to pull them apart and winding around my waist to hold me still. My neck strains as I try to see what's caught me, but it's too dark, and my light is buried too deep, lulled to sleep by the cool sensation creeping over my skin. I struggle a moment, then still as a low voice speaks close to my ear.

"Careful, darling. You'll bruise."

Twisted horns cross my vision, ducking down between my legs. I try again to see the creature that's caught me, now kneeling before me. But before I can, hands grip my ass, dragging dulled claws down the backs of my thighs, where they grip me tight and hold fast.

Realization dawns.

I've been caught in the demon's trap. His trap.

I tell myself to flee, to run, to strike. But the urge dissolves as a warm, wet heat invades my body, parting my tender flesh and

forging a path toward heaven. My legs buckle, but his shadows are holding me up, and a name leaves my mouth in a rush of air.
"Apollo..."

Moonlight streams in through the windows, illuminating the sweat on my brow as I startle awake. Pushing at the blankets, I survey my surroundings. Only, there is no blanket, and I'm not alone this evening.

Apollo lies beside me, face down, with an arm flung across my stomach and his tail wound loosely around my calf. His shadows have wrapped me in a cocoon, moving as I do and clinging to me like skin.

I sit up slowly, trying to right myself as I peel my body out of his grasp, but he stirs, gripping my waist, and memories of his whispered words wash up from the depths of my mind like a dream.

Are you hot, darling?

His slow, deep voice, ordinarily so gruff, echoes in my mind, and I still.

That was no dream. He was talking to me with that voice. Not his usual rough tone of anger or the signature snark with which he calls me "darling." No, that time, it was soft, gentle—a quiet caress in the dark of his room. A shiver runs down my spine, and my cheeks warm as I let my thoughts wander away from me, focusing on his cool touch and deep breathing.

I glance at him, his restful face now pressed to his pillow, and shift, testing the strength of his hold while doing my best to ignore the sensation of his shadows. But my light courses lower as his magic flows over me, and I'm forced to shut my eyes as I pull the pieces of my mind together.

Apollo is nothing but a mark, I remind myself, prying my arms out of his grasp slower than the glaciers in Uranom.

But the reminder does little to cool the fire stoking in my core, and I can't seem to escape his scent even as I untangle the last of my limbs from his magic. I duck into the washroom and pull his nightshirt from my body, hoping to rid myself of the images still lingering from my dream. Frustrated, I toss it to the side. But standing naked in the open only leaves me feeling exposed, and I rush to dress myself.

I dress simply, unwilling to risk waking him. When I'm finished, I slink across the room, cracking the heavy wooden door just enough to squeeze through.

The foyer sits empty, not a guard in sight, and I have to smother a loud laugh behind my hand. Whatever training the Lunar legion is receiving must be rather lackluster.

I chuckle softly, thinking of the look on Apollo's face when he finds me missing and no guard to know where I've gone.

Part of me is disappointed that I was able to slip past him so easily, but another part, the part that I'm trying desperately to ignore, is excited for the moment he finds me. Because, whether I want to or not, I enjoy arguing with Apollo. He does not treat me as if I am incapable of withstanding his wrath because I am a woman. And he does not yield to me out of lust. Instead, he shouts at me, and he threatens me—even though his threats all appear to be empty.

The viper in me finds it thrilling, and as I wander through the castle halls, I think of how best I can torture him when he does find me.

I meander for a long while, moving from empty room to empty room, finding nothing of interest in any of them. Dozens of empty bed chambers, almost as many empty parlors, and at least three libraries. And yet he *still* demands I remain in his chambers.

Beast, I think to myself, grinning as I cross the catwalk into the east wing.

Apollo has forbidden me from this wing, and until last evening, I hadn't seen a single inch of it. But now that I am not pressed beneath the thumb of his guards, I am intent on seeing what he is so desperate to hide from me.

I poke my head into the various rooms, finding more of the same. More empty parlors, more empty chambers, and the little dining room we'd shared last night. I continue yanking open every door until I find one that doesn't open. It's locked.

I step back to look at it.

It's beautifully decorated. Intricate florals adorn the front, with a gilded handle and moonlight pouring from beneath the doorjamb. Whoever painted it was a master of the craft. There is a delicate gold filigree curling up from the bottom, lacing with darkly colored flowers and leaves nestled into the grooves of the woodwork. A careful imitation of Mother Luna sits in the center, bathing the dark florals in a faint blue hue and casting painted shadows in all the right places.

As I stand gawking at the artwork before me, shouts echo through the corridor—several of them calling out my name. One distinctly accented voice rises above all the others, sending a thrill up my spine.

"Celeste!" Apollo's voice thunders in the distance. "Come, *darling*! Before I get angry!"

His voice is strained, thick with frustration, and when he calls me darling, it isn't like the tender tone he'd whispered to me last night.

I step into the recessed doorway, hoping the shadowed archway will cover me as I work the lock. Pressing a hand to the wood, I push to test its strength. When it doesn't rattle beneath my palm, I pull the needlepoint blade from my bodice and work swiftly.

Booted feet march across the stone, and the cool wind that breezes through the corridor provides me with the added urgency I need. Hurriedly, I jam the end of my knife into the mechanism, twisting until the bolt clicks. It turns over with a clunk and echoes softly throughout the cavernous room on the other side.

I shut the door behind me. Pressing my ear to the wood, and wait until the sound of Apollo's voice is too faint to make out before sagging against the door.

My breath rushes out of me as I take in the space in front of me.

The dark grey stone of Castle La Luna is abandoned at the door. Replaced entirely by a smooth, iridescent, alabaster marble devoid of veining of any kind. Only pure, white stone sprawling out in every direction—moonstone. A grand window, with the signature, pointed arch, takes up the entirety of the wall opposite me, stretching from the floor to the buttressed ceiling. Through it, Luna is framed like one of the many art pieces that line the walls, and her light shines through, shimmering with pearlescent colors that shift across the stone beneath my feet. But the true beauty of this room is not in the floor or through the windows. It's on the walls.

Beautiful paintings on stretched canvas cover every inch. In every size and color. Images of Mother Luna, moody florals, bright moonlit scenes, and portraits of strangers stare back at me. Each of them more vibrant than the next.

My head cranes to take it in, and I find myself creeping forward, hesitant to mar the flawless floor. I make a beeline for the bench in the center of the room. It faces the gigantic window with an easel propped between its absent artist and their muse. I drop down onto it as my eyes settle on the image of a woman in front of me. The picture is so vivid I'm tempted to ask her who she is. It's one of the bigger canvases, and her white hair seems to catch the light like Evalina's, but her eyes look like mine. Bright with golden light and full of magic.

I find myself staring, watching the moonlight illuminate the brushstrokes until I can see that every line is painted with intention.

There is no secret here. None worth hiding, at least. But as I stare at the masterpieces on the wall, I can't say I'm disappointed.

CHAPTER 17

APOLLO

—

"Where is she?"

The words tear from my throat as Lucious cowers before me. His mouth hangs open as he shifts on his feet, unwilling to meet my eyes. My shadows surge from the floor, filling the foyer with the smoke of my magic and crowding out the moonlight. My patience grows thinner with every moment he does not explain himself, and I bark out a command.

"Speak!" I demand as my claws dig into my palms.

Last night, I slept more soundly than I had in a full turn of the Moon. But, as with all matters that deal in Celeste, the blessing came with a punishment of its own.

I woke to a cold bed. Which, ordinarily, would not have been cause for concern if it weren't for the woman I'd been sharing it with—who is now nowhere to be found.

Her side of the bed lay vacant, and I'd nearly torn the door from its hinges when I realized she had gone. I searched the chamber thoroughly before stepping into the hall to find Lucious standing at attention, looking completely unaware.

He's now dripping sweat onto my floors, and if he doesn't speak quickly, he is at risk of finding his way into my dungeon.

My arms cross to keep from throttling him as he begins to splutter.

"She-she...have left...before I-I-I returned to..." he says, unable to meet my gaze.

Between his stammering and his nervous glances, his lips are difficult to read, and my frustration mounts as I struggle to understand him.

"Enough!" I shout, closing my eyes and pinching the space between my brows.

I recall very little of last night. Beyond my failure at the charge and Evalina's sharp words, there is only warmth, a deep sleep, and the faint memory of Celeste's passing touches as she rested beside me. But I do vaguely remember dismissing Lucious.

"Come." I grit the word between my teeth. Practically chewing it up and spitting it back out at him. "She cannot have gotten far."

"But-but—" he begins, and I hold up a hand, cutting off his words.

"Lucious," I tell him quietly. "Please, no more."

He stares at me, eyes wide with quiet shock, but he nods once, and I think I see some of the fear lift from his shoulders.

He joins the search for my wretched "bride," and when we come across Evalina, she insists upon "helping."

I try not to be curt with them. It is not their fault I have lost her. But I can't help but trudge around the castle with smoke billowing out of my robes and shadows trailing behind me like extra tails as I shout her name. Men and women bow as I sweep past them, but I don't acknowledge them. My thoughts are of Celeste and the treacherous little snake that she is.

I have underestimated her—gravely.

First, she slips out into the night unnoticed, and now she wanders in broad moonlight unbeknownst to her guard.

It cannot stand.

I will find her, and I will not dismiss this transgression as easily as her sweetly heated words.

Do you think she fled from you? Evalina asks, signing quickly when Lucious breaks off down a separate corridor.

Her question is innocent enough, but she does not know the weight it carries.

Rather than answer her, I break away to continue the search on my own, shouting out for Celeste until I can feel my voice begin to grate.

Before I decide to send for the nighthounds, I see a faint light —soft and yellow, seeping from beneath the door to the gallery. The door is locked, but the light emanating from the other side is unmistakable.

Just like a Solarian to ignore the boundary placed in front of them.

I slip a shadow through the keyhole, swinging the door open as I prepare to berate her. But the fire in my chest burns down to embers when I see her soft light filling the room along with the faint glisten of tears on her cheeks.

She's emitting a warm glow from her head to her toes as she sits in front of the easel, gazing up at the canvases to my right, and she makes no move to acknowledge my presence as I come to stand beside her.

"What are you doing in here, Celeste?" My words are slow and tired, exhausted from the effort of trying to hold her to the standards I maintain for everyone else.

She doesn't look at me as she signs.

The door was unlocked, she explains. Then slower, *Sorry.*

I watch her chest heave as she draws in a ragged breath and drops her head, brunette curls shielding her face from view.

"No, it wasn't. And no, you're not," I challenge, crossing my arms over my chest to keep from pushing her hair out of her face so I can see the light in her eyes. But I don't need to. My accusation catches her attention, and she turns her face up at me with a fierce frown.

Pardon? she asks.

"It wasn't unlocked. And you're not sorry," I correct her.

Her mouth opens to contradict me, but I stop her. I do not have the patience to listen to her lies.

"I'm looking for a reason not to tie you up in shadows. Lying will not help matters any. Now, I will ask you once more. What are you doing in here?"

Light moves behind her eyes, though I can't be sure if it's excitement or anger that makes her magic stir.

Does it matter? she signs. Her hands move easily, unbothered, and my eyes roll in response.

This woman may be the death of me. Between the seekers from the previous night and everyone's persistent need to disregard orders, I may soon reach my limit. As she blinks her big, warm eyes up at me, I can't do much more than grunt at her. So that's what I do.

I grunt my discontent and drop down beside her, nudging her with my knee so I can fit on the other half of the too-small bench. It's barely enough for me alone, and her full hips mean we both sit with our thighs pressed together and a leg hanging off the edge. But she doesn't seem to mind my nearness. I lean back on my hands and drape my tail over the edge as I follow her eyes to the canvas she's studying.

It's a self-portrait of Mother. One of the finer ones. Of the many images of Mother that are hung on these walls, this was Father's favorite. She had captured the moonlight almost perfectly. So precise, I often find myself studying the technique but still unable to replicate it.

Who is she? Celeste signs softly after a few moments of silence.

I have to force air into my lungs before I answer. "That is my mother. Queen Artera of La Luna."

"But she's—" Celeste starts.

"Solarian?" I finish, guessing why she's been staring at the portrait for so long.

Mother had painted sunlight in her eyes for this particular self-portrait. It's the only one to show her half-solar heritage and yet another reason this door remains locked.

Celeste is staring at me now. Eyes wide and mouth open.

She studies me as though she will find sunlight lurking behind my eyes.

"Only half," I add. "She wasn't a Solarian celestial, but she painted the light in her eyes, anyway. I never asked her why," I say, shrugging.

"But that means you-you're—"

"Yes, darling," I mutter. Her light sparks at my name for her, and I take it she's adjusting to her new title. "My father decided it'd be best if no one knew. I'm already quite different, and times were harsher when they were married. He did not think our people would approve."

I expect her to put up a fuss about my secret, but she only nods as if she fully understands the sacrifices that are made in the name of the crown.

"I was admiring," she confesses after a long while. *"They're the most beautiful works I've ever seen."*

I shift, uncomfortable with her examining.

There are hundreds of canvases on these walls. Decades of work on display. But it's not meant for her to see. It's not meant for anyone to see really. I consider dragging her from the room before she can look too long and decide they are nothing more than the reflections of a madman, but I know it would be no use.

"In that case, you mustn't see much art," I say.

She laughs a little, and I feel a small pang of hatred for her serpent that I cannot hear it.

"Who made these?" she asks, gesturing around the room, eyes gleaming as they catch the moonlight.

I hesitate to tell her, but the look in her eyes is wanting, and it pulls the confession from my mouth before I can stop it.

"I did," I say, watching as surprise sweeps across her face.

"All of them?" she signs in disbelief, her head swiveling to take it in once more.

"Some are the work of my late mother, but the rest...yes. They are mine."

Her curls sweep over her shoulder as she turns back to me, eyes filled with light.

"Is that what pains you?" she asks. *"You miss her?"*

I recoil at her question, unable to help the shocked expression that crosses my face, and she rushes to correct herself.

"Oh, no. I only meant that beauty like this is usually born of... pain."

"And what would you *know of pain?"* I ask.

A dark look creeps across her sunlit face, dimming the light in her eyes, and she doesn't meet my gaze when she signs. *"More than you suspect, I can assure you."*

Anger rises in me, and I resist the overwhelming urge to drape her in shadow. To shield her from all who might harm her as a thought settles into my stomach like a lump of coal.

If she is right, then a great deal of pain must have been wrought to birth a beauty like Celeste.

"Whose hands have brought you pain?" I ask, careful with my words. I want an answer. None of her carefully crafted half-truths.

She jerks back a little, frowning up at me as if I've grown too bold.

"What do you care?" she counters, her tongue lashing out from between her teeth as she signs quickly.

I picture someone laying their hands on her warm, brown skin, and my horns ache with a need to spear the offender.

"I care very much." More than I should.

The anger in her expression crumbles to confusion, and she eyes me skeptically.

Why? she signs.

Because the mere thought of another's hands on her, be it pleasure or pain, makes me want to wring the life from them with my shadows.

The thought rips through me at a staggering speed, and I must work to keep it from leaving my mouth. The realization is a troubling one. One I'm not yet ready to confront. So instead, I tell her, "You are a woman of La Luna now...for now. I will not stand for the abuse of my people."

"Including Renwick?" she quips, smirking at me.

"Yes," I answer without pause.

This is not a lie. Renwick may grate on my nerves, but he is family. And I would lay waste to any who would harm him. Shrea and Evalina are no different.

Celeste breathes out a strained sigh like she's trying to clear a path for the words but finding it difficult. Eventually, she rolls her shoulders back and signs in response.

My family, she confesses. *My family are the ones who bring me pain.*

"Why?"

Her shoulders shrug, and her golden eyes find the floor. *"I'm not really sure anymore. I used to think I knew. I used to think it was to make me stronger. To make my family stronger. But now..."* She quiets, finding my gaze. *"I thought I knew a lot of things before I met..."* She pauses, choosing her words carefully. *"Before I came to La Luna."*

"Like?"

She balks, and the little crinkle between her brows grows stern. *"Like...well, like you...I think they're wrong about you."*

I smile at her, enjoying the sunblush that rises along her neck as she looks at me.

"Darling, I can assure you, I am not the man you think I am."

Her eyes narrow as if she finds that hard to believe.

"Perhaps. But you aren't the monster you believe you are either—even if you mean to be." She shrugs, and her simple words make me want to hold her close.

But before I can open my mouth to contradict her, she juts out her chin and asks, *"If it isn't pain, what is it?"*

I stare at her for a moment, unsurprised by how persistent she is, and we sit in silence until my heart speaks on my behalf and gives her yet another piece of itself without my permission.

"It's anger," I say.

Then another piece breaks off, and another, and another.

"When I lost Mother and my hearing, I was quite angry. I kept asking myself *why*. Why would the Great Mother deal me such a deck? I was young, too young to understand. So I thought, 'I must have done something to deserve this.' Perhaps Luna was angry with me...for the demon that I am."

Celeste settles her hand on my knee, and sunlight leaks out beneath her fingers as her lips move, mouthing my name.

"I spent a long while trying to fight it. Taking it out on those around me. Until one day, Father locked me in here and told me I wasn't to come out until I found what I was looking for. This gallery was not made for me. It was a gift from Father to my mother. But she never had the chance to fill it. I thought he was being cruel, locking me in here with her memory. I realize now he did me a kindness. It was a week before I picked up a brush. They all started like that."

I point to a small canvas near the door. It looks hurried and messy—and angry. You can see it in the brushstrokes. Each one haphazardly splashed across the canvas simply for the sake of it.

Celeste hides a grin behind her free hand, and I laugh a little.

"It is ugly, I know. But it serves as a good reminder. Now, each time I finish one, I leave a little of my anger on the canvas until eventually..." I point toward a large canvas hanging just beside

Mother's portrait. It's a colorful rendition of Mother Luna, framed through the window beside us, and the closest thing to perfection that I've ever created. "Until there's nothing left."

Celeste's hand pulls away so she may sign to me, and I am loathe to admit I feel a loss when her light leaves my skin.

"So you aren't angry anymore?" she asks.

Her gentle, naïve question brings a smile to my face, and I peer down at her, tipping her chin up with a claw until my horns form a shadow over her face.

"Oh no, darling, I'm quite angry. Now I just have somewhere to put it."

I expect her to pull away from me, step out of the demon's grasp and move back into the light. But she only blinks, eyes filled with pain—for me, of all creatures.

"What happened?"

"The Serpent happened," I answer.

She flinches at that, but her face remains gripped between my fingers, and I can't help but stroke her cheek. Her beautiful face looks agonized as she meets my eyes, and my frustration bubbles up as she passes me a half-pitying glance.

"Do not dare look at me like that," I grunt. "Or I won't tell you a piece more. I can bear the guilty looks from strangers, even Renwick or Evalina, but not you. Understood?"

Her shoulders stiffen with defiance, but she nods, and I release her. But only because this story is difficult to tell, and I will not risk harming her in the process.

"During the Celestial Wars, before the Council was formed, my father took our legion to war with the Serpent. My mother and I journeyed to the border towns after a Solarian raid. Father was called away to the southeastern border, where the sunlight was beginning to erode the magic that covers the Lunar territories, so we went to help our people evacuate.

"We were helping to clear out a schoolhouse when a preplanted charge was activated. Very few children survived. Mother covered as many as she could. But moonlight is no good against the Sun. I tried to save them. But my shadows were untrained, weak, and I could only shield so many. I wouldn't even be here without her. My ears rang for nights afterward. When it finally stopped, it was almost silent. It's been quiet ever since. Although, I can hear some tones in this ear," I say, pointing to the right side of my head. "But this one," I add, waving to my left. "Nothing."

Without warning, Celeste flings her arms around my neck, burying her face against my chest and mumbling into my cloak. My arms go around her instinctively, and for a brief moment, I forget that Celeste Solém is not mine.

My hands find her thighs, and I pull her long legs around my hips, gripping her through the thin fabric of her dress as I hold her fixed in my lap. I bury my face in her curls, breathing in her scent and trying desperately not to crush her as I press her curves close. But I can't help myself.

She is so soft in my hands, like night-nettle when it's hidden its thorns, and I want nothing more than to touch her everywhere. So when she tips her head back, offering me the one thing I've been thinking about since the scouts dragged her into my throne room, I do not hesitate.

I take her soft mouth, and when she opens for me, I am lost in her.

The sweet heat of her kiss seeps into my bones, driving all sense from my mind, and I find myself chasing her flavor, kissing her hard and holding her tight. My hands roam freely, gripping her ass, fisting her curls, and cupping her full breasts as I fail to rein in my desire. But she does not seem to mind. She sits like a jewel in my lap, glinting in the darkened room, grinding against the erection she's brought to life while gripping my horns in her hands.

She tastes exactly as I imagined. Sweet like honey but spicy, and I wonder if the juice between her thighs is of a similar flavor. I can feel the heat growing strong between her legs, warming my stomach as she moves on top of me, and I long to run my tongue between her wet folds. I long to feel her sweet honey on my lips. But for now, I will settle for her kiss because it is more than I could have ever hoped for.

Chapter 18

Celeste

—

Betrayer!

The Serpent's voice keeps trying to shout at me. But the longer I sit locked in Apollo's arms, the quieter it gets and the less important it seems.

All thought of our playful teasing vanishes. The argument I prepared for when he came bursting in has disappeared, and all I can do is cling to him.

His mouth is on me, drinking in my quiet moans. For a while, I try to stifle them, but then I remember Apollo cannot hear me, and I leave my body to its own devices.

I had no intention of giving myself to him. Not tonight, not ever. But the moment I saw the hurt in his eyes, I knew I was right.

Apollo is not a beast, or a demon, or a monster, or whatever creature he considers himself. He is a man. Plain as day. With a gentle heart, made hard by the weight of life. And as badly as he wants me to believe otherwise, I can see it. Perhaps not on his face, but embedded in every brushstroke, on every canvas. Pain and hurt, wrought by the Serpent's hands.

His hearing.

His mother.

And if I knew the Serpent well enough, his father too.

King Sevah had not passed from age. He may have been one of the oldest reigning rulers, but he certainly wasn't shaking hands with the Great Mother. Not yet. I do not doubt the Serpent had a hand in his demise. If only to make a place for me at La Luna. Just like my sisters—Dawn, Helie, Aurora.

I picture Apollo, young and fearful, clutching at his mother's body as the moonlight leaves her eyes, and I wonder what he might have been like before. Was he happy? Was he less guarded with that big, beautiful laugh? Did he have the same permanent frown on his perfectly chiseled brow?

He deserved better. They both did. They *all* did.

To think the Serpent would bring down children in the name of victory.

For the first time in my many years, and in my many, many marks, I feel shame. Shame at my involvement. Shame in the crest I wear. Shame in the name "Viper." My family has taken everything from Apollo. And I am meant to take more—the last thing he has left.

His life.

My stomach turns as I think of what he would say if I were to reveal myself. He speaks of defending me, but only because he does not know me. If he truly knew me, he would leave me for the seekers.

That reminder seems to right my mind, and I pull away from him, staring into his dark eyes as he breathes a heavy sigh of relief and groans, "My darling."

But I can't be his darling, and I certainly can't sit planted in his lap forever.

I squirm, trying to move back to the bench beside him, but I'm caught in his shadows, and I struggle against them before Apollo tsks, "Easy darling, you'll bruise."

Heat blossoms in my stomach, and I'm suddenly painfully aware of the hard length of his cock pressing against me.

"Apollo, I can't—" I begin, my head too clouded with his electrifying fragrance to remember to sign for him. But I don't get very far before a single shadow drapes across my lips, silencing me.

"Of course, we can," he says, ducking his horns until our lips meet.

"But I—" I mutter against his mouth as he drags me back in.

My light warms beneath his touch, surging through me as his lips find my neck and chest. And my body welcomes him even though I don't mean to.

I grip a single horn, rubbing the smooth, polished surface from base to tip, and a deep growl rumbles in Apollo's chest. His claws find purchase in my hair. They drag across my scalp as he gathers a fistful of curls, balling them in his hand and forcing my head back to claim my mouth. I meet his need with equal measure, inching my hand beneath the collar of his shirt and spreading my light across his chest. A smile tugs at my lips as I enjoy the strangled groan that draws from him.

His fangs scrape gently over my bottom lip as his cool tongue fills my mouth, seeking to devour me whole. I have half a mind to let him. But the Serpent's voice is getting harder to ignore, and I jerk back, pushing at him.

He releases me, but he does not free me from my place on his lap, and I mutter a few curses under my breath.

Apollo's magic balloons into a cloud around us, threatening to blot out the light as he grunts, "I may not be able to hear you, but I do know when a woman speaks ill of me."

I meet his gaze head-on, still pushing at his hands. *"I said you're quite persistent for a man who doesn't even want me."*

His eyes grow dark as he reads my words, and his voice is grave when he speaks. "Who told you I do not want you?"

Claws dig into my sides as he continues to hold me to him.

"You did!" I blurt. *"Every time you curse my name when you*

think I'm not listening. Or when you growl your discontent at finding me in your bed. Or when you choose the barracks over simply lying beside me! I am not a fool, Apollo. Anyone can see it."

I squirm as I sign, trying and failing to free myself from his hold. His shadows are squeezing me now—in every place they meet my skin. My legs, my hips, my thighs, and I push at him, trying to find room to breathe, but he is relentless.

"Those are your reasons?" he asks, his long, elegant fangs gleaming in the light as he smiles down at me.

I nod, wondering why he acts as if they aren't good reasons. Then, without another word, he begins to laugh. Not the short, clipped, half-hearted chuckle he offers everyone else, but that full-throated, deep, thunderous laugh that vibrates my entire body and settles right between my thighs.

"You treacherous little thing," he says, his deep voice warm in my ear. "It is precisely because I want you that I curse your name. That I cannot bear the sight of you in my bed. And that I'd rather lie alone than with you." He pulls me impossibly close, fixing me over his straining erection. "Can you not see what you do to me? Every moment I am near you, the closer I am to disregarding all logic and claiming you over and over until your legs turn to clay and my name is the only word you can form on your lips."

His claws grip my hips, and moisture gathers between my legs.

"Is that what you want?" he asks, deadly serious.

What I want? I've never thought about what *I* want. Only what the Serpent wants. What the Serpent *demands*. And the Serpent only ever demands blood.

I shift under Apollo's watchful gaze. He's staring at me as if he's merely waiting for the words to leave my mouth, and I realize quickly that the answer is "yes." Even though I spend the next few moments trying to get the word "no" to form on my lips. In the end, I can only nod.

He wastes no time. No sooner do I make my decision than I am strung up in shadow. They twist around my limbs, parting my legs and holding me upright while Apollo rises from his seat, leaving me suspended in front of him just as I dreamt he would.

I don't fight against the dark tendrils. Not because I can't, but because I don't want to. The cool sensation feels like a salve on my skin, and it eases my doubts even as the voice in my head continues its barrage of *Betrayer! Betrayer! Betrayer!*

Apollo's hands find my hips as he steps in close, dragging up my dress until I'm exposed from the waist down. He claws his way through the simple cloth panties before running a thick knuckle through my wet folds. The sensation is overwhelming, and I jerk against his shadows as I try to close my legs. But Apollo tightens his hold on me, and I watch with half-hooded eyes as he sucks his finger, a low groan echoing through the room.

"Luna save me," he says gruffly, stepping back to look at me. "You are the sweetest poison I have ever known."

The little voice sounds again, but I don't have the presence of mind to be ashamed. It's been lost to Apollo's touch, and all I can do is fist my hands and grasp uselessly at my bonds while he presses his thumb to my clit and rubs slow, methodical circles.

His name leaves my lips in a needy gasp, but I don't think he notices as he leans forward and whispers, "I'm going to give you what you want, darling. And then I'm going to take what I need."

His voice creeps over my skin, sending another rush of fluid pouring from me, and I fight his hold as he continues a torturous path with his fingers.

He spreads me wide, careful that his claws do not prick me, and strokes me over and over until I'm pleading for release.

The feeling comes in a rush, surging from my core and pulsing between my thighs. Like lightning touching down, his touch makes me shatter, and the ecstasy rolls through me until I am left sagging against his shadows.

Apollo wraps his arms around my waist, and I brace myself for the length of his thick shaft, but it doesn't come. Instead, he cradles me close, freeing me from his shadows and setting me gently on my feet.

"Easy," he says as I sway, trying to catch my balance.

I frown up at him, confused.

"What about what you need?" I ask, signing slowly.

"What I need is not in this room." I try to peel apart from him, but he holds me close, clawing at me. "What I need is consequence. You have flouted too many rules, my love." He pulls my dress back down around my hips. "You defy my every order. You shout at me without repercussion. You broke into my gallery." He waves vaguely, as if the list is endless. "And I do not know how you managed to slip past Lucious last night, but don't think I hadn't noticed." My mouth opens in defense, but he continues without pause, "I cannot stand for it any longer. Punishment is in order."

CHAPTER 19

CELESTE

A pollo maintains a firm grip on my hand as he leads me through the darkened castle, and I follow along with a mild caution, taking comfort in the blade in my bodice. He refused to tell me anything of this punishment of his, but as we cross the moonlit grounds, his plan becomes clear.

The training ring comes into sight as we round the barracks, and I have to keep myself from sprinting the rest of the way. I've seen it many times in passing. Admittedly, I've found myself wishing I could join in, but instead, I've only watched from a distance, silently cheering alongside the soldiers, muttering encouragement and the names of people I don't know but pick out from the crowd.

Usually, I just root for Apollo's opponents out of spite. But they never win. He's much too fast.

He's a brutal kind of beast in the ring. Different than the man walking beside me now, different even than the man I first saw in the throne room. Ruthless and unyielding—body moving like a ghost, sifting in and out of sight as his opponents' hesitant steps cost them valuable time.

He is a worthy opponent, without question, and I squeeze his fingers, excited by the prospect of sparring with him. Even if it is intended to be my punishment.

He mistakes my anticipation for nervousness and peers down at me as we stop in front of the railing.

"Those beautiful eyes will not help you now, darling. Not this time," he says, though it sounds as if he's trying to convince himself rather than me.

Evalina stands in the center of the ring, surveying the matches happening around the arena while cadets sit perched atop the railing, waiting to cycle in. I hop up onto the first rung, studying the legionnaires as Apollo stands close behind me. Most of them are too young to be of much skill, certainly no match for the Solarian army, but a fair few look formidable enough.

Apollo's voice startles me out of my staring and he leans into me, pressing his chest to my back.

"You want to defy me?" he whispers. "This is the place for it."

He gives me no chance to protest.

He hoists me onto the top rung before I can object, and then he clears the railing in a single leap. His eyes gleam as he turns back to me—bright with excitement, and I'm curious about what he has in mind. He doesn't know my skill, but he's not so monstrous he would cut down an untrained woman. So there must be something else he has in mind.

He steps forward, placing his hands on either side of me, gripping the railing to box me in with his arms. "I am going to give you a single cut for your transgressions. Just one," he says holding up a singular claw. "But it only seems fair that I give you the opportunity to avoid it."

He smiles down at me, clearly eager at the prospect of chasing after me.

I'm more than happy to let him. It will be a long while before he catches me. I am the fastest of all my sisters, and I have only been bested by one.

Apollo studies my face before settling on my lips again, and I can't help but tease him.

"You'll have to catch me first, *darling*."

His fangs flash as his smile widens.

"I plan to," he says before gripping my waist and pulling me into the ring with him.

I follow him to the center, where Evalina waits with a grimace on her pretty face.

"Apollo, what is this?" she asks, gesturing at me. "We do not have time for your games."

"No games, General. Celeste is here to learn a lesson."

Evalina does not vacate the center of the ring. Instead, she eyes me skeptically for a long while before she groans, "Fine. Clear the ring!"

The legionnaires stop in an instant, cutting their scrapping short. They hustle up and over the railing until we are the only three left standing. Apollo breaks away first, tossing his dark cloak aside. I move to follow, but a familiar hand latches around my arm, holding me back.

When I turn, Evalina is glaring at me with her signature frown, but it eases as she glances at Apollo and then whispers, "Do not underestimate his tail."

"No cheating!" Apollo barks.

Evalina and I roll our eyes at him before she hurries off, trying to stifle a laugh.

I meet Apollo in the middle, standing a few paces apart. Around us, the cadets have taken up their posts to watch the "demon" fight. Apollo stares at me, eyes narrowing as if he can see the viper uncoiling deep inside, and his stance shifts, suddenly aware that I plan to make this difficult for him.

He bows. I don't.

It isn't the viper's way. With the Serpent, respect is earned with blood, not status. But Apollo doesn't seem to mind. He almost seems to excite as I defy him so openly.

His chest puffs out, his eyes darken, and shadows leech from beneath his feet, bleeding across the packed dirt as if the battle has already begun. But none of it compares to the sight of him growing stiff in his pants. He makes no move to hide his desire, and I can't help but stare at the thick imprint between his legs as I circle him. He is well endowed—this I already know, but a whisper of possession creeps into my mind as I see him standing so brazenly before his legion.

His eyes follow me, but he doesn't turn when I disappear behind his back. And as I reappear in front of him, he isn't watching my feet for a warning. Instead, he's holding my gaze, and I can see the quiet grin whisper across his lips before he darts after me.

He comes at me in a blur of claws and teeth, tangled in shadow. His dark aura surrounds him, making him appear more celestial than I've seen before—utterly captivating.

In the haze of his magnificence, I forget myself, watching in awe as he speeds toward me. But before he can reach me, I step sideways, barely clearing his claws. I spin, trying to find him in the dark night that blankets the ring. Dozens of faces stare back at me, but none of them are Apollo's.

I close my eyes, listening closely for the shuffle of his step, and before he's able to land a blow, I hear the crunch of gravel close behind. This time when I turn, Apollo is there, eyes black as night and shadow billowing out of him. He keeps them to himself, opting instead to lash out with his claws. He swings at me, aiming for my chest. But I move equal and opposite to him, shifting my weight in an instant to propel me backward before cutting to the side.

He smiles and we dance for a while.

Apollo is brutal up close. From a distance, he looks like pure grace when he fights—a big, elegant body slipping from sight, cutting fast, and retreating in a blur. But when I sweep into striking range, I can see the power ripple through him, surging from his center and radiating out like the shock of a solar charge.

Power—pure and hungry.

Like a nightmare come to life, *a beautiful nightmare.*

Now I understand why they call him a demon.

His eyes swirl with excitement when he nears, but I continue to dance just beyond his reach, watching his frustration grow as I evade him. But soon, we both grow bored, and Apollo stops teasing.

He barrels forward, winking out of sight as his shadows swallow him, shielding himself from view. I listen closely for the sound of his movement, but this time I am too slow. I only hear the dirt beneath our feet when he's standing right in front of me.

His shadows clear in an instant, and Apollo's towering form looms as he reaches for me. I keep my light sealed away, unwilling to reveal my power to him and the entire legion. Instead, I duck beneath his outstretched arms, punching him hard in the stomach to throw him off balance. He stumbles back a single step, eyes wide and shadows blazing. An ear-splitting cheer erupts around us, reminding me that Apollo and I are not alone in this ring.

The cadets begin to hoot and holler, but none quite as loud as Raye. I hear her shouting my name over the chorus of trills. I spot her craning over the railing, punching her fist in the air as Evalina stands stoically behind her, watching.

I pay them no mind. Apollo is still hunting me as I make my retreat, and I don't have time for distraction. I don't stop until I reach the far side of the ring. When I turn, Apollo stands like a god at the other end—shoulders thrust back, fangs bared, and shadows swirling around his towering horns.

"Are you scared, darling?" he calls over the chorus of people.

I shake my head, shouting in return, "Never!"

"Then stop running, my little star!"

His words weigh on my chest, worming their way into my

brain before plunging between my thighs and threatening to send me to my knees. I can see the bright smile on his face, and my grip on my emotions loosens. My light burning hot as the lines I've drawn begin to blur. But I don't stop to consider my actions as my legs carry me forward.

Apollo meets me head-on, arms outstretched, his claws aimed like a blade at my throat. Before he can catch me, I push off the ground, lifting over his head like a pinwheel. His gaze follows me, but he's too grounded to do anything about it. He doesn't fight like I do, so he merely watches as I soar over him.

I barely clear his horns, but when his head arches back, I reach out a hand, scraping a singular nail across his cheek. Blood draws forth, and I watch his eyes go black as my body prepares to meet the Earth.

But my landing never comes. And suddenly, Apollo's no longer in view. He's moved under me, and as I twist in the air, firm arms and cool shadows wrap around my waist, pulling me into his chest.

My momentum carries through us, and we collapse in a heap, rolling across the dirt until I'm pinned beneath him, locked in his grip.

He's grinning like a maniac as I blink up at him, fangs shining in the light now burning through my chest.

"Caught you," he whispers.

"And yet, no cut?" I tease.

"I wouldn't be so sure about that," he says, reaching under my dress to wiggle his fingers through a small tear.

There is a smear of blood beneath the fabric. When I look back at him, his tail sweeps leisurely through the air, the small, barbed tip flecked with my blood.

"We're even then," I tell him, as a droplet of blood drips from his face, landing on my forehead and sliding back into my hair.

He brushes it away with a frown, then touches his cheek, realizing for the first time the damage I've inflicted. It's a fine cut, the same as mine, starting in the center of his cheek and arching up toward his ear.

I brace myself for the familiar anger of a man bested by a woman. I've seen it reflected in the eyes of my marks more times than I can count. Even in death, they cling to their arrogance. But this time, it doesn't come.

Apollo laughs, that rumbling laugh that makes my stomach clench and my heart slow. It's full and loud, and I can feel it vibrate through me where our chests meet. I shrink back, unsure what to make of this reaction. But as I press myself into the dirt, he follows, crashing his lips against mine and kissing me like he's trying to keep me from floating away.

My eyes slide shut as his big hand moves to my waist, pinning me in place. His cool fingers trail across my stomach, tracing my waist chain before he grips it in a tight fist and uses it to arch my body closer. The shocking length of his erection presses against me, and I moan deep in my chest, moving my hands to his hair without thought. He takes my weight, lifting me from the floor to hold me to him. And when his fangs graze my lips, asking me to open, I do. Not just my mouth and my body, but my heart.

I can feel it splinter apart as I try to reconcile the sensations running through me.

Pleasure. Pain. Need. And the foreign taste of fear climbing up my throat.

All of it knots together in my gut as the viper and my heart wage a bloody war. And for the first time since its conception, the viper loses, leaving me to face Apollo alone.

He's all hands and cool lips—touching, feeling, searching. Whatever he's searching for, I want him to find it and take it—no —I want to *give* it to him. But before I can, the crowded cadets erupt in loud trills, cheering for their king who's claimed his conquest. Except Apollo doesn't stop.

I don't know if it's because he cannot hear them or because he doesn't care, but he doesn't pull away until he's had his fill and we're both breathing ragged.

"Celeste." His voice comes close. A whisper of air between the soft kisses he presses to my neck, but I don't open my eyes.

I'm not ready to step out of this moment. I've forgotten who I am and why I'm here, and I'm not ready to confront the reality of the viper who fell for the demon.

But Apollo is used to getting his way, and he pulls back to hover over me as he demands, "Celeste, open your eyes."

His voice is soft, like honey dripping over my skin, and I pry open my eyes reluctantly, bracing for the crushing weight of reality. But all I see is the dim glow of my light bouncing across Apollo's pained expression.

A bubble of shadow covers us like a dome, locking in my light and blocking out the prying eyes of the entire Lunar legion.

"Did you let me catch you?" he asks, his eyes searching my face as always.

I want to tell him yes. But that would be a lie. And for some reason, I don't want to lie to him. Not anymore.

Truthfully, he caught me on his own, and a burning shame courses through my chest as a stone settles in my stomach. I prepare to face the consequences of my failure. Because falling for your mark is certainly a failure. One I will pay for dearly. If not by the Serpent's hand, then by my own.

Apollo's low, commanding tone interrupts my fears. "Darling?"

No, I didn't let him win. But the words won't come out. Unable to confess it, I opt for a different truth.

"I'm not in the habit of submitting to men."

Apollo's eyes fill with quiet pride as he watches me.

"How about demons?" he asks, kissing me roughly and gripping my body tight.

As I give myself to him, all I can think is *the Serpent is going to kill me.*

CHAPTER 20

APOLLO

I'm lost in her light. Or perhaps I have been found? I cannot be sure.

All I am sure of is that Celeste Solém has been sent to La Luna to destroy me. And I may just let her. Because her light is too brilliant for me to dare look away.

In all my time, I have not witnessed a fighter so graceful, leaving the comfort of soil to fight from the sky like a vulture picking off its prey as it ambles around on the ground. I know she didn't give me her all, and I tried for restraint, but the moment her feet left the ground, I lost all sense. It took everything in me not to claim her right there in the dirt.

I can still taste her on my tongue, like spiced amber and a warm wind. My shadows stir, and my tail flicks uncontrollably across the floor at the memory of her supple body pressed to my chest. Her light wandering across my arms while her fingers played with my horns.

My cock has been stiff ever since. So much so it's beginning to ache, and the glimmer of her hair in the low light of the castle only makes it worse.

What are you looking at? she signs, turning to me with a small frown on her face. It isn't anger or frustration this time, just curiosity and mild confusion at finding me moseying a few paces behind her.

I let her trail ahead for the simple joy of watching her hips sway in the close-fitting dress. But now that she's facing me, I can't help but notice *everything*. Her warm eyes, her soft skin, her full mouth...heavens, her mouth. And most magnificent of all, that stroke of bold defiance she wields like a sword.

"A star, I think."

Her light flares, blushing up to her ears before she can quiet it.

"Where did you learn to do that?" I ask, but my question strikes a chord in her, and she buries her light quickly, fixing her lips to lie to me.

Her eyes are trained on the floor as she contemplates her answer.

Eventually, she signs, *My mother does not believe in weakness.* But I know that isn't the whole of it. It never is with her.

"Come on, darling. You know all my secrets. Isn't it time I know some of yours?"

Her eyes warm to a golden-brown color and I wish to capture it in my hands, or on my canvas, just so I may stare at it as long as I'd like. But she soon returns to her unease, and I try again.

"You don't have to hide from me," I add.

"Hide?" she snaps, hands flying as I dare to question her strength. But she must forget that I am not someone she can dissuade with her sharp words. We are beyond that now.

"Yes, darling. *Hide.* I am deaf, not blind. I can see that you withhold your truths. What I can't see is why?"

"I-I," she stammers.

For the first time since I laid eyes on her, I see her truly falter. She hesitates, shifting from foot to foot, and I'm shocked by the woman I see standing before me. So bold, yet somehow so unsure. Like two sides of the rarest coin.

I reach out a shadow to soothe her, and she leans into the dark tendril until whatever lie she was prepared to tell crumbles.

"Apollo...I...I can't."

"Why? Why not?"

But she does not speak. Instead, she aims to distract me with her touch.

Her eyes hood as she stalks forward with a singular purpose. I think about telling her to stop, demanding she explain herself. But I can't move an inch as she reaches up on her toes to grip my right horn and pull my lips down to hers.

I kiss her because I am incapable of denying her, but when her hand strokes up and down, I release a low growl in warning. As always, she does not heed my orders, and I worry I may spill my seed here in the hall. Yet still, I do not stop her. Instead, I contemplate stripping her bare and carrying her to our chamber shrouded in shadow. But then the familiar click of light-footed steps comes rippling down the hall.

I know Celeste hears it too when she pulls her hand free, leaving me desperate for her touch and angry at Renwick's impeccable timing. She peaks around my shoulder as he skids to a halt beside us and tries to separate from me. But I'm weak-willed and slow to release her. So rather than give in to her demands, I grip her tighter, resting my hand along her hip, where I can feel her light's warmth.

"What do you need, Renwick?" I ask, turning on him to see he's already chattering away.

Celeste begins a swift translation, signing for me without question.

"You have guests, your majesty. From the Council," she translates, eyes widening as she peers up at me. *"They are here to see that you intend to marry the Lady Solém. They have requested an audience...immediately."*

Chapter 21

Celeste

—

I change quickly before heading for the dining room. Ordinarily, I wouldn't care too much about the tear in my dress or the dirt smudging the hem, but I need a moment to clear my mind. My skin feels raw, and my lips are flushed from Apollo's ravishing, not to mention the liquid heat now smeared across the inside of my thighs.

It's a betrayal of the highest order—to *give* yourself to a mark. Seduction in the name of your objective is one thing. Love is another entirely.

It's foolish and dangerous. But I don't care. Because Apollo's touch feels better than any victory I've ever known.

I hear him pacing just beyond the door, and when I step into the foyer, he turns on me with worry carved into his brow. The stress in his shoulders seems to ease as he eyes me up and down.

"I may need to release Silas from his duties as the royal tailor," he says dryly.

"What? Why?"

"It seems he may be trying to kill me too."

I don't get the chance to ask him what he means by that as he takes my hand firmly in his and sets a fast pace across the castle.

When we reach the northwest dining room, Renwick is standing outside the doors, sweating. As soon as he pulls them open, my heart threatens to burst out of my chest and land beating and bloody on the stone beneath our feet. I lean heavily on Apollo, hoping to remain upright. The prick of his claws digs into my sides as he adjusts to my added weight, but he doesn't falter as we listen to Renwick make unnecessary introductions.

"Your highness, my lady, King Aros and Queen Davina of House Mars. Aros, Davina, his highness, Prince Apollo and his Lady Celeste of House Luna."

Renwick's introduction is brief, but I don't need it. I know better than anyone who stands across from me.

Her hair is shorter than I remember, perhaps a bit darker from the lack of sun. Her soft, pointed face holds a bright and easy grin as she curtseys in front of me. An unmovable façade stares back at me as our eyes meet, and I bow deeply. Deeper than I should for a woman who is of equal standing, but her reputation precedes her, and my excitement overcomes me.

I've never met Queen Davina of Mars before, but I have met Princess Dawn of Solaria, the first viper, my eldest sister by twenty-eight years. The only person to ever mark me—aside from Apollo. My fingers stroke the faint scar that starts above my brow and disappears into my hair as I remember the sting of her blade. And all I can muster is a soft smile to keep from divulging our secret.

It's been at least a year since I've seen another viper. A debrief will be in order.

Apollo and Aros bow to one another before greeting their respective ladies. Aros makes a show of gripping my hand in his and bringing his lips to my knuckles. His kiss is long, and his skin is rough. Apollo grows agitated as he takes his time releasing me.

Shadows wind around my body, staking an open claim before he uses one to pull my hand free.

Apollo greets Dawn with much less fervor, taking her hand and placing a brief kiss on the back, at which she bows politely.

He does not remark on her appearance. He has no reason to. We look nothing alike. The subtle almond shape of our eyes and the deep cupid's bow in our lips are the only things we both inherited from the Serpent. Aside from the bloodlust and a bone-breaking resilience. The remainder of her is distinctly Venutian. Long, blond hair drips down her back in soft waves, pale as Mother Venus's. Her skin is a few shades lighter than mine, but the thing that truly sets us apart is our eyes. Whereas mine streak toward the center in various colors, Dawn peers at me with her milky white gaze, solid and flat, with just the faintest hint of brown around the rim to hint at her Solarian half. She beams at me with the grace of a queen, and before I can say anything in greeting, Apollo's voice jerks me back into my senses.

"Come," he directs a little too loudly for the space we're in. I squeeze his hand gently as we all move toward the table. It's an imperceptible touch, but I know Dawn sees it. She sees everything.

But does she see *me*? Like Apollo does?

I hope not.

Apollo leads us into the dining room, where a smaller table has been placed in the center. It isn't the usual setting. It's much too small for comfortable dining—the glasses too close together and the chairs too uncomfortable for a lengthy conversation. It's nothing less than intentional, designed to ensure conversation moves quickly to the point and guests are well within sight at all times. Tactful. An approach I would have used myself. But it also means I am sitting much too close to Aros, who insists on pushing his elbows past his own setting into mine while he leers at me over his sharp nose.

Everything about him is cut on a harsh line, his jaw, his nose, his eyes—distinctly Martian. Even his skin seems harsh, not as soft as the rest of us, thicker, a protection against the flames of the Martian territories.

But the most severe part of him, by far, are his eyes. The heavy red rim and yellow center are like a blazing fire, burning so hot it's a wonder they don't melt out of his skull. Part of me wants to get a closer look, but each time I glance over, he's already staring at me, so I settle for pinning my eyes on Dawn.

"Apollo, how did you manage such a Solarian beauty?" Aros asks, ogling me out of the corner of his eye.

I glance at Apollo quickly in case he needs my help to carry the conversation.

But he doesn't miss a beat as he says, "A gift from Mother Sun, I believe."

Dawn's eyes flare in subtle surprise, and I know Apollo has caught it when his full lips twitch in amusement.

"You speak praises of the Sun? Has Luna fallen from the sky?" Aros asks, glancing up at the ceiling as if it may cave in on itself at the mere thought.

Apollo laughs, that dry chuckle I've grown used to.

"How could I not when she has birthed such a creature?"

Aros gapes at him, eyes wide, his knuckles turning white against the knife he holds. I watch it in my periphery, unable to fully relax as he threatens to snap it in two. Dawn does the same, though her eyes hardly leave mine. Every once in a while, they dart to where my hand rests beneath Apollo's, but I don't remove it. For all she knows, I am a viper with her mark, just as she is, nothing more.

"I'm surprised the Serpent hasn't come to claim her for himself. She is a prize, to be sure," Aros speaks in a low, threatening tone that makes my skin itch.

I contemplate stabbing him with my table knife but I doubt it would be well received.

Apollo brushes my curls over my shoulder, making space for

his big hand on the back of my neck. He grips me lightly, stroking his thumb just beneath my ear.

"He'll have to kill me first," he declares.

I lean into his grasp, selling the lie, and when I glance at Apollo he is watching me with dark eyes. My light stirs in my stomach, and the longer he holds me, the less sure I am of whom I'm lying to. Aros or myself.

The flame in Aros's eyes grows as if he is considering taking on Apollo's challenge himself.

"Am I truly meant to believe a beauty such as she has chosen a beast like you?" Aros sneers, playing on Apollo's insecurities.

He says nothing until Aros has the gall to add, "She mustn't be very bright then, must she?"

Aros chuckles to himself as Dawn flinches at his comment, and before I can open my mouth, the room goes dark.

Shadows pour from every darkened corner, covering the wide windows and smothering the dinner table. Aros responds in kind. Fire sparks in his eyes and ignites on his fingertips as he sits, grinning, waiting for Apollo to make a move. But Apollo is not so brash. His soft blue eyes have been swallowed by shadow, and his voice is even when he speaks.

"I will not claim to know why she has chosen me, but so long as she does, I will not tolerate insult or injury to her," he says, his dark eyes fixed on me though his words are for Aros only. "Should you speak ill of my bride again, this *beast* will send you back to the Council with a message scrawled in your blood and your head in your wife's hands," he finishes, smiling wide, fangs glinting in the candlelight.

No sooner than Apollo punctuates his threat do white-hot flames engulf the Martian king. They swallow him from head to toe, burning bright, and I can feel the heat from where he sits, though it doesn't seem to burn the chair beneath him or the clothes he wears.

Aros moves to stand, a stern glower on his face. I think he may strike, but Dawn catches his hand, and he stills. His flame gradually dimming. Slowly, he lowers himself back onto his seat, all the while gripping Dawn with a ferocity to rival Apollo's shadows still twisted around my legs.

With a hearty laugh, he douses his flame.

"Praise to the heavens for the blessing of beautiful women!" he shouts, lifting a wine-filled goblet high into the air.

Dawn's eyes dart to her plate, but Aros pulls her out of her seat, dragging her into his lap before she can resist. I'm not sure she would have even if she could. The viper in her knows better than to resist the desires of her mark.

In this regard, I may be the greatest viper to ever live, as I'm starting to think I couldn't deny the touch of Apollo's shadows, even if I wanted to.

"Though there are none so beautiful as mine. Mane oof fier en jair lein ish reiven der liegen dien Mars." *With a fire between her thighs to rival the lakes of Mars*, Aros declares.

A raging blush rises along Dawn's neck as he places swift kisses on her arms.

I don't think he knows I can understand him. I'm not sure he would care even if he did. I almost laugh, watching Dawn squirm in her husband's arms. Between the two of us, we could kill them both in a single breath, but here we sit like decorations—roses sat in a vase along the table.

"My deepest apologies, demon," Aros says, locking his arms around Dawn to keep her planted in his lap. "I had to be sure this wasn't a farce. The Council would not take kindly to being tricked in such a way. They will be glad to hear of your decision. When do you plan to wed?"

I'm still trying to decide if Dawn's blush is real when I realize Apollo hasn't answered.

I glance at him, but he's already looking at me, and my heart hammers as I realize he's lost the conversation. He doesn't know what's been asked. Aros's face is still buried in Dawn's hair, covering his lips from view.

Apollo and I exchange a knowing look, and I don't hesitate. I close the space between us, fisting his shirt in my hands and crushing my lips against his. His arms fold in around me, and his shadows move past my legs, encircling my waist as he pulls me close with a grunt. I kiss him openly, adding a soft whimper that I know he cannot feel, but Aros will hear. It catches his attention, and the absence of Apollo's answer is forgotten.

"Forgive me," I say, pulling back and feigning embarrassment. "I grow excited thinking about it. We'll be wed at the next full moon. Tomorrow evening."

I keep my eyes trained on Apollo's, and a smile whispers across his lips as he grows bold and adds, "You are welcome to join our festivities."

We both look to Aros then, watching to be sure he does not suspect us. His eyes shift back and forth between Apollo and me before he declares, "Thank you, but we cannot. We are headed home from quite a lengthy visit to Solaria. My darling flame is eager to return to our children." He glances at Dawn, and she meets his gaze with a soft smile that I know to be disingenuous. "We only agreed to stop in your territories as a favor to the Council. We will be on our way this evening."

Apollo and I do not question Aros's lies. Instead, I take my opening.

"In that case, Davina, would you like to see the gardens before you go? You cannot claim to have visited La Luna until you've seen them." I try for a pleasant smile, hoping that my unusually cheery tone will tell Dawn that her answer must be yes.

Aros's hand twitches against her hip, barely discernable but an unmistakable sign of alarm. Apollo steps in before he can object on her behalf.

"Yes, you must see them. Celeste can take you. They're just beyond this corridor. Won't take long."

I don't question why he is so eager to give me time alone with Dawn. Or, rather, for him to have a moment alone with Aros. I have more important concerns.

"Well..." Dawn wavers and I try to bake the urgency into my eyes without looking as if I've gone mad. "Alright, but it'll have to be a quick one."

She untangles herself from Aros's grip before he can say anything more. We both slip from the room as quickly as we can without causing suspicion. But as soon as the door slides shut Dawn crushes me in her arms. I wheeze as I try to catch my breath, and she pulls back, smiling down at me.

"I was starting to think you didn't recognize me," she says. "I shifted my hair and eyes so long ago, I couldn't remember if you'd seen them before." She drops her shift briefly, warming her eyes until they look more like mine and darkening her hair to a more golden blond than the silky platinum she was sporting a moment ago. She chuckles, replacing her façade with ease.

"Of course not," I whisper. "How could I forget my own sister? Come, we can talk outside."

"He doesn't require you to have an escort?" she asks as we hurry through the hall hand-in-hand.

I shrug. "No."

I don't bother to tell her that just this morning, the answer was yes. After all, something has changed since then. A lot has changed since then.

We don't stop until we're standing on the terrace overlooking the castle garden. But neither of us are the slightest bit interested in flowers. Dawn turns to me, gripping me by the shoulders and squeezing me lightly.

"Goodness, you've grown so much. I've missed you." She pulls me in for another fierce hug. "I miss everyone," she mutters, and when she pulls back, I can see the toll the viper has taken on her.

"Have you seen the others?" I ask.

"Only Helie, a few years ago. But the Satúran king does not

travel with his wives, and I haven't been back since. She seemed to be alright, though. As well as any of us can be."

I have no doubt my circumstances are more favorable than Helie's. Her mission is particularly unpleasant. She was sent as a concubine to the Satúran King some thirty years ago—a foul man with a taste for being too rough with his women. None of us envied her. I often pray that she will receive her order to strike, if only so she may be free of him. But it has yet to come.

"How are you? How are your children?" I ask, trying to keep my voice low in case there are any groundskeepers still milling about at this hour.

Dawn's face blossoms into unbridled joy, and she begins to gush, "Oh, Celeste, they're just lovely. You would adore them."

Her eyes brighten as she tells me of their skill and how much they take after their father.

"For a while there we thought Phoenix wasn't blessed by Mother Mars. But you should see him now. He's almost caught up to Ember."

She goes on for a while, and I listen to every minute detail, trying to soak it in.

"And Aros?" I ask after she's finished. "Is he fair with you?"

Dawn catches the meaning in my eye, and she chuckles softly, a blush creeping up her neck.

"He can be a bit forward, but he's never been anything but... kind." Her eyes find the floor, smiling softly. "He's usually quite gentle, really."

I watch her for a moment as she rights herself, smothering the blush back down and crossing her arms in front of her.

"You love him," I say.

I'm not asking. I can see it on her face. But she shakes her head anyway.

"No. No, I'm simply playing my part. As the Serpent demands."

"Dawn, you don't have to lie to me. I understand. You've been there so long. I could only imagine—"

She pries herself from my grip.

"No, Celeste. No, you don't understand. You couldn't possibly," her voice grows stern, and I'm reminded briefly of the times she scolded me for my form when we were young. "You've only been here but a month. You don't know how it feels, waiting and waiting for the moment the Serpent gives the order. You don't know what it's like, waiting year after year for the call to come. For twenty-five years, I hadn't seen another viper. Haven't seen my family. *Twenty-five*." A distant longing takes up the space in her eyes as she remembers a time since passed. "It's torture. And not even the worst kind." Her gaze finds mine as she asks, "Do you know what I think about at night?"

I shake my head, too nervous of upsetting her further to answer aloud.

"I think about my children. What will come of them when I leave? What do you think they do to the children of a traitor?" she asks. It's rhetorical, but I know she truly wishes she had an answer. "And what's worse—what will come of them if I'm found out? Will Aros rip them from me? Am I doomed to leave them motherless either way?" Her eyes close, and her shift flickers as her magic strains to hold on under the weight of her anxiety. "I wouldn't wish this upon anyone. But you're a lucky one, I suppose. You won't be here much longer."

"What do you mean?"

"The Serpent sent me with a message for you," Dawn whispers, stepping in close. "Striking orders."

I think the ground beneath my feet begins to shake, but really it's just my knees trying and failing to keep me standing. Suddenly they feel weak, and my head spins as if the world has been tilted on its side. I don't have time to steady myself as Dawn gives me my orders.

"The Serpent will arrive in one week's time. Solaria will move against La Luna."

"But...but the wedding. The Council has no reason to allow such action. The treaty hasn't been broken."

"Do you think the Serpent cares about the Council's treaty?" Dawn asks, chuckling at me.

I'm too embarrassed to admit that I thought the answer may be yes. Instead, I stand paralyzed as Dawn seals my fate.

"You must kill the demon before the army reaches the border."

CHAPTER 22

APOLLO

When Celeste and Davina return, I do not miss the fact that Celeste's light has grown dimmer. It had been burning bright ever since we left the ring, near white, and now it has returned to a dull yellow that glows softly in her chest, almost completely dark.

She tries her best not to display it, but I can see something has upset her. I spend the remainder of our meal with a possessive grip on her thigh, wishing I could shield her from whatever foul mood Davina caused.

She keeps a close watch on Celeste, eyeing the place my shadows rest around her arms, and shifting between us every once in a while. Celeste doesn't try to pry herself from my grasp. She lets my hands and my shadows linger until Aros declares that they must be leaving.

Renwick arrives to escort them back to their carriage, and I'm grateful when Aros does not reach for Celeste's hand as he bids us goodbye. I keep her close as we return to our chamber.

She walks beside me with ribbons of night laced around her

legs, and I don't free her from them until the door swings shut behind us.

Watching Aros fawn over her nearly drove me to violence, and I am eager to claim her as I should have the moment I first laid eyes on her. I snatch up her hand as she tries to move past me, reeling her in until I can feel her supple curves pressed tight against my chest.

Her eyes slide closed as she offers me her sweet poison, and I wrap her in my arms. Drinking it freely and kissing her hard. Perhaps harder than I should, but I know she can handle it. The Great Mother would not have sent her to me if she couldn't.

She melts in my hands, her light rising up as she yields to me, but when I pull back to see its beauty, it still does not reach her eyes.

"My darling star, what is wrong?"

She only blinks up at me with those big golden eyes. *"I should gather my things."*

"Pardon?"

"My things," she repeats.

I am not a fool. I know what she is suggesting. But she must have hit her head during our sparring session. Or perhaps Aros is right. Perhaps she is not so bright if she truly believes she can ever be free of me now. I belong to her now. My heart belongs to her. As we stand here, I can see it beating between her soft, brown fingers. There is no freedom from this, from her. And if she thinks otherwise, she'll have to say it aloud.

"I'm not sure I know what you mean," I tell her.

"Apollo..." she starts. *"You do not need me any longer. The Council is too busy with their own misgivings to send another member to confirm our union. Aros and Davina will tell them what they've seen tonight, and they will be satisfied that the treaty is not broken."* She shrugs. *"There's nothing more for me to do."*

"I can think of a few things. More than a few."

She shakes her head. *"No, you don't understand..."*

"What? What don't I understand?"

Celeste shifts, biting her lip and crossing and uncrossing her arms as she takes the time to choose her words. Her fists clench, and I can see the moment she settles on what to say. But she doesn't speak as she signs.

You shouldn't have chosen me, Apollo. You should have sent me away as soon as you met me. She pauses, shutting her eyes briefly. *If you knew me,* truly *knew me, you would not want me, Apollo.*

She signs the words with the same swift skill as always, but they come slower than usual, and it's clear it pains her. My tail flicks in irritation as I watch her eyes draw down in shame.

"I do know you," I challenge. "I know your spirit is fearless and full of virtue. That you love your freedom more than you love most things. That you will fight for what you hold most dear."

Her eyes warm as she shakes her head. I'm prepared to tell her that is all I need to know, but she is quick with a response.

No, you don't, she signs. *Because if you knew me...you would kill me.*

My face twists at her words. The mere thought is sickening. To see her light washed away after searching for her for so long? So long I'd nearly given up? Only a fool would do such a thing.

"You must think very highly of me if you believe I am capable of turning away from you. If I have learned anything these past weeks, it is that I am not."

Her eyes find the floor, and she signs silently, *Apollo—your people would demand it. They would not want me by your side. They would call for my head.* Your *head even.*

She backs away from me, but my shadows meet her first, winding around her waist and pulling her in close. She pushes at them, but her hands swipe uselessly through them, and her light heats as she grows frustrated.

"They already do," I say. "My own people flee from me. They run from the Demon of La Luna even as I spend every *waking* moment trying to remedy it. Trying to do right by them. To *save* them. Everything I do, I do in their name."

She opens her sweet mouth to defy me, but I step in close, wedging her hands against my chest so she can't say anything more. It is a mistake I know I ought not to make. My shadows writhe as soon as her light hits my skin, and in the back of my mind, I worry I will not be able to separate from her.

"But when it comes to you, and *only* you, I will not. I refuse. In you, I am selfish." As if confirming my helplessness, my hand reaches out to stroke her jaw, desperate to touch her. "I would not give you up if the Great Mother herself demanded it."

Her sunset eyes burn bright, and for once in her life, she seems to be at a loss for words.

"You are mine. Now and always. Regardless of what my people may decide. And I am yours despite what you may think."

I watch as her eyes search my face, and I can feel my breath still in my chest as I wait for her answer.

In this moment, I am not a demon. I am not even a king. I am just a man asking his light to follow him into the dark.

Celeste wavers, staring into my eyes as if she is in desperate need.

"Apollo..." she mouths, her eyes growing brighter.

She rises on her toes and snakes her arms around my neck, pulling me down the rest of the way to meet her.

I greet her slowly, her lips grazing mine as her soft tongue plays along the seam of my mouth. Her hand trails down to my stomach, pausing at the waist of my pants, testing.

I cannot say a word to stop her. So when her fingers reach the curls beneath my belt, my hips jerk forward, wanting, and my sweet star abides.

Her fingers encircle my length as best she can, and my head pitches forward, knocking my horns into the door as her warm hand plays at the base of my cock. A heavy growl follows as she plunges down, gripping it in her little fist and forging it into iron.

My eyes slide shut as she strokes me, blinding me with her touch.

She continues teasing, gripping, and squeezing, and I'm forced to anchor myself against the door. The wooden frame splinters under the weight of my desire as I claw at it. And I nearly snap it in two when her mouth drops open in a breathy sigh, my name quiet on her lips. But as I've said, I am selfish when it comes to her, and before I can spill my seed across her warm fingers, I lift her from the floor, gripping her thick thighs as she wraps her legs around my waist.

I lay her on the bed beneath me, standing between her knees to pin her in place, as my fingers grasp her hips.

"I'm going to fuck you now, darling. And I'm not going to stop unless you tell me to."

Her face twists, shocked but pleased, and I take it she is deciding whether I should be permitted to speak to her this way.

I doubt any other man can.

I consider it a great triumph when she does not scold me for my forward words. Instead, she nods, eyes shut and panting as I slip my hand into her bodice.

Her breathing grows quick as I squeeze her pillowy breasts. But her eyes snap open as my fingers close around the small blade that she keeps tucked between them. With wide eyes she watches me pull it free.

"Did you think I did not know about your hiding place?" I ask. "Don't worry. You may keep it. I only need it a moment."

I take the blade to my right hand and cut back my claws, blunting them each in turn until my hand no longer bears the threatening tips. Then I repeat the process with my left. When I'm finished, Celeste is still staring at me in mild shock, but her surprise subsides as I reach between her legs to tear through her panties and part her swollen flesh.

Her cunt is flush with desire, and she spreads her legs wider as I stroke her wet folds and watch her eyes roll back.

Words form on her lips, but I'm too distracted by the light behind her eyes to know what she's saying. Its warmth covers my face, and I think I'd like to bathe in it, to bathe in the heat of her body.

I work a soft moan out of her, pressing my finger to her entrance and teasing her clit with my thumb. When I slide a digit inside of her, her body clenches tight around me, and my cock weeps, spilling into my pants. But I don't care. There will be plenty left for her to claim, should she want it.

I push her body to its limit, stroking her with a fierce need. Her fearless spirit meets my fervent lust, and her breath grows ragged as she nears her peak. Her thighs begin to quiver against my hand, and her mouth stops forming words, only lapping at my tongue, which I have to fight not to send swimming down her throat.

Her sunlight reaches up to the ceiling, spreading from her head to her toes and bleeding out into the sheets around her. The golden rays tangle with the smoke of my shadows, creating twisted images that dance across the walls as her core clenches around my fingers over and over. Until she lay panting beneath me. But I don't stop.

I peel her out of the tight-fitting dress to stare at her bare body. Her dark nipples point up toward the ceiling as she arches into my palms, silently pleading for more.

It takes everything in me not to spear into her then and there. I long for the comfort of her body. So much so that I ache. I want to feel the warmth of her light wrapped around my cock and see the sunlight pour out in ecstasy. But first I must taste the heat between her legs.

I kneel before her, tossing her legs over my shoulders, and she rises to her elbows, eyeing me closely.

I'm struck by the beautiful blush creeping up her face. It's a color I haven't seen on her before. A soft white light fills her cheeks as her heart begins to beat faster. I can feel it hammering beneath my fingertips, and her excitement overwhelms me. I can't resist the urge to kiss her. It's quick. A small one placed along the inside of her thigh before I grip her ass in my hands.

"I would like to taste what is mine," I tell her.

The blush intensifies while her heart feels as if it is trying to escape her body. Her legs part even further, and the scent of her heat blossoms into a cloud of salty, sweet fragrance.

Now it's my heart's turn to attempt an escape. I've dreamt of this moment each night since I saw her lying in my bed, those dark curls sprawled across my pillow.

I lay my hand across her soft belly, offering it to her.

"Two taps if you'd like me to slow. Three if you'd like me to stop. One if you'd like me to start again."

Her eyes search my face with soft confusion pulling her brows together.

"My darling star, it's important I know you understand these signals. I may not see your words when we are together."

Her frown deepens as if I've misunderstood her apprehension.

And what if I want you to go faster? she asks, a sweet troublesome grin spreading across her face.

I trace a slow circle between her breasts in demonstration, and she nods.

She inhales sharply as my tongue rolls out to sweep between her folds, and her hands dart into my hair, gripping me by the horns. She uses them to steady herself, and I groan low in my chest, peeling her hands from around the base and placing them back on the bed beside her.

She signs, eyeing me mischievously, *Does that feel good for you?*

"Yes, my darling. And if you don't stop, this will be a shorter endeavor than I intended."

She giggles, looking more innocent than she has a right to, and I send my shadows around her knees, holding her open as I feast on her sweet nectar.

My hands are full of her plush body, gripping her hips and

palming her tender breasts. Each time I roll her nipples between my fingers, she bucks beneath me, and I can feel the muffled vibration of her cries as she makes her pleasure known. I lick and tease and suck until her legs quiver atop my shoulders, but I can't seem to stop.

Her taste is divine. And the sweet liquid that rushes to meet me only grows more flavorful with each passing second.

When she traces a slow circle along my shoulder, I slip my fingers into her, groaning against her wet skin as she tightens around me. Her nails scrape against my arms as I drive her to her peak, and her thighs clamp around my head when she finds her release.

I look up to see her smiling brightly and signing my name with half-hooded lids. She is a vision spread wide across my bed and tangled in my shadows.

Please, she signs, desperate.

The simple gesture breaks me, and I find myself standing between her slicked legs, poised to enter before she can even catch her breath.

I free myself as she flops back to the bed. Her legs part, inviting me in, and I do not hesitate.

I push into her without another word.

Her nails burrow into my skin as her body stretches to accommodate me, pulling me in deeper until I'm seated at the hilt, and she is taking every inch.

She shifts, adjusting to the sensation of me filling her, and I cannot bear to lie still. I thrust into her slowly, then harder as she traces more circles across my back.

My star is a greedy little thing. But I am happy to accommodate, and I make my home in her body, watching her shake and shatter beneath me over and over. This time when her hands go to my head, I do not stop her. Instead, my pace grows brutal as she rubs my horns, squeezing each time she returns to the base.

My hands look for purchase on her hips, but I worry I am

already too rough with her, and they wander over her until I find the gold chain still stretched across her stomach.

"I believe you lied to me to me, darling," I tease. Celeste's eyes fly open, growing wide with mild panic, shining up at me as her breasts heave with shallow breaths. "There seems to be a clear purpose for these," I tell her, curling my fingers around the chain.

I take hold, fisting it tight and using it to pull her body back around my shaft as I spear into her once more.

Her mouth falls open in a desperate gasp that I'm sure is music to the ears, but I would not know.

"By the Moon, I wish I could hear that," I tell her quietly.

Her hands move deftly in the space between us. *Who says you can't?*

My movement slows as I frown down at her. "How could I ever—"

But I don't get the chance to ask. Before I can finish my sentence, Celeste pries my fingers from around her waist chain and drags my hand up her body until it rests on the smooth column of her neck. She smiles a little devious smile before wrapping my fingers around her throat.

My eyes go wide.

"Celeste—"

I'm prepared to chastise her for being so careless in the presence of the demon. She does not know what she does to me, and I fear she is wandering too close to the limits I've set.

I open my mouth to tell her as much, but the words are cut off as her lips part, and a deep vibration echoes through her, traveling up her throat and out her mouth but also through my fingers.

I squeeze involuntarily, chasing the feeling of her soft cries. When she makes no sound, I stroke into her, deep and rough, until I can feel her body clamping down around me, drawing me deeper.

I watch as my name pours from her lips.

It is my undoing. My magic acts on its own, sending shadows twisting around her arms and legs and snaking through her hair.

But my hands can only hold her, and she cries out again as my hot, slick seed pours into her. Her body answers the call of my own and tightens and releases, pulsing like a heartbeat deep inside.

Anger spreads through my body, rippling out from my chest like a heatwave as I think about what's been stolen from me. "If I ever see the Serpent, rest assured, I will cut him down for having stolen such sweet sounds from me."

Shh, no talk of the Serpent now, she signs, and I obey. Discarding my anger in favor of her sweet light.

CHAPTER 23

CELESTE

———

Tomorrow, I tell myself. Tomorrow I will abandon this man and this bed. And my mission. I will take my failure and pray that the Serpent shows me mercy. Because I cannot kill him. I won't kill him. He is too precious to me, the only man I've ever loved and the only one who sees me. Not the viper, but *me*. I cannot allow the Serpent to take anything more from him. Certainly not by my hand.

Tomorrow.

But for now, I will give myself this one moment with him.

Apollo continues to thrust into me until my hips grow sore from being spread wide, and even then, he does not stop. He merely lays me on my side and wedges himself between my thighs from behind.

The feeling is overwhelming, and all I can do is surrender to his shadows wrapped around my waist, helpless to the tortured cries of pleasure rushing from my mouth.

He works my body expertly, as though he's been here a thousand times before. Not just with *any* woman, but been here, with *me*, a thousand times.

His hands are where I want them before I even know that's where I want them. His lips find mine every chance he gets, and his pace is perfect, hitting every scorching inch of me. Even his tail is exactly where I need it to be, wrapped tight around my ankle and holding me open. Best of all, his fingers lay splayed across my throat, capturing every sound I make. And he answers with his own growls of pleasure that run up my spine before settling in my ears.

It's everything I've ever wanted, and he continues teasing and touching and stroking until I'm desperate for him to release me.

"Please. I can't handle another," I sign, stringing together symbols that I'm only half certain form a full sentence. In the end, it doesn't matter because Apollo only grunts and says, "This one's not for you."

Liquid rushes from me, pouring down my thighs. And I can't help the strangled cry that escapes me. By the gleeful look on his face, I think Apollo can just barely hear it.

Good to know.

My body shatters once more, and I can only faintly recall what he'd said at the start. I try to find the words to tell him to stop, but my mind can't seem to catch up. Or rather, it doesn't want to. Soon, the feeling grows unbearable, and my light begins to burn hot wherever Apollo's hands land, but it does not deter him. He continues to thrust into me mercilessly, and all I can say is his name.

My eyes pry open between my bouts of heavy breathing to see him looming over me, propped on an elbow with shadows twisting around my arms and legs, holding me open and bending my body to his will. His muscles pulse as his shadows move in a frenzy. His horns stand grand on his head, and I want so badly to feel their smooth texture beneath my palms. But he shows me no mercy, and I'm left clinging to him as I go hurtling into another sun-shattering orgasm.

When we've finished, and my muscles no longer feel strong enough to lift a hair, he pulls me to his chest, pressing my cheek to his heart while stroking my back with shadow. But he doesn't vacate the space he's filled deep in my core, and I sit there for a long while, trying not to think about the fact that I may never know a joy like this ever again.

Apollo's confession was like a dream come to life, and now that the haze of our lovemaking is lifting, I know it will slip through my fingers.

As if sensing my rising tension, he brushes a thumb across my cheek, tilting my face up to meet his eyes. "Darling, you worry too much. You are here, and that is all that matters."

I sit up so he can see me, but I don't attempt to move from his lap.

"*Your people will never accept me,*" I tell him, trying again to convince him to let me go. I cannot stay here and continue this farce, and it will be easier if we are in agreement.

He grunts his discontent as I return to the topic of our impending doom.

"In time, they will," he insists.

"*Your own mother saw fit to hide her heritage. What makes you think they could forgive hundreds of years of terror?*"

Apollo shakes his head, pressing a finger to my lips.

"We are not so different. Solarians and Lunars. Many of my people have forgotten that. But our history is shared. My father was too blinded by hate to show them. But I am not. I will remind them."

"*A history of* bloodshed," I correct.

"Is that what your serpent has told you?" he asks, frowning down at me.

That's exactly what the Serpent told me.

Based on the incredulous look he's giving me, I suddenly feel as if that is the incorrect answer.

When I don't speak, Apollo smiles. But it isn't earnest or even amused. It just seems...sad.

"It is a history of bloodshed, yes. But it is also a history of love," he says in a gentle, caressing tone. "The Serpent would like us all to forget because it makes it easier for him to carry out his plans. But there are those who remember that Mother Sun and Mother Luna are not enemies." His gaze flits from my eyes to my mouth, then back again. "Some of us know the truth. We know that the Sun and the Moon...are lovers."

My face must be scrunched in confusion because Apollo chuckles at me, smoothing his thumb between my brows.

"The Serpent would have your head for saying such a thing," I tell him.

He laughs as if he relishes the idea of the Serpent making an attempt on his life, and I don't doubt that he does.

"For telling the truth?" he asks. "Darling, your sun and my moon are not at war with one another. They never have been. And never will be. Because they are nothing more than lovers separated by the stars. The old histories tell of a time when the celestial plane was whole, but it makes no mention of a war between the Sun and Moon. They tell only of two lovers driven apart by fear."

I realize I'm sitting up now, propped in his lap, as his hands wander around my hips and thighs. But his eyes are fixed on mine, and when the next words leave his mouth, I'm forced to question everything I've ever known.

"When the celestial plane was divided, the Sun and Moon desired to remain as one, but the other mothers believed they would be too great a force should they decide to act against the rest. So they drove them apart. Mother Sun was sent to one end." He pauses to point at the east wall of our darkened room. "Mother Luna, the other."

I shake my head, unwilling to believe him, but he continues despite my protest.

"And now, every morning, and every evening, one rises without the other, and she races across the sky." Apollo's finger trails up and over until he's pointing west. "Searching for her love. Over and over and over, but never coming closer." A shadow curls under my chin, and he directs my sight to the picturesque image of Mother Luna just beyond our window, dipping below the horizon. "Even now, she pleads for the warmth of the day. But they will never know one another again. They are destined to be alone because of fear. It is a tragedy of celestial measures," he says, and when I look at him, I can see the disappointment in his eyes.

"Then why do you fight?" I ask. *"If our people are meant to be together, why not let the Sun cross your borders? Why not take down your wards."*

"Because my people cannot withstand Mother Sun's rays, not anymore. There was a time, long ago, before the Serpent, before the Rising Suns won the crown, when they could walk among the light as you do. Now, it is too strong for even the best of us. My shadows protect me from its effects, but my people cannot be exposed for long. It drives them to madness, to violence, and death."

"Sunsickness," I mutter, remembering the empty eyes and angry faces of the men in the market square, and Apollo's insistence that I not wander too close to them.

"And who is to say the Serpent will stop with La Luna," he adds, but he's not looking at me anymore. His head is leaning against the headboard, eyes fixed on the ceiling as if this is a thought that pains him greatly. "The Serpent does not care if we live or die. He craves power more than anything. And I don't think he will stop until there is *only* sun across every plane, as it is in Solaria. A never-ending day for all eternity. *Enlightenment,* as he calls it. And if La Luna will not stand in his way, who will?"

My mind reels as I try to reconcile Apollo's words. He has no reason to lie to me, and his assessment of the Serpent is true enough.

This is what I've been fighting for? Genocide? *This* is my mission?

"So, you don't hate the Sun?" I ask. My voice is unexpectedly quiet, but he reads my words with ease.

Apollo doesn't hesitate before reaching out a hand to press his fingers to my collarbone and brush them down my bare arm. My light rises to the surface, trailing after his touch. "No, Celeste." His deep voice feels rich in my ear, my name even richer. I'm forced to quiet my light as it brightens deep in my core. "The Sun is not my enemy. But the Serpent who wields her light so brutally? May he hope he never crosses my path."

Unease knots in my stomach, a sickening feeling I've never known. But I swallow it down and straighten my shoulders, looking up at Apollo. His smile widens until his fangs are gleaming in the moonlight, and as he kisses me, I decide to enjoy it, at least until tomorrow. After that, I know my time for joy will be over.

Because when else would the heavenly mother bless me with a moment such as this? After lurking in the moonlight to bring La Luna to its knees? After the Serpent is sated? Once I'm holding Apollo's head in my hands?

Will I feel joy then?

I might have...before. Before I knew him. Before I knew the lengths the Serpent was willing to go in the name of Enlightenment. But now, I'm almost certain it may kill me.

I am better off returning to the Serpent empty-handed. Heaven knows I will find no mercy there, but at least I'll die knowing I did not betray my own heart.

Perhaps that is the penance I must pay for my deceit.

CHAPTER 24

APOLLO

"*ove!*" Evalina shouts as the riders streak by in a rush. "Move them east!"

She stands across the clearing, idling in the shadow of the tree line as she barks her orders. There's a great distance between us, but with the charge in the center and its flares lashing out in every direction, I can see her face clearly. A vein of anger has pushed itself to the surface of her forehead as she strains to make herself heard, shouting over the wailing screech of seekers. I watch as my legion scrambles around her, rushing from side to side.

She's leading the push this evening. This final effort was her demand, so she shall lead us toward either victory or failure. Whatever the Great Mother may have for us.

I left Celeste to rest peacefully in our bed after another maddening round of lovemaking. For a while, I worried I was pushing her too hard, but my little star is wilder than even I knew, and she met my every thrust with tooth and nail, clawing at me and nibbling at my skin with her blunt teeth. Eventually, she decided she'd had enough of me, and we lay bare beneath the sheets for a long while.

She fell asleep with her glowing face pressed to my chest, and it'd taken all my strength to pry us apart. To leave the warmth of her body for the cold night and a fight with fate. But she didn't need me tonight, and my men did.

Hoofbeats rock the earth beneath my feet, and I know the seekers are on the move—the riders close on their heels as they force them around the clearing. They've grown bolder these last few nights, edging closer and closer to the charge. Something in its energy has shifted. Though it looks the same, I can feel it.

I'm not sure if Evalina can, but I know the seekers do. The call of its light has pushed them past their own instinct to survive, no longer hesitating when they cross paths with a rider. Already we've lost three men to a seeker drawn to madness. It tore through them, caring nothing of a meal it couldn't eat, but only of the light beyond them. When it reached the charge, it was engulfed almost instantly in a white-hot light, burning its body beyond recognition. Yet still, the pack persists. Even now, the rumble of stampeding horses tells me they are drawing too close. But I remain at the post Evalina has assigned to me.

This idea is madness. As was every plan before this, but this one is particularly senseless. Then again, so was this entire endeavor. From the very moment, Father conjured it in his mind, perhaps. But it doesn't matter. Hopelessness calls for miracles, and all I can hope now is that Luna will grant us one.

I am to stand here until Evalina gives the order. Me and thirty other soldiers, ready to push forward at the call of her voice. This time, I am supposed to cover my soldiers and not the charge. I will drape them in shadow, cover them completely, and together we will attempt to push the charge toward the border.

Madness.

Covering the charge was easier and less reckless. It only required one sacrifice should it end poorly—*me*. Now there are thirty-two of us crowded around the charge, standing much too close for comfort. I watch my men shifting on their feet, unsure.

Across the clearing I can see them huddled together, waiting for Evalina's command to fan out. They busy themselves with idle chatter as they aim to distract one another from the inevitable.

Unless this goes exactly to plan, there are bound to be more injuries. But I will do my best to bear the brunt of them.

"We saw her in the ring," one says. "She fought the prince."

"I heard she landed a cut!" another adds.

"I could see her light. It shines from everywhere," another interjects.

I focus on their faces at the mention of Celeste—the little star swallowed up by the night.

Their faces wear the same open awe that I felt when she danced around me. They were right to be struck with wonder. Any man not in awe of her was too foolish to be trusted.

As I watch them talk of her with such esteem, a new hope creeps into my heart. One where Celeste can rule by my side without question. One where they accept her openly, and she need not hide as Mother had.

"Do you think she...you know..." a soldier asks, glancing at the others. They look at him, puzzled faces frowning at his rambling. "Lights up...when she..." His eyes grow wide, trying to convey his meaning, and they shout in an uproar as knowledge settles behind their eyes.

Several of them laugh. Though one has enough sense to say, "You shouldn't speak of such things. Prince Apollo would not approve."

I chuckle softly. Because I know that the answer to the young man's question is yes. Celeste's light shines like the Sun herself each time I bring her body to its peak—bright light pours from her eyes in a picture of pure ecstasy. I witnessed it many times this evening before unlacing her warm body from mine to trek into the forest.

I am the only one who knows. And it will remain that way until Mother Luna falls from the sky. Even then, the goddess herself could not pry it from me.

I know the men are merely curious. But that doesn't stop me from reaching a shadow around the circle and swatting them all in the back of the head.

"Ah!" they yelp, raising their gazes to search for the culprit. Some of them spin to look through the trees as if a seeker had come up to scold them. Or eat them.

I bark out a laugh, louder this time, and their eyes find me across the clearing, shrinking back into their heads as they realize I "heard" them.

"Pay attention, boys! Wouldn't want the seekers to catch you napping!"

They straighten and step apart just in time for Evalina to shout, "On my count!"

She raises her fist high above her head, preparing to count us down.

I wait, spreading my shadow across the soldiers until they're all covered from head to toe. Some of them flinch as my magic reaches them, but they all stand still as it creeps over their skin, shrouding them in night and shielding them from the light.

Evalina shouts, but I cannot hear it, and I focus on her hands, waiting until she holds up a single finger, at which point the legion begins to move. They take hesitant steps forward, inching toward the charge.

"Rest assured, I will not let you perish!" I tell them, and their steps become more sure, steady, and quick.

I think Evalina is shouting more directions because the soldiers spread further apart, spacing themselves evenly until they stand just before the charge. They look like demons as they surround it, dark creatures of the night covered in black shadow. I watch them closely as they plant their hands to the charge, pushing with every ounce of strength they can muster.

The charge seems to creak and groan as my shadows meet the surface, but before I can call for a halt, I see it roll. Just barely. A fraction of an inch.

The charge reacts, defending itself as if it knows our intentions. Several flares snap free, whipping through the air and aiming for my soldiers, but my shadows hold strong. Even as it touches down, they continue their course, pressing onward and rolling the charge one inch at a time. Evalina moves beside me. Arms crossed, a haughty look of satisfaction on her smug face. I roll my eyes at her,

"Do not distract me," I growl, but she ignores me to join the others. I keep watch over them all as they continue toward the edge of the clearing.

I try to focus on the duty in front of me, but beside me, the trees are shaking as the thunder of horses draws nearer. I chance a glance over my shoulder just in time to see a seeker, big, and black as night, barreling into the clearing with several riders following close behind. They shout and point while two of them race after the maddened creature with ropes that we know will do nothing. It is lost to thirst. Its hollow eye sockets are glowing with light, and its path is fixed on the charge. Standing between it and its goal are Evalina and thirty of my legion's finest.

"*Evalina!*" I shout, but she doesn't turn in time.

It scrapes a claw down her front as she spins, sending her flying backward. The seeker continues on its course, latching onto a single flare, only to explode in an instant, overwhelmed by the light.

My breath slows as I watch Evalina's body hurtling toward the charge's core. I yank the line back, pushing their shadow-covered bodies into the trees, abandoning our minor success for their survival. For all the hope this was worth, my legion is worth much more—Evalina chief among them.

A seeker's claw is one thing, but a solar burn is another

entirely. On her current course, she will hit the core head-first, and her life will burn away in an instant.

She is falling fast, and I pull my shadows free, shouting for the soldiers to flee. I can't be concerned with them if I am going to catch her. I know I won't reach her in time, but my shadows might.

I reel them in, gathering them into a wide net and sending them flying across the clearing. Evalina's mouth hangs open at an unnatural angle, gaping with a scream I can't hear. Her legs are pointed toward the sky, and her arms flail beneath her. Her eyes watch my shadows as if she is reaching for them, but I know she isn't. Her body is already limp, the moondust coursing through her blood, leaving her helpless against her trajectory.

My shadows find her arms, swallowing her and covering her from head to waist. But before I can shield the rest, a flare twists free from the domed top, snapping out between us.

Hot, white light sears my eyes as it floods the field in front of me.

A burning pain rips its way down my back, and my body goes rigid, leaving me in a heap as a seeker tears past. I crumple to the earth as my legs go numb.

But I can still feel the riders racing around me when my eyes slide shut. I find a face buried in the pain—staring up at me with a smile as bright as the Sun.

And the only prayer I can think to say is, "Celeste…"

CHAPTER 25

CELESTE

Wet leaves slosh underfoot as I race past the training grounds, paying no mind to the armory, and heading straight for the stables. My light zips through me in a frenzy, igniting every muscle until I feel certain they will vibrate out of my skin. The sound of blood rushing to my head is drowned out only by the persistent drumming of my heart as my feet meet the earth and I hurtle toward the one place I know I shouldn't. Not if I want to keep my light. But Apollo's voice came like a whisper, crawling into my mind and calling me out of my sleep—desperate and pleading. For *me*. And all I could do was answer.

I hardly took a moment to dress myself. The only things I could find were boots to cover my feet and one of Apollo's nightshirts, now whipping around my thighs as my legs set a splintering pace. The ground shakes beneath my feet, like thunder rolling through the dirt, and I push myself harder.

Strega is already stamping out a frantic beat as I burst into the stable. I ignore the saddle and sling myself over his bare back in one leap, fisting his mane between my fingers as we take off toward the trees.

The telltale screech of a seeker pierces the wind ripping around my face, and Strega presses harder.

They are on us the moment we break through the tree line, scratching, clawing, and screeching close behind. I place a hand on Strega's chest, flattening myself against his back and passing my light between us, boosting his own and giving him the force to move quicker. My curls thrash against my face as we cut through the dark wood. I can hear riders rounding behind me and the unmistakable sound of life bleeding out of bodies, human and seeker alike. I send my blade flying into the hollowed eye of a passing seeker as it chases after a young legionnaire, but I don't slow. Apollo's voice is still calling me, and I won't stop until I find him.

I point Strega in the direction of the solar charge, cutting a familiar path through the trees and hardly slowing even as its light comes into view. It looks dim at a distance, the thick darkness swallowing it up like a sponge, but as I draw nearer, I can see it is anything but. It sits like a glowing sphere on the edge of the clearing, further than it had been before, bleeding into the sky above. Only it isn't the same orange-red orb I'd seen. It's since turned a pale, frosted-white hue, and as we approach, I can see the flecks of blue snapping out at every angle. Flares threatening to eat up the surrounding trees.

Strega doesn't stop as we come upon it. I jump from his back, rolling across the dirt, before springing to my feet and racing across the clearing. Soldiers stand in small pockets, engaging a few seekers as they try to make their retreat, and I bark out an order, "Strega will draw them into the forest! Follow him! The riders are four hundred paces east! Tell them to circle back to collect the others! I will cover you!"

Several of them pause to gape at me.

I know what I look like. My celestial form took hold during my wild ride through the forest, making my skin burn bright. A color close to the charge but not quite. My hair isn't its usual brown anymore. It's stark white along with my eyes, swallowing the red-flecked color until they look like a Venutian's. Blank and full of light. But we don't have time for the shock and awe.

"*Now!*" I shout, unleashing a panel of sunlight to shield them.

They snap back to life, ducking behind my light, sprinting in the opposite direction as Strega cuts in front of them, drawing the seeker's attention.

Strega's light is no longer buried, and they follow him without question.

Praise Luna they aren't intelligent creatures.

"Apollo?" I call out.

I know he cannot hear me, but just saying his name brings me comfort. As if he can't possibly be gone so long as I'm breathing life into it. But my voice hardly sounds like my own as I run through the clearing searching for any sign of him.

I find him crumpled against the earth too close to the base of the charge, eyes shut and shadows pouring out of him. His eyes flutter as he tries to focus on me, and the little voice in my head returns. Only this time, it whispers something new.

Leave him! It hisses. *Let him die. Your job will be done.*

The words burn through me as I stand looking at him.

I could leave him here. Claim another "victory" without lifting a finger. The Serpent would be none the wiser, and my head would remain squarely on my shoulders. But as I stand here, Apollo's deep voice drowns out the little one.

"You cannot be here," he orders, straining to lift his head and hands. "It is not safe for you."

Shadows push at my legs, but the majority of them are occupied with something lying beside him. It looks like a cocoon of sorts, wrapped in his magic and smelling distinctly of charred skin.

"Celeste," he says. "Please."

It is a tone I've never heard from him before, one of pleading, and the note sends a shiver up my spine as my light plunges into my gut.

He's scared.

I don't spend time arguing with him. Instead, I grip him by the arms and drag him from beneath the charge, keeping a close eye on the flares still whipping through the air. His body is heavy, and the added weight of the cocoon he's trailing makes it a difficult task. Sheer strength isn't a viper's skill. We rely on agility and speed to do the Serpent's bidding. So I only manage to drag him halfway to the trees.

"You must leave," he demands, staring into the dark sky.

When he doesn't turn to look at me, I know he's been struck with moondust.

I curse under my breath. A solar burn I can handle, but moondust requires moonlight.

"Where is Evalina?" I ask him, pulling his head into my lap and praying the riders circle back quickly.

His eyes drift slowly to his side, where the cocoon lies in the dirt.

"Craters," I curse again, pulling the Lunar expletive from my mind with little effort.

His lip twitches into a feeble smile. But the emotion is swept up in his words as he says, "You must leave. It is not safe for you. The seekers..."

Tears prick my eyes, and I feel them well before pouring over, displaying my weakness without shame. But I don't care if my tears mean I've failed my objective. If I am a viper no more. I will gladly give up the blade if it means Apollo will see another night.

I watch my tears drip down onto his face, and his eyes grow pained. But I place a hand on his chest as I absentmindedly trail a thumb across his jaw, drawing him into silence.

"They're gone. And I'm stronger than I look, I promise. Don't worry about me," I say, trying my best to keep my mind focused.

I don't tell him that his worry is wasted on me. But when he opens his mouth again, my heart cracks open even wider than it had last night, and I worry I won't be able to put the pieces back together when the time comes.

"You do not get to decide whether or not I may worry about you," he says. Then a little louder, "I refuse to see your light washed away in my name. Please go. Before they return."

His words crush the remaining particles of a girl I no longer know into dust. But rather than sit here arguing, I simply say, "If you get to worry about me, then I get to worry about you."

His eyes flare as I defy him, but he doesn't argue any further. I check him over, looking for any sign of a burn. When I find none, I turn my attention to the cocoon.

There is a sickly sweet, burning scent coming from beneath his shadows, and I brace myself as I sign, *Show me Evalina.*

His lips flatten as he stares at me. I know it pains him to do nothing. I can see it on his face. So I lace our fingers together as I kneel between him and the husk he's wrapped her in.

"I don't know what's underneath. I think she hit the charge before I could cover her fully." His voice sticks in his throat, and he chokes out, "I think she's been burned. I can feel the light beneath my magic. I think it's still searing her."

I know it is. Once a charge finds its victim, the light will continue to penetrate until it dies. Whether it be human, animal, or plant. That's what makes it so particularly devastating. The light crawls across the earth, leaving only corpses behind until a Solarian celestial with enough magic can reel it back. A creation favored by the Solarian kings of old. The source of destruction that claimed Pluto and scattered its people across the planes. A weapon rarely seen since. It is, to put it mildly, all-devouring. But I keep that information to myself.

I nod just once and watch as the casing unfurls. The soft sheen of his shadows dissolves into smoke as they fold back into his limp body. I stifle a gasp as Evalina's light-charred limbs emerge from underneath.

Her mouth opens and closes as if she's trying to speak, but I shush her.

Her entire lower half is burnt to a crisp and four talon marks are engraved into her stomach. The image is familiar. She looks like many of my own marks—*my victims*—after they've had the unfortunate fate of meeting me. Gasping for breath, she moans in pain.

"Tell me," Apollo demands.

"She's going to be alright," I say. I will make sure of it. *"Evalina, I'm going to pull the light from you. You shouldn't feel anything because of the moondust. But I need you to tell me if it hurts. Blink once for no, twice for yes."*

She blinks one time before the moonlight fills her eyes, and she loses consciousness.

I gather my magic, unsure of what to do but feeling as if I have to do something. As I move to lay my hands on her, Apollo shouts at me.

"Celeste! The flares!"

His panic breaks my concentration, and I whirl in time to see a cobalt-blue flare snapping free and swinging through the air.

I spread my arms wide, letting my light pour out into a sheet as the flare touches down where my chest would have been if not for my light now covering me. I take the brunt of the blow, absorbing the light until the bright blue fades to white and the flare dies.

Power charges through me as I work to wrangle the magic into my own. Its energy is strong, and I recognize the signature immediately.

The Serpent's magic greets me like a stinging slap, and I wrestle it down, barely containing it.

"My Lady!" a voice calls, and a rider streaks past with Strega hot on his heels. "We must go! The riders will fall soon. We must leave!"

"Take Apollo!" I shout back, "I'll take Evalina!"

He nods, dropping from his horse with the ease of a well-seasoned rider to haul Apollo over the saddle. I push Evalina onto

Strega's back, face down, and climb up behind her before digging my heels into his sides.

We catapult through the darkness. Several riders join us near the outskirts of the palace grounds and I can hear the rallying cries of those left behind for the sake of others. As we pierce through the trees into the open grasses, I can see that any number of them would've done the same.

Several riders pull back to patrol the boundary line, and I'm thankful for their sacrifice. Every last one of them. Even though I am not deserving of it.

May Luna greet you with open arms, I pray.

"*Raye! Raye!*" My voice strains as I shout my way through the barracks. She *has* to be in here. "Ray—" Panic grips my throat, and my voice catches as I sprint from room to room. I've never been in the residential wing before. I never had reason to. But now... "Raye!"

"Celeste?" Her ordinarily quiet voice answers, loud and clear, somewhere to my right.

I spin, adjusting my course until we run smack into each other, both of us barreling through the halls.

"What's happening? Is it time—"

"Come on!"

Our voices overlap as I snatch up her wrist, tugging her back the way I came. Raye follows in silence. She knows I would not be sprinting across the earth if it weren't for good reason, so she keeps pace, and when I burst through the infirmary doors, she's barely a step behind me.

Half the Lunar legion is packed into the small space, crowding around their brethren. I push through the crowd, dragging Raye behind me, and she gasps as the horrors come into view.

Apollo and Evalina lay beside each other on low cots, flat on their backs, staring up at the ceiling. Well, at least Apollo is. Evalina's eyes are closed, and I feel another wave of panic seize my chest.

Pus is beginning to form in her seeker's wound, and the light from the charge burn is creeping up her thighs, making its way toward her torso. The only thing that comforts me is the shallow rise and fall of her chest, though they come too far apart and too labored. She will not last if we do not move quickly.

"Evalina!" Raye's voice is pained, tight, and pitched too high, even for her. "What happened?" she wails, breaking apart from where our hands are joined and falling to her knees beside Evalina.

For a moment, I think she may cry, but her back straightens as she takes Evalina's limp hand into her own., and I'm reminded that Raye has known her fair share of loss.

I glance down at Apollo, looking for some confirmation of what I should tell her, but he's not looking at me. He's frowning as best he can at Raye's familiar touch and tone, though most of his face is slack.

What should I say? Raye doesn't know what I've seen in the forest. And I cannot reveal to Apollo that I've seen it before. He may speak of loving me despite my secrets, but I think he may be wrong.

Before I can say another word, Apollo saves me from the decision and barks, "What have you brought a handmaiden for? What good will she do?"

I have half a mind to tell him he'd best watch his tone, but as I look at him, all I see is fear. Not fear of pain, not for himself, but fear of loss—of Evalina.

I turn toward Raye, and she's already peering at me through her dark lashes.

Her black hair is pin straight, having not yet been wrangled into her usual braids, and it falls to her waist like a dark curtain.

Her soft upturned eyes are pinched at the corners with a grimace I can feel in my chest. And her once toffee skin is paler now after weeks in the darkness, and as I look at her, she is distinctly Plutonian.

Without so much as a word, she nods, giving me permission to divulge the secret we carry almost as closely as my own.

"Everyone out!" I shout.

My voice doesn't feel as strong as it usually does, and the legion only stares at me unblinking, dazed and confused by my boldness. When no one moves to exit, Apollo lends me his authority.

"You heard your Lady! *Out!*"

Feet shuffle, and murmurs sprout up, but everyone hurries to the door, leaving only the four of us.

I draw in a deep breath, looking to Raye for reassurance, but I can see her throat bobbing up and down as she fights back tears, so I confess it for her.

"Raye is not Solarian," I say. "She is Plutonian. *Blessed* by Pluto."

Apollo's eyes widen, and he fights his limp body, trying to face Raye. Thanks to the moondust, his head only turns a fraction of the way, but I don't need anything more to know the shock he's experiencing.

All Plutonians live in hiding. And for good reason. Their power over the spirit brought destruction to their doorstep. The power to raise the dead and control emotion was a lure too tempting, a weapon in any arsenal. The greed of others, the greed of the Serpent, had brought their house to its knees. And in the name of preservation, they slipped away into the other planes, harboring their celestial magic in secret. A secret Raye guarded with her life. But this called for an exception.

Raye's magic may be untrained, never having successfully resurrected so much as a toad. But if it becomes necessary, I know she'll do her best.

"A necromancer?" Apollo mutters. I nod. And my demon

surprises me when he says nothing more on the subject and simply asks, "Is she truly so badly injured?"

Raye and I both startle as Renwick comes surging through the door with Shrea in tow. Her lightly wrinkled face flits from Evalina to Apollo then back again before she rushes to Apollo's side, hands outstretched and palms gathering moonlight between them.

"Are you mad?" Apollo shouts. His face twitches as if he would back away from her were his limbs within his control.

"Your highness, the crown—" Shrea starts, but Apollo is already shouting over her.

"I don't give a damn about the crown, Shrea! Save Evalina, save your daughter!" he bellows in her face, but she takes no offense.

I drop down on Apollo's cot and lace our fingers too tightly, my grip threatening to sever them as I cut off the blood supply. Shrea squeezes in beside Raye, who only shifts an inch, and smiles up at her with tears in her eyes.

"Celeste, you'll need to remove the sunlight first," Shrea directs. "If I pull the moondust from her now, she'll feel every spark from the flare. Once that's done, I can heal the seeker's wound. And you—" She glances again at Raye, who offers no explanation for her presence.

Shrea doesn't question it. She only nods as if confirming something she's known for quite some time before calling me to her side.

I leave Apollo reluctantly. His shadows move beneath his skin, languid and slow, trailing after my hands, and I wish so badly to take their comfort with me. But I leave it to join Shrea and Raye in a makeshift semi-circle. As we hover over Evalina's lifeless body, we mutter our respective prayers.

"May Luna's light strengthen you," Shrea says.

"May Pluto bring you peace," Raye offers.

I struggle for the words I wish to say. What can Mother Sun offer her when she is the cause of her pain? But I quickly remember the Serpent's signature singing through my bones as the flare hit me.

Mother Sun had nothing to do with this. This was the work of the mundane. Of man. There is nothing celestial about our circumstances.

The thought hardens my resolve, and I lay my hands across Evalina's thighs and whisper, "May Mother Sun guide my light."

We work quickly, and I'm surprised by the healing power of my light—so often used toward a very different end. It pulls the Serpent's energy free while Shrea and Raye work in tandem to bandage and soothe her wounds. It moves through the burn like a salve, stitching some of the broken skin and healing the blisters. She will still scar, perhaps not as badly as before, but she will bear the mark of the Serpent just as so many others do.

Just as Apollo does.

As Raye does.

As I do.

I try not to think about the fact that I have yet to meet a single soul unaffected by the Serpent's bite as Shrea moves on to Apollo. His injuries are easy work by comparison, and he's barking at soldiers before his wound is even stitched closed. Shrea works in a frenzy, following behind him with her hands hovering over his bare back, but she doesn't let him leave her sight until he's bandaged and clean.

When she finishes, he leans over Evalina's shivering form, now wrapped in thick blankets and clutching Raye's hand with a ferocity only matched by Raye herself. She still hasn't opened her eyes, and yet she clings to Raye as if by instinct alone. As Apollo laces his fingers with mine, pulling me close to his chest, I realize how far we've all fallen.

"Thank you." Apollo's words come easy, but they are heavy, burdened by a great weight. He watches Evalina's eyes flutter and shift behind her lids. "Thank you for helping her."

"It is my honor, truly," Raye says.

"The honor is mine," Apollo corrects. "Our houses spent centuries by each other's sides. Do not think that Luna, or her people, have forgotten you and your sacrifices. We will see the house of Pluto again. Until then, the night welcomes you, sister. Your secret is safe with me."

Apollo bows, deeper than I've seen him offer before, and Raye's tears begin anew, just as a fit of foul, shameful jealousy wrings me out like a rag.

If only he could embrace my secrets so easily.

Shrea waits for us at the entrance to the infirmary with a gentle frown taking up the space on her face. A mother's worry. Though, as we draw nearer, I'm unsure who it's for.

"Thank you, dear," she says, clutching my hand between her soft palms.

"Please, do not thank me." I should not be thanked for saving anyone from the plot I've been sent to carry out.

"Nonsense!" Shrea asserts. "She would've been lost without you. They both would have," she adds, glancing at Apollo who makes no attempt to follow our conversation.

He's craning over his shoulder, staring at Evalina. But my light surges at Shrea's words. It heats in my palm, melting into Apollo's and drawing out his shadows. They twist up my wrist, holding me to him and easing the anxiety filling my mind. And this time when he barks, "Come," I do not argue.

Chapter 26

Apollo

———

Shadows cloud my vision as fury overtakes me and I fail to dampen my anger. They pour out of me, spilling across the ground and hovering around Celeste. She walks beside me, shrouded in my dark magic, but I make no attempt to reel it in.

I had much time to consider the reality of our circumstances as I lay defenseless beneath the charge. Much time to think about what I would do if I lived. And two things had settled squarely in my mind.

First, I would obtain answers about the Serpent's plans. One way or another. For the sake of my people.

Second, I would not live without Celeste by my side.

She may be Solarian and she may hold many secrets. But the thought of her was the only thing that kept me breathing as death loomed over me. And now, she is the only thing keeping me from tearing through the castle like a raging bull.

Her sweet sunlight glows in the low light and I stroke her knuckles, savoring the sensation of her magic trailing after me. Surprisingly, she has not asked where we are headed. It is unlike her to follow so dutifully. Ordinarily, I would expect questions to spew from her mouth like a fountain. But tonight, she follows without question, gripping my fingers a little tighter than usual.

I don't ask her why. I know this night has been hard. I will not make it more difficult for her with my questioning. But I will give her comfort in any way I can. So when her steps begin to slow I scoop her up into my arms and carry her the rest of the way. She squirms but I hold fast and she eventually succumbs. Nestling in against my chest as her light dims.

The throne room is empty when we arrive. Save for the two guards that man the entrance and Renwick standing in the center looking worn.

I bark out a brief order as the heavy doors slam shut behind us and I set Celeste on her feet.

"Bring me our guest."

"Very well," Renwick answers. But he idles, standing between me and my throne.

I continue on my path until I come to a stop a few inches from his nose.

"Now," I add when he doesn't move.

Renwick's mouth opens and closes as he glances between me and Celeste.

"Will the Lady Solém be joining you?" he asks.

He doesn't say what he means to say. He doesn't have to. I know he disapproves of her presence. I simply don't care.

Celeste translates his inane question before turning to me, frowning. Her light burns hotter in frustration, but she dampens it quickly. I too try to remain calm, but my answer comes out steeped in ire.

"Celeste has just saved countless Lunar soldiers, your niece, and your king. She stays."

"But-bu-but." Renwick stammers.

I don't give him a chance to finish his sentence. I will not hear it. There is nothing he could say to dissuade me. Celeste is Lunar now, as far as I'm concerned.

"She. Stays." I reiterate, and Renwick bows briefly before exiting swiftly through the tall double doors.

I drop down onto my throne, sitting on the arm as I usually do, and gesture for Celeste to join me.

"Sit," I tell her, more gruffly than I mean to be.

Her eyes grow hesitant as I reach out a hand. When she doesn't take it, I wind a shadow around her waist to yank her forward. She stumbles into my lap and I hold her around her middle, fixing her in place.

"Forgive me," I mutter into her hair, breathing in the scent of her. She smells like smoke, fire, and rain. Like us, and the memory of the bed we shared. "This night has been long. And I cannot bear to part from you. Are you alright? Your silence is beginning to worry me." I ask her, stroking a finger down her cheek.

She twists in my arms, glancing up at me with dim eyes.

I'm fine, she signs.

I know there is more. I can see how tired she is. Her eyes have the same haggard look I feel in my own. But there is something else beneath it. Worry? Fear? Anticipation? I can't be sure. For now, I will not ask. She is whole and that is all that matters.

What are we doing here? she asks.

"I need answers," I say simply.

Renwick returns with more men than I anticipated. Near a dozen guards follow behind him with a shrouded figure slumped between them—our guest hanging limply between two soldiers. They shoulder him as his feet falter, dragging him to the front of the room. His boots scrape across the stone, and I think he may be close to death.

"Hello, my friend," I call as the group stops before me.

The soldiers release him, and he crumples to the earth in a heap of filthy rags.

"The time for silence is over," I tell him. "What do you know of the Serpent's plans?"

Our guest is silent as always, and a guard nudges him with his boot, encouraging him to speak.

"Surely you know something. You bear the build of a soldier."

Silence.

"Have I not been gentle with you?" I ask.

More silence.

"Very well...perhaps it is time we say our goodbyes."

I look to the nearest guard, prepared to give the order when Celeste turns to me, my name on her lips.

"Apollo I—"

But whatever she was about to say is quickly washed away as our guest lifts his head.

"Prinesta?" He mutters. The subtle vibration of his voice so faint I'm not sure the others have caught the name he calls her. It is a Solarian word for 'Princess.'

Celeste's head spins, and she's on her feet before I can stop her.

"Kefu?" she blurts, eyes wide.

"You know this man?" Renwick barks, overstepping his bounds.

Celeste does not answer him. And I don't stop her as she drops to her knees in front of our guest—Kefu rather. Her hands breeze over him and he groans in pain.

"Celeste?" he mutters.

My lip curls as he gropes at her, and I find myself on the edge of my seat. She speaks, but I cannot see what she says. Her back is to me, and she doesn't make space for me to read her, so I am forced to lean over for a glimpse of Kefu's words.

"My sun," he says. Then again, "My sun." And again. Over and over until I'm almost certain they are the only words he knows aside from her name.

He reaches out to hold her face in his hands.

"Celeste...he touches you too freely," I warn through gritted teeth.

She whirls on me.

"What have you done?" she shouts. "Look at him!"

I glance down at Kefu, bloodied and bruised, and I know what it must look like. He is frail and withered, with hardly a drop of light left, babbling like the sunsick. But Celeste does not offer me the chance to explain. She's already turned her back on me.

"Darling," I try, reaching out a shadow.

Kefu shrinks back. Celeste follows, disregarding my words. Her light is burning close beneath her skin, and I can see she's angry even if I can't see her face. She continues speaking to him, but Kefu seems incoherent and I wonder if this is why he was so silent these past weeks. Has his mind been lost to infection?

I watch closely as words spew out of him, reading them even as he mutters and mouths them silently. When Celeste moves to stand, he latches onto her, pulling her back down in front of him. My fists clench, but I stow my magic. She is more than capable of handling him should it be necessary. But her body shows no signs of fear as he leans forward to whisper to her.

"Kill him," he says, mouthing words he does not want me to hear. "Kill him, now."

Nobody moves. Only Celeste and I seem to know what he's said, and she hurries to shush him.

"Shh. Kefu. You're sick. You need rest." She insists. "It's alright. You're safe now."

But Kefu's face swells with rage, and he reaches for her, gripping her by the shoulders.

"Why is he still breathing?" he shouts, surging up from the floor. "Do your duty!"

He shakes her violently. Celeste stumbles back falling onto her butt.

"Why else did they suffer? What did they die for? Kill him!" He demands, and Celeste flinches as spittle flies from his gaping mouth. "What good is a viper who will not strike? Kill him, Princess!"

He bellows in her face, and I realize all too late the mistake I've made in bringing him here.

The throne room erupts into chaos.

My guards, loyal as they are, react without orders. All of them moving in on Celeste and Kefu.

They sprint across the wide-open room. Blades unsheathed and moonlight shining as they prepare to subdue them. They close in on Kefu easily, dragging him kicking and screaming from the room. Leaving myself and the others to handle Celeste.

She is on her feet in a single breath, and my shadows explode as I rise, aiming to shield her from my men. Should any of them lay a hand on her they will regret it for the rest of their days. But she mistakes my action for anger and her magic swirls to life in front of me.

It lashes out, forming stinging flares that she holds steady as the guards creep around her.

They hesitate. They know her strength. They've seen it for themselves. And several of them glance at me for direction, but words are beyond me in this moment.

Celeste is standing in the middle of the throne room, shining brightly as they surround her, and I can see she means to run.

Fear washes over me, and I shout at her.

"Celeste!"

But she is already occupied. The guards stalk forward, and when they reach her, she does not delay. She claims their blades for herself and throws them into the nearest wall. Where they stick and stay as she brings my men down gently. She moves swiftly, but not as I'd expected. Not as ruthlessly as she had with me. She holds back her power, landing blunt blows before downing each soldier with sunlight. Leaving them lying in crumpled heaps around her feet—all of them breathing as if they've fallen into a deep slumber.

As I watch her prepare to run, all I can do is look at her.

Her light is spreading from her head like a golden halo. That same golden yellow I've grown so fond of. I can feel its warmth on my face, and I still want to bathe in it. Even as she stands threatening me with her power.

I search her face, looking for the truth in her eyes, but it is well guarded, and all I see looking back at me is a viper, poised to flee.

But I am incapable of acting against her. Just as I have been from the start.

"Darling..." I mutter. "Please, don't—"

Her light grows in a white-hot flash. Flooding the room and blinding me. I shrink back, shielding my eyes as my shadows lie useless along the ground. And when her magic clears she is gone. The only evidence of her presence is a scorch mark on the stone where she once stood.

Broken shards litter the floor in front of a nearby window and I race toward it. Through it I see her sprinting across the grounds like a star—*my* star—barreling toward the forest's border.

Is she mad?

My heart feels as if it may tear from my chest as I watch her moving closer and closer to the darkened wood.

"Celeste!" Her name tears from my throat in a roar that shakes the ground beneath her.

She stumbles just shy of the trees, rolling across the earth before springing to her feet and continuing.

My anger mounts as I watch her flee from me.

She would rather face the seekers' claws than me?

Rage heats beneath the surface of my skin, and my shadows flow free, clouding my vision as I release an earth-shattering roar.

"You cannot run from me there, darling! I own the night! I will find you!"

My voice carries across the wind, and she turns when it reaches her. But the woman I see is not the woman I've known these past weeks.

She blinks once, and the emotion I thought I knew disappears from her face. She stands with a surety that guts me like a fish, spilling every ounce of hope from my bleeding heart. A heart she still holds in her hands.

I cannot read her. Her eyes have locked me out, and I worry that everything I thought I knew was nothing but the skill of a viper lying in wait.

When she turns from me, I think I feel my heart stop, but before I can be sure, she's gone. Swallowed by the night as she sprints into the trees. And the only way I know it still beats is when it clenches at the faint sound of a seeker screeching its excitement.

Chapter 27

Celeste

How could I have been so foolish?

Apollo's face is burned at the front of my mind as I flee across the grounds.

I knew he was wrong. I knew he would not turn a blind eye to my betrayal. Even if he thought he could, his feelings for the Serpent are too strong. Stronger than whatever affection he may feel for me.

The fury in his eyes was unlike anything I've ever seen. His magic poured out of him like a flood, threatening to swallow the entire room the moment the word "viper" left Kefu's lips.

I should have known better. But I'd made the fatal mistake of lying to myself. And now it may cost me my life—and Kefu's and Raye's.

I shouldn't have left them. I shouldn't have fled. A viper never flees. But seeing Apollo's shadows aimed at me was more than I could handle. And I ran. Into the night, with no direction.

That's not true.

I know where I'm going. I'm just hoping and praying I can come up with something better before I get there.

The castle gates are only a short distance away, but the soldiers are still perched at their stations. And Medina wouldn't dare open them without Apollo's order. Which means there is only one place for me.

The forest.

Fear rolls through my stomach in a wave, and I try to tamp it down. I don't have time for it. Or the luxury of believing it can be avoided. I swore to myself I wouldn't enter this forest again. I already broke that promise when I went chasing after Apollo and his legion. But now I have no choice. For now, it is my only option. It may mean certain death, but not so certain as finding myself back in Apollo's hands. After what I've seen, I wouldn't be surprised if he wanted to place my head on display at the border. A small present for the Serpent's arrival.

I keep myself pointed firmly in the direction of the forest boundary, forcing my legs to move even as my own instinct fights against me.

"Celeste!" Apollo's voice booms, calling for me in the dark, and shaking the ground beneath my feet.

I tumble through the dirt, and I force myself not to look at him as I stand.

"You cannot hide from me there, darling! I own the night! I will find you!"

I spin to see him hanging halfway out of a throne room window. Shadows fly around his head and his face is hard as ice as he pins me with a stony glare.

My heart fractures as I see just how wrong he was. But I force myself onward, ignoring the pain deep in my chest, and calling the viper to the front. My training takes over as I turn and sprint through the trees.

I run with no destination in mind. I try to steer away from the charge, but I entered through a different path, and I can't be sure exactly where I am once the moonlight no longer pierces through the trees. Still, I run. Only stopping to listen for the sound of seekers looming in the dark.

The forest is surprisingly quiet, and I take it the charge is occupying their attention. But I will not chance it. I glance around, looking for even a hint of shelter.

With my light buried and the forest's dark magic, all I can see are trees.

"The trees," I whisper to myself, remembering the way the seekers passed beneath me the night I'd wandered in here, trailing after Apollo.

I find a tree with a wide base, whose branches extend far past the forest floor, and haul myself up. When I reach the top, I prop myself against the trunk and curse silently.

Sunspots!

I should never have come here. Not this night—not ever. Not to La Luna, or these territories, or this sun-forsaken forest.

Suddenly, I wish I were a Mercurian celestial so I could turn back time. I would tell myself not to set foot in Luna, to abandon my duty and run for the Martian mountains. A lifetime spent fleeing from the Serpent is certainly better than my current circumstances.

I *had* planned to leave. But not like this. Not with Apollo's fury hunting me. Not without Raye.

I briefly consider whether fleeing was a sound choice, but then I remember the foul look in his eyes as he shouted after me, and I am sure I made the right choice.

My heart clenches as I remember his sweet words, whispered in the dark of our bed. Promises of loving me. Memories of us tangled in each other and our magic blending together in a haze.

Guilt settles in my stomach like a sickness.

I had spent weeks idling around the Lunar castle, teasing and touching with Apollo. All the while Kefu sat beneath my feet slowly dying. And now he and Raye were left to the whims of Apollo's rage.

I can hardly imagine him laying a hand on Raye. But I'd seen Kefu's condition. If the Great Mother was not already on his doorstep, she soon would be.

What if I was wrong about Apollo? What if he isn't the man I thought he was? Afterall, had I not been warned? Had he not told me so himself?

I cannot leave them behind. Even if the chance is slim, I could never go on knowing I'd abandoned them to save myself from my own foolish choices. Raye would never forgive me, and Kefu deserves more than the cell Apollo will offer him.

I must return for them. And if I must go through Apollo to reach them, then so be it.

CHAPTER 28

APOLLO

Evalina and Renwick sit before me yammering about what to do with Celeste. So far, the list includes hunting her down with nighthounds, abandoning her to the forest, or luring her out with the promise of freeing Kefu and Raye in place of her.

I sit quietly, reading Evalina's signs as they go back and forth in turn.

She's bandaged from the waist down, but Shrea did more work than I anticipated, and Evalina is in a better state than I could have hoped for. She demanded to speak with me as soon as she opened her eyes. She was worried that the charge had swallowed me up, but then she found Celeste missing and Renwick shouting about vipers. And now she is sitting here cursing Celeste to high even.

"Enough," I growl when their shouting starts to grate on me.

I cannot hear them, but I cannot bear much more of this. Each time they speak her name I want to strangle them. I can hardly bear to think of her, let alone the prospect of her lost in the forest forever.

"Sire! I told you she was not to be trusted," Renwick says for the fourth time this evening.

He keeps reminding me of this fact as if it will change something. As if suddenly I will forget her and her image will leave my mind.

"Enough." I try once more, but neither of them are listening to me.

"As if he could've known?" Evalina asks.

"A Solarian!" Renwick answers. "We should have never..."

Words blur as I fail to focus on Evalina's translations and Renwick's thin lips. The scent of Celeste's warm body still clings to my cloak, clouding my mind as blood rushes to my head. A piercing tone rings in my left ear, forcing me to steady myself against the table where we're sitting. Shadows bleed into my eyesight, tainting everything a deep, dark grey and fracturing the only sliver of patience that remains.

"*No! Enough!*" I shout, slamming my fist onto the table, causing the wood to splinter.

Renwick stops speaking before I can tear his tongue from his throat and Evalina's hands fist in her lap.

"We will not hunt her down," I say, speaking to the table.

Evalina gapes at me.

"We must," she insists. "She has seen far too much. Our training, our numbers."

"No," Renwick interjects. "The crown must come first. The prisoner has been rambling about the Serpent's arrival. He claims they will be here within a week. We should forget this nonsense and this woman and focus on securing the border."

The two of them launch back into their squabble. Evalina advocates for finding Celeste and placing her in the dungeons alongside Kefu or cutting her head from her shoulders. Renwick thinks we should be grateful she didn't kill me in my sleep and count our blessings. They continue to talk over one another, arguing as only family can, but eventually, they both quiet, looking at me expectantly.

I suspect they want me to tell them what to do. But I can hardly sort my own thoughts, let alone theirs. My mind is too busy replaying every moment I shared with her. Over and over again, they flash in my head. Memories of her soft light shining up at me, and the image of her sprinting into the darkened wood as I wonder whether it had all been a lie.

My mind is filled with thoughts of her, but I catch the tail end of Renwick's sharp words, claiming that Celeste does not matter.

"She is all that matters," I mutter, and they both stop to look at me. "*Celeste* is second to none. Not you, not Evalina, not my father's hopeless dreams, and not this forsaken crown he so *graciously* placed on my head! I am no king without her. I am hardly even a man."

My confession earns me a concerned look from Renwick and a pitying stare from Evalina.

"*Apollo—*" she starts, preparing herself to convince me otherwise.

"And you!" I turn on her. "How dare you chastise me when your own betrayal is written on your face as clear as craters?" Her mouth flaps open, ready with an excuse. "Spare me, Evalina. You've fallen as far as I have. Would you have done anything differently? For your necromancer? What would you do if it was her?" My hands fly, gesturing to the sudden emptiness I feel weighing on me. Evalina pales, anger and pain swirling in the moonlight behind her eyes as she considers what I'm asking of her. And it's like standing before a mirror—my own emotions staring back at me. Sorrow, loss, rage, agony—everything but even a hint of shame. "That's what I thought," I grunt, sliding deeper into my chair.

"But it does not matter. Celeste is gone," I say after I've had a moment to find myself. "Do not be so foolish as to believe you will find her. The vipers are well trained. If she does not wish to be found, she will not be."

Evalina nods, and they do not question me.

"We will evacuate the castle," I command. "I will not disregard Kefu's ravings as nonsense. If what he says is true, we must be prepared. Move the legion into the dungeons. There is room enough for them there. And send a riders' squadron to the nearest villages. Tell them to move South as soon as possible. If the charge ignites, it will swallow everything from here to Le Aleen. They cannot be here."

"What shall we do with the prisoner? Should we place him back in his cell?" Renwick asks.

"I do not care. We will all be residents of the dungeons soon enough."

"*Should we...send for a healer?*" Evalina asks, hesitant.

Renwick whirls on her, shocked by her suggestion, and I shake my head.

"I had Shrea tend to him the night he arrived," I tell her. "There is nothing we can do for him. He needs a Solarian healer. Moonlight will not cure his ailments."

Renwick's neck nearly snaps as he turns back to look at me and I growl deep in my chest.

"Renwick, if you continue this way you will injure yourself."

Evalina smothers a laugh behind her hand, and Renwick settles.

"*What about the legion?*" she asks.

"Prepare for battle."

Renwick nods, taking his orders and exiting the room with no further argument. But Evalina remains seated before me, eyeing me with a soft look I have only seen from her a few times before.

"*I'm sorry,*" she signs, unable to meet my eyes.

"For?"

"*For my blindness. I should have seen it. If I wasn't so caught up with...*" She pauses, and I know she is thinking of Raye. "*I should have seen it.*"

"Don't be foolish," I tell her. "I'm not sure it would have turned out any differently if you had."

"Do you think she'll come back?" she asks, rising from her seat and using the back of her chair to keep herself upright. *"The vipers never abandon their marks."*

I stand, moving to her side to offer her my arm.

"I'm counting on it."

CHAPTER 29

CELESTE

—

I spend a couple of nights perched in the tree working up the courage to return to La Luna. Every so often, I venture down to the forest floor in search of something edible, but everything here is too foreign for me to be sure it won't kill me in a single bite. And eventually, I decide I can no longer delay the inevitable.

The longer I sit here, the longer Raye and Kefu must suffer. And the longer I have to imagine all the possibilities when I finally find them. So when the forest seems too quiet, and I haven't heard the seekers for quite a while, I drop to the earth, sprinting for the boundary a few yards ahead.

When I reach the tree line, I expect the scouts to be at their stations, with an arrow marked for me. But there is no one to be found as I inch past their posts.

Not only are the scouts gone, there are no guards, no groundskeepers, not even a chambermaid lurking about. La Luna looks utterly abandoned, and I soon realize there is no one to be found *anywhere*.

A stone drops in my stomach as I continue up the castle steps and through the unmanned doors.

My footsteps feel loud as I walk cautiously through the empty corridors, passing over barren catwalks and poking my head into rooms where I think Apollo may be hiding—if he is here at all.

I start with the throne room, but it is just as bare as the rest. I try the dining rooms, the library, and our chamber—*his* chamber, doing my best to ignore the sight of his bed, though it looks to be untouched from the last I saw it. I shut the door quickly, moving to the barracks before I realize there is only one place I have yet to check.

The gallery is unlocked when I arrive, propped open just a crack, with darkness seeping out from beneath the door. I push it open with a ribbon of light, careful not to cross the threshold. The pristine, moonstone floor has been covered in shadow, and it moves, ebbing and flowing like the waves of a black sea. It parts for me, and when I step into the room, I see him.

He sits before his easel, facing the window, painting a portrait of a woman with big curly hair and full lips. The rest of her isn't completed yet, so she sits faceless in front of him as he continues making lazy brushstrokes across the canvas.

"Has my viper come for her prey?"

He doesn't turn to face me. Instead, his shadows carve a path, weaving through the big empty space until I'm standing in front of him.

"*Where is Raye?*" I ask, avoiding his pointed question.

"With Evalina," he says, refusing to meet my eyes and watching my hands only.

"*Is she safe?*" I spit.

"If you think I would lay a hand to her, you mustn't know me at all."

I take that as a yes and disregard his comment. It doesn't matter if I know him anymore, because I've already seen the wrath he holds for me.

"And Kefu?" I ask.

Apollo's shadows twitch at my mention of him, and his dark eyes settle on my face, glaring at me.

"He is alive if that is what you are asking, my darling."

My light heats, rising to the surface in a white-hot rush.

"I am not yours, Apollo. I never was." I lie, hoping it may save me from the pain. But he only aims to make it hurt more.

"Oh, weren't you?" he quips, smirking at me from where he sits. "In fact, I believe you were mine right here," he says, patting the bench beside him. "And over there," he adds, gesturing at the floor beneath my feet. "And I believe you will be mine again before we are through."

I grit my teeth, pushing the memory of his hands roaming my naked body from my mind.

"What makes you think I would ever let you touch me again?" I snap.

"Because you love me," he says simply, and I have to fight to keep my jaw from cracking as my teeth clench.

"No. I don't."

Another lie. One I must believe if I have any hope of surviving this with my heart intact.

Apollo rises from his seat, leaning across the space between us until his horns are hovering close to my face. I take a singular step back, and he follows.

"I don't believe you," he whispers, sending a chill from my head to my toes.

But I will not let him distract me as he plans my demise.

"How does it feel?" I ask. *"Knowing that you believed every lie you were sold?"*

A sly look crosses his face, but he straightens to his full height, peering down at me over his nose as he bares his fangs.

"I considered that, for a long while. The prospect that every word was truly a lie. But I know you. I know your sweet body. And your light cannot lie to me," he says. A shadow reaches out, brushing across my stomach, and my magic follows his path, swirling beneath my skin even as I try to stifle it. "The only lie you're telling is the one you tell yourself."

I shake my head, not only because I'm trying to remember that he's wrong. That he's not the man I thought I knew. But because I'm hoping it will clear the images from my head. But it doesn't seem to work, and I'm bombarded with flashes of memories. Of us.

Apollo's hands gripping my hips as he moves inside me. His cool shadows brushing my hair over my shoulder. The bass in his voice as he threatens the Martian king in my honor.

But then I'm hit with a harsher memory.

His snarling face and the heavy threat he laid as I fled into the night.

"And what about the lies you tell?" I hiss, and he frowns.

"I have never once lied to you."

"Didn't you?" My voice feels rough as I swallow down a stiff lump. Didn't he say he would not turn away from me? Didn't he say he would love me regardless? And yet, here we are.

My light gathers in my chest, and I let it rise until I'm standing before him, beaming.

He does not back away. Instead, he lifts his shadows from the floor, letting them swell around him like a dark cloud, meeting my magic with his own. He smiles at me, grinning with genuine excitement.

I step forward, shoving him hard in the chest and burning him with my palms. He pulls away from me as I unleash my light. I wield it like a whip overhead, flying through the air and cracking down in front of him. But he is swift, and he blocks my blows with shadows, standing fixed in place even as I attempt to drive him backward.

"There she is!" he shouts.

His shadows whip back and forth, blocking my sunlight at every turn.

"Come on, my darling star." He nods, waving me forward. "You want my head? It's yours. Come and take it."

His arms spread wide as he offers himself to me, and my chest heaves, choking back a sob.

"Don't!" I shout in frustration. *"Don't do that! Don't pretend like you still love me."*

I rush toward him, but he doesn't move an inch. Instead, he waits until I reach him and captures me by the wrists. Pulling me in close as I continue my barrage, beating on his chest senselessly. And my anger quickly turns to pleading.

"Don't." I sob. "Don't. Just tell me the truth! Tell me you hate me."

"I can't." Apollo grunts, his chest heaving. "I can't," he chokes out again. "I won't! If you mean to kill me, you will have to do it knowing how much I love you."

His eyes are a soft blue hue, filled with sadness as he peers at me. But my heart has already been broken, and I lash out, trying to shield it from further damage.

"I never loved you," I mutter.

Apollo jerks back as if I slapped him. His nostrils flare as I push him to his limit, and his eyes turn ink-black as his shadows lick at my ankles.

Before I can even think to react, he drives me backward, stepping quickly, lifting me from the floor with his shadows until I'm pinned against the window.

He pins my hands above my head, slamming them hard into the glass.

His eyes darken with fury and his chest presses into me as he takes a deep breath. He is close enough to taste, to strike, but my body won't move. My legs are locked in place, and my magic grows dim, sinking into my stomach. He bends down until his lips graze my ear and his big horns scrape against the glass.

"Say it again," he grunts, his voice deep as he whispers the words to me.

A chill runs across my body, and I think I see his lips turn up in a smile, but his face is too close for me to be sure. His shadows find their way to my legs, winding up my body and roping around me as his arms do the same. I thrash against him, fighting for my freedom, but my heart isn't in it.

"I never loved y—"

My words are cut off as his tongue finds its way into my mouth, kissing me hard and taking more than it gives.

This kiss isn't like the others. It's rough and wild, almost angry, and I find myself leaning into it.

When he pulls away too soon, I can feel my traitorous light pulsing between my legs.

"You cannot lie to me, Celeste." He groans, pressing his hard body into me. "I know you. I always have. From the first night, I knew the Serpent had sent you."

My breath hitches at his words.

"I hoped you would tell me. I did not think we would come to this. Even if it did, I never cared. Because you are mine. Viper or not. Solarian or not. From the moment you set foot in my throne room, you were mine. And I am nothing without you. So, kill me if you must," he whispers, licking at the shell of my ear then dragging his fangs across my jaw. "Because I will not be the one to snuff out your light."

Apollo breaks away, but I can't find the strength to stand. In an instant, he's all that's holding me up as the tears I've been holding back pour down my cheeks.

"What?" I ask.

"My name," he explains. "You always use the military hand sign. Never the standard one."

He demonstrates briefly and the air rushes out of my lungs.

"And you said nothing?"

Apollo shrugs.

"I am a simple man, Celeste. All I've ever wanted is someone to hold. To be loved without fear. And I have told you. I am selfish when it comes to you. I *will* love you. Even if it is the death of me."

Tears spill down my face as he watches me.

"But...the throne room. I saw it. The rage on your face—"

"You ran," he says, offering no further explanation.

It isn't needed. The pain in his eyes tell me all I need to know.

I'd fled just as all the others had. Ran from the demon into the night. And it had broken him.

I slump in his shadows, letting the fight trickle out of me.

"I'm sorry."

I wish I could sign the words to him, but he's still pinning my hands to the window and leering at me with his arms crossed. So I repeat the words in the hope that the simple admission will make the pain of my betrayal go away.

"I'm sorry."

He presses his forehead to my own, gripping me with his rough hands as he whispers, "I do not want your apologies. I want the truth."

"Apollo..." I breathe, and his head dips down until his lips brush against my own.

"The truth, Celeste."

He pulls back to look at me, releasing my hands from his shadows' hold. Those soft, blue eyes bore into me, waiting for the inevitable, and I sit there in silence until I can't hold it in any longer.

"I love you," I confess. *"I do. I shouldn't, but I do. More than I ever thought possible. I love the touch of your shadows. I love the feel of your horns beneath my hands. I love it when your tail wraps around my leg. I love the husk in your voice when you call me darling."* I pause, pulling in a shallow breath. *"I love the night because it's where you are. I love the demon, and I love the man. I love you, Apollo."*

A small smile tugs at his lips as he stands before me, holding me gently, and when he speaks, his voice is soothing.

"I know, my darling. I know."

His fingers find their way into my hair, and he grips it tightly, jerking me forward before I can say anything more. I reach up on my toes to yank him down to meet me, and when our lips touch, I can feel the weight of my duty lift from my shoulders like dust in the wind.

He plants soft kisses everywhere he can reach. My chest, my cheeks, my arms, and when he's finished, he holds me close, claws poking into me. But I don't care. I have missed the touch of his cool skin, and I will take it in any way I can.

As if sensing my need, his fingers come around my throat, gentle and caressing, pulling his name from my lips as his shadows caress my breasts.

"Again," he demands, and I'm helpless to his command as I call out his name.

He groans in response, and I reach for his horns so I can hear it again. But he stops me, gripping my wrists and wedging my hands between us.

"I'm still angry, darling," he whispers, pulling his shadows tight around my arms and legs. "No matter how many portraits I paint of you, I'm still angry." He growls, reaching between my legs. "There must be consequence." His voice is throaty as he brushes the remnants of my tears from my cheeks before kissing me softly. "Do you understand?"

I nod as his hands find the hem of my skirt, pulling it from around my hips.

"You're going to come, and you're going to count until I tell you to stop," he whispers before burying his face between my breasts and licking his way up to my collarbones. His fangs snag against my shirt as he nips at me and slowly begins to peel away the filthy fabric, baring my body for his pleasure and laying me down on the cold tile.

I gaze up to see a freshly painted mural on the ceiling. There is a woman painted in the center with dark skin, sunset eyes, and light dripping from her fingertips. Behind her, the Sun shines brightly. Orange and red rays bleeding across the ceiling toward every corner of the room. And as I tilt my head, I recognize my face staring back at me.

My eyes slide shut as Apollo strums my body to completion. His shadows gather to mix with the rays of my light, and I watch them tangle together in the air above us as my core clenches and releases before shattering into a million pieces.

He pauses his ministrations to look at me expectantly.

"One." I breathe.

Just in time for him to start again.

CHAPTER NINETY

CHAPTER 30

APOLLO

———

Celeste's punishment doesn't come without some of my own. She counts aloud each time her body hurtles past its breaking point, and on the way down, she makes a cut into my skin, dragging her nails across whatever space she can find. I can feel the sting of seven cuts along my back, arms, and thighs, but I don't stop.

"Celeste. Look at me."

Her eyes are cinched tight as she meets my every thrust, but I want her to see what she's done to me. I want her to know that I am undone at her fingertips.

"Celeste." My voice is harsh now, desperate for her to look upon me once more.

I think her body must understand my need. As she pries her eyes open, all I see is the bright light of her magic staring back at me. Her mouth hangs open as if to speak, but I cut it off, working another earth-shattering orgasm from between her legs. Her body spasms and her hands scrape uselessly for purchase against the cool tile before she remembers I am there to anchor her, and her hands dig into my skin, hot and searing.

"How many?" I ask.

Her lip quivers, fighting for the words.

"Eight," she mouths, a tear rolling down her sunlit cheek while she flops to the floor, boneless.

I bring my lips to her face, kissing up the salty tears and hissing between my teeth as she places a cut along my side.

"You have two more," I demand. It is not a question; it is a fact.

I've decided she will feel as I felt. Her pleasure for my pain.

I push her to the point of madness, watching as the tears well in her eyes and her lips beg for me to give her another sweet release. She clings to me as I abide, taking her punishment and dealing it out in equal measure.

I fill her until I can feel my own seed crowding me out, but she mewls for more, locking her ankles around my hips and tracing consistent circles across my back. So I barrel into her again and again until I bear the evidence of her ecstasy across my chest in the shape of one more cut.

When I peel her from the floor, she grips a singular horn as I twist beneath her, setting her sopping wet core over my abdomen. Her slick heat drips down between her thighs as her body expels the excess, seeping onto my stomach in a rush. She moves, spreading it further up my chest until her knees frame my head, and she has my horns in her hands, pinning me to the floor.

"One more, my little star." She nods. "Sit."

She obeys much too quickly, and I stifle a laugh. She is eager for my mouth against her core. Greedy thing.

My shadows unfurl from their place across the ground, wrapping around her wrists and jerking her hands free.

I can feel my name rumble through her as she shouts it into the heavens. And I only let go of her once she's sated, panting hard.

She slides down, joining me on the floor, and together we stare at the picture on the ceiling.

"Do you like it?" I ask, unsure I truly want to know her answer.

"*I love it,*" she signs, and I don't care if she means it or not.

"It was all I could manage after you left," I confess, running a hand up her thigh. "But I can't quite get your light right."

The colors are warmer than they should be, and I couldn't achieve the faint iridescence that Mother had somehow painted in her portraits. Regardless, it is now the greatest work I've managed to date.

"*It's perfect,*" she tells me, rolling onto her side.

She lays curled against me, draped in shadow as her light bleeds out of her hands to settle onto me. I revel in it, holding her close and planting a kiss on the top of her head. Her hair is thick with sweat from our lovemaking, but I breathe her in anyway. Savoring the scent of us now imprinted on her skin.

We lay there for a long while until Celeste sits up in a rush, clutching at her bare chest with eyes wide and mouth slightly ajar.

"What is it?" I ask, brushing my hand down her arm.

"*We need to go,*" she says. "*We won't have much time. The Serpent will be here in four days. It isn't enough time.*"

"Time for what?" I ask, sitting up and stroking a hand down her smooth back.

"*To prepare.*"

She rushes to pull on the pieces of her tattered clothes, and I snatch them from her with a shadow before she can think to cover herself. But she's quick as always, and she turns on me, eyes heating with light ready to scold me. I don't let her get very far.

"Darling, do you take me for a fool?" I ask, grinning and standing up to face her. Her eyes narrow as she tries to ascertain where I'm going with my questioning. "I had little expectation that the Serpent would honor the treaty when he learned of our marriage. I knew he would come. My people have planned for this very moment for decades. Father knew what needed to be done. I assure you we are more prepared than you may think."

"But the charge—"

"The nearest villages have been evacuated, and the legion has moved to the dungeons. They are ready to fight to the end," I tell her.

"The Serpent will not stop until your head is on a pike," she warns.

"Then I shall have his head first," I declare.

Celeste merely frowns at me.

"I find that difficult to believe, darling.*"* She hisses the name at me playfully. *"Considering you don't even know who the Serpent is."*

I eye her skeptically, and she adds, *"Apollo, the Serpent is not a man. The Serpent is a woman."*

Our entrance into the dungeons is not without some fanfare.

The soldiers all gawk at Celeste as they usually do, only this time, they are a bit less guarded about their distaste for her presence. They make way for her regardless, and I follow close behind as she uses her magic to light our path.

It's a tight fit with the entire legion stuffed into the already suffocating rooms, and I do my best to create space for her as we move through the winding passageways. A makeshift war room has been constructed out of one of the bigger cells, and Shrea, Renwick, Evalina, and Raye all stand waiting with grimaces on their faces as we enter.

Raye squeals immediately, rushing for Celeste and crushing her in a bone-breaking hug so fierce I think I may need to pry her off. But Evalina is close behind, hobbling forward and pulling Raye back after a few moments. The smile on my little star's face tells me she doesn't mind at all, and they fall into an easy, high-pitched conversation as we all move toward the table in the center.

Kefu sits in the corner wilting. I decided a cell was no longer necessary. The man doesn't seem to have long left, and he's fallen back into silence after quite a lengthy outburst. He manages to offer Celeste a brief bow, and I'm grateful when she doesn't greet him with the same fervor she does Raye. He is no threat to me, but after watching him throttle her, I am hesitant to have her near him.

Shrea sits beside Kefu, watching over him, and she rises to greet us both. She makes a point of squeezing me and signing, *"Good choice."* While Renwick only bows and makes the wise decision to keep his mouth closed.

There are two other members of my legion hovering in the corners. My lead rider, Captain Lupin, and my head scout, Captain Everet. Everet eyes Celeste skeptically, but he doesn't attempt to leave, and Lupin stares harder than I would like as Celeste settles into her seat. He steps forward with an outstretched palm, aiming for Celeste, and I slip a shadow between them, keeping him at arm's length.

"Oh, forgive me, your highness," he murmurs, but he isn't talking to me. He's speaking to Celeste, and she frowns at him in confusion.

Lupin looks at me questioning, but I don't catch his meaning, so I gesture for him to continue while keeping my shadow firmly planted so he doesn't get too close. "I do not mean to be rude. It's just..." He passes another glance in my direction.

"Speak plainly, captain. Celeste is Lunar now. You may treat her as such."

Lupin nods and straightens, feeling surer of himself.

"We saw you..." he begins. "Riding through the forest, I mean. That night, at the charge." Celeste nods but does not interrupt. "I wanted to say thank you. Our men would have perished if it were not for you."

Celeste's sunblush makes an appearance, and I can tell she's trying to dampen it when she offers Lupin a terse smile and says, "It is I who should be thanking you. Apollo and Evalina would never have made it out if you hadn't returned for us."

Lupin seems to work up a blush of his own, and I move to stand beside Celeste, watching him closely.

"I've never seen such expert command of a horse. I was wondering if you could...if you could show us how you achieve it?"

Celeste turns to me with a question in her eyes.

I saw little of Celeste's riding that night. I was too busy trying to keep Evalina from going up in flames, but I do remember the look of her streaking by in a white blur. It was impressive in any regard, but bareback especially. I have no doubt she knows a great many things that she can share with us. She is one of the finest warriors in these nine planes, and I will never discourage her from it.

I slip a hand beneath her curls laying it on the back of her neck and squeezing gently. She stares at me waiting, and I merely answer, "This legion will be yours as well. If you have guidance to give, I welcome it."

"Should I..." she asks, gesturing vaguely with her hands, asking me if it is safe to sign here.

I glance at Lupin, who still isn't paying me any mind, and then at Everet and Raye. Both of them are presently preoccupied. Raye with Evalina, and Everet with the dirt under his nails.

"Their king is a demon, and their queen shall be a viper." I shrug. "I doubt my deafness will push them past their limits."

Everet, Raye, and Lupin all turn to look at me, but their curious stares do not last long.

"*I do not command Strega,*" Celeste says. "*I cannot. He is Celestial.*"

Lupin's eyes bulge. Admittedly, my own grip on her tightens in surprise.

A celestial breed is nearly impossible to break, let alone ride as seamlessly as Celeste does.

"It takes more than skill to move as one with any horse, celestial or otherwise," Celeste adds, and I can feel the confidence pouring out of her as she steps into a space she knows, the space where her power lies. *"And believe me…you will need to move in unison against the Solarian riders. Not just with the horse, but with each other. I disrupted your formation quite easily. But the Solarians will not move past you. They will move through you."*

For the next few hours, Celeste provides a comprehensive and well-honed assessment of our forces. We all wince when she points out our flaws, but her criticism is warranted, despite what we'd like to think. So no one dares to interrupt her as she provides us with sound suggestions and valuable insight into the Solarian army.

Their forces are comprised only of Solarian celestials. Which bodes well for us once they enter the forest. The horses are standard, which means our riders will be able to keep pace with them easily. And their combat training is mostly focused on close range, given their numbers allow for such sacrifices to be made, but their archers are nearly non-existent.

We decide to focus our efforts on the scouts, setting them at the front of the line rather than the rear, as we usually would for additional coverage. The healers will be stationed nearby. With the seekers occupied, they should be free of their nuisance. But a small team of soldiers will go with them as additional security.

When Celeste finishes, we have accounted for all aspects but one. The charge.

"I will handle the charge," she declares. *"And the Serpent."*

"Absolutely not," I demand. "It is much too dangerous."

"Only a Solarian celestial can reabsorb the charge. And it's made of the Serpent's light. She will have to reach it if she wants to ignite it. I will reabsorb the charge and see to it she never has the chance to create one again."

Celeste's reasoning is sound, as much as I hate to admit it. She is the only one here who can subdue the Serpent's magic, and the only one who the Serpent will at least hesitate to slaughter.

"Very well. But I will not allow you to go alone," I insist.

She eyes me, prepared to argue.

"She will not hesitate to cut down your men. And I cannot protect them from the flares if I'm meant to stop the Serpent."

"I was not referring to my legion," I correct.

CHAPTER 31

CELESTE

———

"Take these," Apollo directs as he grips me by the arm and places dual blades in my hands.

We're standing in a makeshift supply room, and he and Evalina are pulling out various items, doling them out amongst the captains. Raye stands off to the side, pouting as Evalina refuses to hand her so much as a rock.

She argued for hours until she was blue in the face, and her voice grew coarse, insisting that she be permitted to ride with the rest of the legion, but Evalina was hearing none of it. I watch as Raye sucks in a breath, preparing herself for one last-ditch effort.

"Celeste gets to go!" She huffs, causing several passing soldiers to peer into the room with questioning eyes as they pass.

"Celeste is well-trained. One of the most elite assassins in all of Celestia." Evalina grunts and Raye's face grows a ruddy color as her eyes find the floor. "Your magic is untrained, my love. If you get spooked, it could infect the legion. We can't have them running off."

"I would not run off!" Raye pouts, earning a stern glare from Apollo as my translation catches up with the conversation.

"Enough," he barks, and Raye grows still. "You can go with the Shrea and the other healers."

Evalina's head snaps around, prepared to argue further, but Apollo cuts in.

"That is where she will be of most use. Her ability to soothe emotion is a valuable one. The healer's station is safe and far removed from the battle. She will not be able to infect the others, and her desire to 'help' shall be satisfied."

Evalina's mouth slides shut, but I can see the moonlight brighten in her eyes and then go a little brighter as Raye sticks out her tongue in victory.

I watch as the two of them embrace in a gentle kiss, and I decide I'm grateful to them both for the distraction.

Since I set foot in the dungeons, my mind has been filled with worry. Worry about whether I will be of any use, worry at whether this *mission* is of any use. Worry that Kefu will die lightless, lost in his own mind. I'd tried to help him. But whatever sickness had befallen him is far beyond my ability. All I could do was ease his pain, and hope I can find a Solarian healer before the Great Mother collects him.

As I weigh the blades Apollo handed me, I feel a little more myself.

"They're made of moonstone and laced with moondust," he says, watching me spin them around the handle a couple of times. "Unrefined. Lighter than any other blade. They'll do well with how much you move."

He's right. They're perfect for a close field of engagement. Short enough to be concealed but long enough to strike within an arm's length. They're short and narrow and shining like they'd been cast just this morning.

"I take it you don't need instruction on their use," he says dryly, eyeing me with a small smile. But his sarcastic remark earns him a quick burn to the arm as my magic reaches up to swat at him. He hisses, shrinking back and mocking injury.

"*Thank you*," I sign, stowing them with the other items I've selected. "*Were you so certain of my return to the night?*"

He brushes a shadow across my cheek.

"Of course. Where else does a star belong?" he says, handing me a legionnaire uniform.

It's a near-perfect match to Apollo's armor. The same dark midnight shade and carefully crafted leatherwork. Although his looks as if it is alive, crawling across his skin. It's made of a thick hide, dull and matte, like smoke. But he's laid his shadows on top, covering himself in a living shield. Mine is cut precisely to my measurements, designed to wear like a second skin—a firm confirmation of his declaration.

"And darling..." Apollo calls. "You favor your right foot."

"I do not!" I assert, jerking back. I try to make space between us but my right foot is tangled in his shadows, turning my contradiction to dust. He pulls gently at my ankle, throwing me off balance and catching me with a stiff arm around my waist.

"Yes, you do," he says, kissing me feverishly. "But do not worry, I will be at your left."

____

Our trek to the charge is easier than any journey I've ever had through the forest. The riders and scouts moved out days ago, clearing the path of seekers and driving them to the border. The legion had followed close behind, setting up battlements along the border. Apollo insisted on sending the bulk of them to the northeast. He was certain the Serpent's agitation to the south was merely a diversion. Which I all but confirmed it based on my knowledge of the Serpent's tactics.

We'd agreed Apollo would escort me to the charge, but once we were at the clearing, he would rejoin the other forces. Even so, he demanded a small battalion accompany us to the clearing, insisting that I would be of no use if a stray seeker downed me before we reached it. He was right, of course, but even knowing that, as we make our way out of the dungeons and into the forest, I can't help but feel like I am walking them to their deaths.

The feeling quickly grows into instinct as we pass through the darkened wood, and a deafening boom echoes far ahead.

Apollo's shadows drape over me as we duck, shielding ourselves against the base of the trees. Another explosion sounds, igniting somewhere up north, but smaller than the last.

"They've reached the border!" I shout, signing as Apollo's eyes settle on my face.

He nods, looping his arms around my shoulders and waiting until the tremor stops.

Go! I sign. *The clearing isn't far! They will need you!*

"No, I will not leave you," he declares, his voice loud in my ear as the piercing shock of another charge explodes up range.

"No! We agreed," I shout back.

The Serpent has taken enough from me, he signs. *I will not let her take you too!*

He gives me no opportunity to argue before we're sprinting through the trees. The soldiers break apart, flanking us as we head toward the clearing. I can hear the seekers' calls mixing with the sound of exploding sunlight, and I only hope they are too occupied to think twice about us.

We move toward the charge, forcing ourselves to ignore the pained cries of dying soldiers and the tremors moving through the ground.

When we reach our destination, the charge appears to be just as we left it, but I know we are not alone.

I cannot see her, but I can feel her.

Her magic pulses through the air like a magnetic wind and I

raise a hand, asking the legion to hold. Before I can send them running in the other direction, I see her step from behind the charge, a single hand trailing around its wide base, sparking sunlight as she moves.

"Celeste," she says in greeting.

I flinch when my name leaves her mouth.

"Mother," I spit, watching as her face twists in anger.

I've always resembled her more closely than my sisters. As the only full-blooded Solarian, I've inherited more of her than any other. And as I watch her magic swirling menacingly, I can't help but wonder if this is what it feels like to be on the receiving end of my sunlight.

"What have I said about calling me that?" she sneers, light exploding from behind her like wings. They bleed into the surrounding space, and I almost have to shield my eyes before she reins it in. "I see you've brought me a gift."

Her voice is smooth and confident, but my hands fist at my sides as I shout back. "You cannot have this land. Turn back. There is nothing for you here!"

Mother's eyes hood as she cocks her head.

"Don't be foolish, Celeste. This dark little crater is nothing but a smudge on a map. It's him I want," she calls, unleashing her light to point over my shoulder where Apollo stands, shadows ripping through the air in a frenzy.

The soldiers react despite my orders to flee. But their mistake is quickly realized. In an instant, a string of light flies toward them, snapping like a whip and knocking the soldiers back. Apollo's shadows move to intercept, but the Serpent is faster than any celestial I've known, Apollo included, and he doesn't reach them in time.

Her light touches down, racing through them like flares, and their screams fill the night air as I shout.

"*No!*"

Apollo roars as their screams die out and the light burns

through their bodies. But Mother pays them no mind. Instead, she opens her arms wide and smiles at me.

"Oh, darling," she coos. "You've done spectacularly." I frown, jerking back at her abrupt change of tone. "So well," she adds, blinking at me with soft eyes I have never seen before.

I have to fight my instinct to run, sprinting in the other direction as her sunlight curls up to stroke my cheek.

"I'm not going to let you ignite this charge," I mutter through gritted teeth.

She cackles. Always the same bitter sound. Like daggers scraping on stone, dragging and straining.

"Let me? My dear, you forget to whom you speak. Besides, I don't need the charge. I have you."

Before I can ask her what she means, her sunlight ropes around my neck, lifting me from the forest floor and squeezing until stars burst before my eyes.

"Celeste!" Apollo shouts for me, but he is still as Mother places her hand on the charge.

It swells, growing right before our eyes and the light begins to burn hotter, causing sweat to drip between my shoulder blades as I struggle against her hold.

Her magic tightens and I stop fighting in hopes she may let me live a while longer.

"Now," she says. "I would prefer not to waste an entire legion of Lunars, but I will if I must."

Apollo's face grows dark, and his shadows shrink as Mother levels her threat.

"Good, now that that's out of the way. Why don't you take a knee to make this easier for me?" Mother gestures dramatically toward the grass beneath her feet, and Apollo snarls. She chuckles again when he doesn't move. "Come now, demon. Your viper is mine. There's no need to draw this out."

Mother's words cut deep, and I can see the pain rise to the front as Apollo's shadows start to bleed into his eyes.

"She is not yours to take!" Apollo shouts, and Mother's light grows hot against my skin.

My feet scramble, trying to find purchase, but she is holding me high by the throat, roped in sunlight, squeezing the air from my lungs.

"Oh, but isn't she!" she shouts back. "I made her! She is my creation! And I will do with her what I please!" Apollo's eyes, already pitch black, narrow at her. Mother's anger turns fierce, her magic shifting to a blinding color. "Foolish, petulant, ungrateful child—playing with shadows," she hisses. "She is nothing more than what I made. *For you!*"

Apollo stills, and I can see his shadows recoil as he reads the words on her lips.

"For me?" he asks, his voice barely audible.

"Oh my." Mother tsks. "Did you think you awakened something in her?" She laughs again, louder this time. "No, no, dear. You see, *I* molded her. *All* of her. Even that bone-breaking defiance you love so dearly. *I* placed it there. I did that. She's your star because *I* made her one." Apollo's expression grows thunderous when she plucks out the nickname he gave me as if it were nothing. A meager fact that she had already factored into this plan long ago. As if she'd known every word spoken and every touch would lead us directly to this point. "Look at what you do for her." Mother waves a hand at his fallen soldiers. "Your legion withers under the weight of your love for her. She is your perfect poison. And she has brought you to your knees quicker than any blade ever could."

An aching shame devours me as I realize I have just handed Apollo to her on a platter.

It never mattered if I killed him or not. The Serpent had a fail-safe for every outcome. Yet something tells me this is the one she had planned from the start.

I squirm, trying and failing to shout for Apollo to abandon me. But my head feels full of air and Mother's light is burning so bright it's beginning to sear my skin.

"Well, demon? Will you kneel for her?"

Apollo's eyes find my face, and I shake my head, unable to speak my desperate pleas aloud.

"My darling star," he calls, holding my gaze. "My legion will go on without me. But I cannot continue without you. I refuse."

"Please, Apollo don't—" My voice chokes as Mother tightens her hold even further.

"I love you, Celeste."

His eyes lighten to their true color. That beautiful ocean blue that tells me he is happy to give himself in my place. And my heart splinters into a thousand pieces as he nods, stowing his shadows and kneeling in the grass.

He does not look away from me as his hands fist the damp earth. I thrash once again, but it's no use. Mother is holding me firm, and my body is growing weak as she strangles me. Tears streak down my face, and my light leaks out of me as quiet sobs rack my body.

My magic lashes out instinctively, aiming for Mother's head, but she has the charge at her command and she blocks my every blow with ease.

"Please," I beg, but I don't think any sound comes out.

I want to shut my eyes, but I can't bring myself to look away as she raises her hand. A blade of light comes to life in her palm and I plead with whatever gods are listening.

"Quiet, dear," Mother snarls, and I watch her light creep across the earth, aiming for Apollo.

Before her rays can reach him, a stream of moonlight strikes between us, aiming for Mother's eyes.

My heart hammers in my chest as I see Evalina streaking across the clearing through the grass, moonlight bursting from every pore. She limps as she runs, but there is a fury in her eyes, a rage and determination that's almost palpable.

I twist in Mother's hold, taking the moment of distraction to free myself, and Apollo is already doing the same.

His shadows rush forward, and he unleashes them in a cloud. He aims for the ribbon of sunlight Mother is using to keep me suspended. His shadows crack between us, severing the light and sending me flying toward the charge.

I raise my hands as I prepare myself to meet its power. Apollo reaches to catch me. But from my vantage point above them all, I can see what he does not.

Evalina is on a lethal trajectory, aiming for the space between Mother and Apollo. He's too preoccupied to see that Mother has already abandoned me to take his head. Her light will reach him before I land, and his shadows will not be fast enough to catch me.

I try to shout for him to leave me. For Evalina to stop. To save themselves. But they cannot hear me. Or my voice is not working. I'm not sure which one. I don't have time to contemplate it before my body meets the charge and Mother's light consumes me.

It burns across my body, engulfing me in a burning pain—the power too great. Like walking through flames.

I think I may be screaming, but I can't know for certain. All I know is pain as I pry my eyes open, looking for a way out. But the Serpent's magic is barreling through me, and I cannot think as it overwhelms my mind.

I can feel the charge growing, preparing to detonate, and my body begins to break under the pressure. Until all I can do is watch.

Through the light, I can see the blurred images of people. There is a man, or a monster, lying in the grass, and a woman standing over him. While another lays beside him. There is a dark mark crawling across the earth. Like blood, but thicker.

My heart breaks, but I'm not sure why. I can't remember who these people are, but I know they are important to me. I reach for the memories, but my mind fractures under the weight of pain. A tortured scream escapes me as my eyes slide shut and a vision fills my mind.

Night lifts up from the earth to crawl over me.

A man like a god, with a crown of horns and wings like a bat, spread wide, beating as he hovers in the sky.

The god of night. He has come for me.

He must have heard my pleas.

My hand stretches out to him. But I cannot reach him before the sunlight surges. It barrels through me one final time, and suddenly I'm swallowed by darkness.

CHAPTER 32

CELESTE

arkness. Everywhere.

> *In my mind, in my heart, in my spirit. It infects me. Crawling through me and spreading through my every atom.*

Buried beneath it there is a voice calling my name, but I can't find it. Even as it grows desperate and pleading. I try to answer, but I make no noise, and they can't seem to hear me. But the darkness is drawing nearer. And eventually, I do not fight the cool sensation that washes over me.

"Darling?" a smooth, deep voice whispers, stroking a hand down my cheek. "Celeste?"

I turn, looking for the voice.

It's the same one from the darkness and I don't want to lose it this time. My vision blurs as I blink my eyes open in the harsh light to find a man crouching beside me.

"You need rest," he says firmly as if I'm thinking about defying him.

But I'm not. My body aches all over, and I feel hotter than usual. Too hot.

As if sensing my discomfort the man pulls the blankets from my legs, and a bright light shines up, reflecting across the ceiling. I lift my hand, trying to shield my eyes from the harsh light, but it follows me, streaming across my face as I wave my hand in front of me.

"Your magic absorbed the light of the charge when you fell in," the man says, but I can't manage an answer.

Every thought feels like walking through mud and I'm not sure what he's talking about. Or who he is. My eyes won't focus long enough to see his face clearly, but I know he has followed me from the dark. So I don't fight him as he drapes me in a cold essence, covering me in blackness from head to toe.

"Your body is trying to digest it," he says. "Shrea thinks the heat will die down once you've made the magic yours. My shadows will keep you cool until then."

I blink, incapable of words. But the name reminds me of a different woman. This one is stone-faced and beautiful, younger with a coarse personality and a knack for insubordination.

Another name bubbles up from the depths of my mind and I can't help but mouth, "Evalina?"

The man shakes his head, and I think I see tears welling in his eyes, but I don't have the strength to reach up and soothe him. Instead, my mind falters, and my eyes flutter shut even though I fight it. And the darkness claims me again.

———

"Be quiet! She's sleeping!" A sharp voice calls me out of the darkness, and I blink awake, half expecting Evalina to be standing over me. But as the blur clears from my eyes, I see Raye frowning and blocking the path of Renwick and Shrea. "Just leave her alone."

"Raye?"

My voice is hardly a whisper, but she turns for me, eyes rounding with tearful joy as they land on me.

"Oh, praise Pluto!" she cries, launching herself forward and wrapping her arms around me.

I struggle beneath her, trying to sit up. She eventually pulls away, helping me to an upright position.

"Oh, thank the heavens. I was so worried."

Her ordinarily cheery voice is weighted by sadness, and I suddenly remember a man beside me with tears in his eyes.

My mind was not its own last I remember. It was filled with sunlight and dark images of death and dying. But I remember the man standing over me, his smooth voice calling my name. Apollo's voice. And the darkness that filled his face when I asked about Evalina.

"Raye, I'm so...so sorry," I sputter, but she waves me off.

"Don't. Or we'll all start crying," she says gruffly.

I reach out a hand, noticing the oddly bright color has subsided as I pull my legs over the edge of the cot. It is not without great difficulty, and before I can think to stand, Shrea and Raye flank either side of me.

"Where is Apollo?" I ask once they've righted me.

"Celeste..." Raye says. There is a warning tone in her voice and panic settles into my heart.

"*Where* is he, Raye?"

"He's not..." She pauses, looking to Shrea for reassurance.

Shrea nods, and when Raye looks back at me she is a little more herself.

"He isn't how you remember," she insists.

CHAPTER 33

APOLLO

———

My horns feel heavy as I kneel in the dirt. They dip lower than they had before, and I'm still not used to the added weight as I stand. So my steps feel equally as heavy as I wind my way through the rows of freshly churned soil.

I pause over each of them and press a hand to the earth, blessing each grave as I pass. It is a slow endeavor, but one I must complete.

More soldiers were lost than we expected. It took a long while for news of the Serpent's disappearance to reach the border. I don't remember much after Celeste went flying into the charge. My shadows had taken over instantly, and the surge of power had drained me almost entirely. Once the charge had been subdued I was unconscious for an entire day. With Evalina gone, the fighting went on for a while longer. By the time the Solarians pulled back, there were already too many Lunar bodies littering the earth. So I take my time as I thank them, and when I come to the place where

Evalina has been laid, I kneel before her, unable to stop the shadows that pour from me.

They bleed onto the ground, seeping into the soil as if I can reach through to the other side and tear her spirit free. For a moment, I am lost in the feeling, and I can't help but press my claws into the dirt as I curse the Great Mother. But she is quick to forgive as a bright ray of light floods my vision, crowding out my sorrows.

Celeste kneels beside me, propped up by Shrea and Raye, glowing a dim golden color.

Her magic beams, a sad smile on her sweet face, and I can't help my shadows as they reach for her. I crave the touch of her light.

To see her smiling up at me now is a gift I wasn't sure the Great Mother would grant me.

For three weeks she'd been asleep, burning hot as the Sun herself, and for two of them, I sat beside her, covering her in shadow. She's been wrapped in them from the moment the charge fell. Even as I lay unconscious, she lay beside me in a cocoon of my magic's making, keeping the charge's power from tearing through her. Shrea recommended I keep her draped in it to prevent her from reaching a temperature she would not survive.

"Darling, you shouldn't be here," I tell her. But even in the state she's in, she refuses to heed my orders.

"*You shouldn't have to do this alone,*" she declares, stubborn as ever. "And besides, I wanted to see for myself."

She smiles sweetly, staring openly at my blood-red eyes and the dark markings now covering my face.

I don't try to hide from her. I know she will not run from me. My star is well-equipped to love a monster like me.

She reaches out a hand to stroke a wing. They're tucked tight against my back, but the tops of them peak out over my shoulders and I can feel the gentle warmth of her light as she brushes her hand across the leathery texture.

"I thought you didn't have a second form," she sasses.

"I'm still not sure I do," I say. "This seems to be just as permanent as the last one." I shrug, feeling the weight of my wings as I stretch them open wide. But Celeste is frowning at me with a curious look.

"I wouldn't be so sure about that, my love."

She gestures at my horns and I reach up to feel for them. They're shorter than they have been these last few weeks. I shake my head noticing the absence of their heavy weight. And before I can say anything else, the pressure on my back dissipates, dissolving into me, until I'm able to sit a little straighter.

"But..." I gape at her, gripping my shrinking horns and feeling around my shoulders to find my wings now gone. "What?"

She laughs.

"A celestial form only arises in a time of great need," she answers. *"When our gods answer our prayers and provide us the strength we need to survive. It only departs when we no longer need it."*

I can only stare at her—this brave woman, so bold, so beautiful, so perfect.

"I guess your god cares for you after all," she says. *"Perhaps you've just been praying to the wrong one."* She teases me, stroking a horn, and I can't help but hold her close.

I reel her into a crushing kiss, holding her body tight as she opens for me, and I only stop when she taps me three times.

"We'll do it together," she says.

She grips my hand and uses me as an anchor as she struggles to keep herself upright.

I don't bother to tell her she shouldn't strain herself. I merely take her weight and prop her up.

Her light swells beneath her palms and I watch as she lays her magic over the earth as I do the same with my shadows.

Together we bless Evalina's spirit, and when her fingers lace

with mine, I take comfort in knowing I will never face fate alone
again.

CHAPTER 34

APOLLO

———

"A*pollo*?" Celeste signs my name, hands illuminated by her eyes as she stretches across our bed.

Her face holds a question as her fingers move slowly, too tired for their normal speed and surety, and I watch her with a patience I didn't know I possessed.

I nod just once, encouraging her. Her hands move, and I can see my heart beating between her fingers as she signs, "*What do you imagine I sound like?*"

No one's ever asked me such a thing, but I know my answer immediately.

I don't need to imagine, I begin, and her light dims a little. *I know exactly what you sound like.*

She frowns and I place a swift kiss between her brows before I continue.

"Your pitch is high, like a songbird, but only when you lie."

A sunblush rises in her cheeks.

"Otherwise, it's low, languid, like a river, never rushed."

I drag my thumb down her bare arm to demonstrate, moving slowly from her shoulder to her wrist.

"Your laugh is surprisingly light for someone with such worry on her shoulders."

She doesn't bristle at that. Though she seems surprised at my mention of it. I suspect others are too easily distracted by her beauty to see the subtle tension mounting.

I reach around her neck and squeeze lightly causing her to moan as some of it dissipates.

"It carries like flowers in the breeze. But when you're angry..." Her eyes had fluttered shut, but she pries them open to hear the rest. "I just know that tongue of yours cuts like a knife."

Her soft smile dissolves into quiet giggles as she burrows her face into my chest. I think perhaps she is done for this evening, but when she pulls back, she is poised with another question.

"Do you miss it?" she asks. *"The noise?"*

Her eyes are bright with an innocent curiosity, and I trace a thumb across her lips, enjoying the warmth that rises to the surface.

"Do all Solarian women ask as many questions as you do?"

"I wouldn't know," she signs, turning her nose up at me.

My eyes roll, but I can't help the smile pulling over my fangs. She is so radiant in the dark light of our bed. I would answer any question, no matter how many or how odd. She could ask it of my cold, dead corpse, and I would find a way to answer from beyond this plane.

"If so, I think one shall be enough," I tease. But my darling star is not one for such jokes, and she grips me by the horn, signing proudly with her free hand.

"As if I would ever allow you to have another."

"I have no need for another," I tell her, pulling her in close and kissing her tenderly.

———

R. A. MOREAU

KEEP READING FOR A SNEAK PEEK AT BOOK 2!

CELESTIAL BODIES: THE WHITE DRAGON'S WIDOW

Aros

"My sweet flame, will you please drop your shift? The Demon of La Luna has greater things on his mind than your true face."

Davina crosses her arms in defiance, jutting her nose out toward the window. It's angular and pointed. Not at all the one I'm looking for.

"Not until we are within our own borders," she says.

"Please, my love. I miss your warm eyes. I do not want to look at these blank ones any longer."

Her brow lifts, and she glares at me from across the carriage. Her milky-white gaze grows blank as she blinks, somehow shifting her eyes to appear more vacant just to punish me.

"I wouldn't have known it from the way you were watching Celeste all evening."

Her ordinarily soft voice feels loud in the small space. Made louder by the sting of pointed words. And I realize she will not come easy tonight.

She is angry with me. I know this.

I was not myself at dinner. My curiosity got the best of me, and I'd spent too much time staring at the demon's so-called bride. Now I am paying for it dearly, though it is no surprise.

My flame has always been a jealous one. Never one for wandering eyes. In fact, I'm almost certain she would prefer I was blind.

But then who would there be to look upon her beauty? Because surely, I would slay any other man who tries.

Their blood would fill the halls of Mount Cinis, a muffled voice echoes in my mind, and I smother it back.

"Davina..." I begin again. "I was not looking at the demon's bride with envy or desire. Surely, you know that?"

She eyes me skeptically but does not turn away from the window. Instead, we sit in silence—her long legs crossed at her ankles, and her hands fisted in her lap. That is, until the carriage begins to rock, jerk, and jump along the uneven path.

Davina startles as we cross over rough stones, reaching out to steady herself. I seize the opportunity, gripping her by the hand to balance her. Yet still, she will not look at me.

So few travel to La Luna that it makes for a difficult journey, made all the more trying without my flame by my side.

"Do you want me to beg?" I ask. "Because I will."

We kneel to no one, the voice echoes.

My frustration sparks as he rears his ugly head, but I ignore it.

My flame is smiling once again. Her eyes are bright with quiet amusement. I can see she tries to smother it. But it's too late. I am already dropping to my knees on the carriage floor.

"Please," I beg, fisting her skirts in my hands. "It is a torture too unkind. Have I not suffered enough?"

Her shift falters, and for a brief moment, the woman beneath her facade is revealed. The one I'm desperate to look upon—my wife.

It's been too long since I've seen her face—her true face—and I will not wait any longer. The image she wears outside our home is beautiful—tall, blond, and utterly Venutian—but she is not the one I crave. She is not the one I need.

I lay my head in her lap, burying my face as I pretend to weep.

"Please, oh benevolent one, free me from this torment."

At last, she laughs. That same sweet sound that's been my only vice for the last one hundred years.

"You are a fool, Aros," she says, smirking at me as she brushes a hand across my cheek.

I pull her down into my lap and kiss her until my flames grow hungry. Until they leech out of me, crawling up her legs and across her body, enveloping her from her head to her toes.

My flames do not burn her. They never could. Not even if I wanted them to. I have given myself to her so thoroughly that my magic is now hers as much as it is mine. So she merely sits contentedly in a blazing blue light as I worship her.

I place kisses in every place I can reach. Her face, her neck, her arms. Even her hair.

It is still the white gold color that is so common with Venutian women, and I frown at it, curling a thick piece around my finger.

"Fix this," I command her. "I want my wife back."

Her eyes level on me, and I half expect her to take up her shift again. But the color slowly recedes, revealing her natural shade. A dark, curly blond that reminds me of a freshly planted ash tree before it's gone grey. It is the perfect tone for her brown skin, and as she releases her magic, my wife comes back into view.

"Thank you," I say, dropping another swift kiss on her shoulder.

"Do not thank me," she says haughtily. "I did not drop it for you. I am simply too tired to carry on."

"Ah, in that case, I shall thank you for your sacrifice."

I squeeze her around her middle, and she squeals. A girlish sound I'm sure would send others into shock.

This Davina is a rare sight. For all but me, that is.

For me, this is the only woman I have ever known. A bright and vivacious spirit, with a knack for dragging men to their knees.

She kisses me gently, no longer angry at my transgressions, but I cannot allow even a shred of doubt in her mind. So as I hold her close, pressing my forehead to hers, I remind her who she is.

"You are my only love," I recite, "until the last embers burn."

"And the flames turn to ash," she answers—as she always has.

Or until her bones lie buried beneath the mountain, the voice declares, and I can't help myself as I bark back, "Be silent!"

Davina does not flinch. She's grown used to my outbursts after all this time.

"Can you hear him?" she asks.

I nod.

"What does he say?"

"Nothing that I would have you hear."

Her eyes turn downward as a sad frown takes up space on her beautiful face, and I curse the madman within for stripping her of her joy.

I have never understood how there could be a part of me that does not love her to its very core. She is the fire that keeps my spirit warm. The only hand I trust to steady my own, and yet, the voice grows louder each day.

"It's getting worse," she whispers.

"Yes."

I cannot lie to her. She has seen it for herself. He lurks ever closer to the surface, growing bolder with each passing moment.

He even threatened to reveal himself in front of the demon and his bride. All that talk of sending my flame home with my head in her hands sparked a fit of anger unlike any other. The haze of rage had driven him to the front. Thankfully, Davina was there to calm me. Without her, La Luna might have been reduced to a pile of ash. And then where would we be? At war with the moon?

That was a circumstance we could not afford.

I try to reassure her.

"He will not rise, my love."

Davina's brows pinch together, doubtful.

"You never used to hear him so clearly before," she adds. "What if he gets stronger? What if he takes hold and you become lost in your own mind? What if he—" Davina's face twists as her words break off, and her golden eyes glisten with unshed tears.

Until tonight, I had never seen eyes like hers. That golden hue that glitters like diamonds in the light. But the demon's bride, Celeste, bears a similar color. In truth, that is why I was staring at her so intently. But it is all but forgotten as I see Davina looking at me now.

Her look of worry nearly spears me. I know she worries that he will overtake me. That I'll be trapped forever in the fog of my own mind, as my father was. And his father before him. But I do not care what comes of me. My only worry is that he will not be as kind to her as I am.

Assuredly, she will be the first to go, he confirms.

I ignore him and his bloodlust. The more I think about him, the louder his voice becomes.

"Let's not discuss this now. We will meet with the healer when we return to Cinis."

She shifts, unhappy with my persistence in avoiding this discussion. This is not the first it has come up these last few moons, and it most certainly will not be the last. Not if she has anything to do with it.

"Until then, let us enjoy our time alone."

A small mischievous smile spreads across her face, and with that confirmation, I draw her into my lap, wrapping my arms around her to hold her close.

She hesitates, muttering, "But...the driver."

I glance through the small window set high into the carriage to see our stagecoach sitting alert in his seat. If he can hear us, he shows no sign of it.

"He is discreet. And I will melt his eyes in his skull should he see even an inch of you."

Davina giggles her sweet, innocent laugh.

"Open," I tell her, nudging her knees apart.

My cock swells as she obeys, but it will be disappointed this evening. My only intention is to please her. To right my wrongs and show her how thoroughly she possesses me.

Beneath the layers of her dress, I find her body wet and ready to welcome me, and I tend to her for the remainder of our journey, only stopping when we reach the castle gates.

The carriage comes to a jerking halt, and I am loath to abandon her. But the feeling dissipates as Ember yanks the door open, shouting, "Finally!"

Her face is screwed up in irritation, and she glares at us both as we step down from the cabin.

"Must you leave for so long?" she sasses. "They nearly burned the entire mountain down!"

Ember groans, jerking a thumb in the direction of her brothers, who have hardly noticed our return and are too busy wrestling one another in the dirt to mutter anything other than a muffled, "Hello, Father."

"Boys! Say hello to your mother before I char your behinds." My voice echoes across the courtyard, bouncing back threefold, and they rise suddenly from the dirt, jumping up to greet her.

Without hesitation, Ember launches into a long list of the events we've missed.

Apparently, Kai has been working on his dragon's breath, and after nearly eighty years of practice, he has finally managed to spit a blue flame. He beams with pride as he demonstrates, burning the banner beside the castle entrance to a crisp.

He'll make a fine dragon, the voice says.

"Yes, he will," I mutter under my breath.

"No one cares about your shoddy dragon's breath!" Phoenix declares. "Not when *I've* perfected my flame arrows!"

Phoenix pulls his palms apart like an archer settling into position, and a needlepoint flame stretches to life between his hands. It goes flying a moment later, landing square between the eyes of the metal dragon's head hung above the gates.

Kai grumbles, and Ember laughs as Phoenix takes his victory lap. The three of them make enough noise to wake the entire village.

Watching them, I cannot help but notice how much they favor their mother.

Golden brown skin, upturned eyes, and a smattering of freckles across their noses. Each of them is a near copy of the other. Made every bit in her image.

When I first laid eyes on them, I half wondered if she'd done it on purpose. Perhaps she'd used her magic to mold them into her likeness. But then, I saw their flame-filled eyes and the dark mop of hair on top of their little heads, and I knew they were nothing more than what Mother Mars had intended.

Gravel crunches beneath my feet as we pass through the iron gates and into the central courtyard. A blazing heat swells from the stone pit in the center, and I stop before it, passing my hand through the flames.

"Have you been feeding it?" I ask.

"Yes, Father." Kai groans, rolling his eyes. "Every day. As we always do."

"Good. This flame has been burning longer than any of us has been breathing. I will not have our family be the ones to douse it."

This time, they all roll their eyes, Davina included.

"Yes, Father," Ember echoes.

I spit my flame into it, offering my mana to Mother Mars, and the children follow suit, adding to its strength. Having no fire of her own, Davina tosses a lump of coal from the bucket along the edge to feed it.

The flame burns hotter, reaching up toward the sky, as it takes on new life.

Before it dies down to its ordinary simmer, the boys have already disappeared, and Ember is dragging Davina through the north archway. She passes me an apologetic shrug before they sprint giggling down the empty corridor. A smile creeps across my face, even as I find myself standing alone in the shadow of the blazing fire.

How easily forgotten you are...

"Stop your whining," I bark back. "Before I put us both out of our misery."

My voice fills the courtyard, and I'm grateful there are no others around to witness my slow descent into madness.

Ha! He laughs. *You wouldn't dare abandon them.*

He's wrong, of course. I wouldn't hesitate to lay us both to rest if it meant they were safe from him. But I don't bother correcting him. There is no use in answering. He only ever spews the same vile hatred. So instead, I focus on silencing him.

I begin my count at six hundred, as Mother taught me. And I work backward as I make my way toward my study. By the time I reach two hundred, I'm in the west wing. And before I reach double digits, I am passing through the Hall of Ancestors.

I avert my gaze as I pass beneath the portraits on the wall.

It's an old Martian custom, born of ancient legends. Stories that warn of the dangers of looking upon the dead. Most claimed that should the spirits see you, they would steal your flame for themselves, so desperate to escape the cold clutches of death.

I know it's nothing more than superstition. But I am not one to test matters of Mother Mars. So I abide by the custom, lowering my eyes as I pass, giving the dead their dignity.

The voice inside is silent by the time I reach single digits, but that peace is soon shattered by the soft light seeping from beneath the door to my study.

I still, watching it closely. It doesn't flicker like a flame, and there are no shadows dancing in it. It is flat and bright like the artificial light they are so fond of in Terra or the unwavering light of the sun. That tells me there is something other than a Martian on the other side.

I swing the door open, flame at the ready, and what I find waiting is something akin to a miracle.

Or rather, a tragedy.

"Hello, Aros," the woman beside the hearth hisses quietly.

The fire in the hearth has been doused, and she sits with her face shrouded in darkness, the only light coming from her outstretched palm.

I do not need the light to know who sits before me. The irritating grate of her voice is familiar enough.

"Serpent," I mutter by way of greeting.

I do not bother hiding my distaste. It is nothing new between us.

I light a fire quickly. One big enough to crowd out her sunlight and force her from the shadows. But I realize too late there is a reason she is lurking in the dark.

A curious mark stains the right side of her body, black and writhing. Like a living burn, her skin is charred. Oozing and crusted with deep ravines crawling along the surface.

An ugly sight if I ever saw one.

"I see your meeting with the Demon did not go according to plan."

The Serpent's face remains blank as I shut the door behind me, lest Davina come wandering through the halls.

"A minor setback." She waves a hand vaguely as if the dark shadow crawling up her arm is nothing more than a flea.

"I take it he lives then?"

"The beast still breathes," she answers, hiding her mangled arm beneath her robes. "For now."

I make my way around the room, keeping her square within my sight. "If you have come here looking for sympathy, rest assured, you will not find it here."

She does not balk at my admission.

We are well acquainted with one another. She knows the kingdom of Mars would rejoice in her demise. Secrets are the only thing that binds us together.

"I do not need your sympathy," she snaps, her face bright with sunlight.

I smother a smirk.

The demon has riled her well.

"Then what is it that you want from me?" I ask, growing more impatient with every breath I watch her take.

She laughs—loud—and the screeching pitch makes my teeth feel hollow in my mouth.

"I am not here for *you*," she declares. "I am here for the great White Dragon of the West."

Finally.

The voice within ignites.

Someone with sense!

———

ALSO BY R. A. MOREAU

COMING SOON

CELESTIAL BODIES:

THE WHITE DRAGON'S WIDOW

Dr. Jekyll and Mr. Hyde meets *Mr. and Mrs. Smith* in this thrilling dark fantasy romance. Unleash the monster within in this action-packed tale of two lovers pitted against each other and a battle for the fate of the Martian kingdom.

AVAILABLE NOW

THE FALL OF SOULS

A reimagined tale of Egyptian gods and goddesses in a one-of-a-kind adult fantasy romance filled with passion, secrets, and betrayal.

ABOUT THE AUTHOR

R. A. Moreau focuses her work on Black romances in fantastical settings of both fantasy and the paranormal. She hopes that by sharing her work, more women will have the opportunity to see themselves in the stories they love.

When she isn't working, she loves spending time with her two dogs and eating more bread than any healthcare professional would recommend.

SOCIALS

www.moreauwrites.com